FIVE KEYS

Rose Mary Long

authorHOUSE®

AuthorHouse™
1663 Liberty Drive
Bloomington, IN 47403
www.authorhouse.com
Phone: 1 (800) 839-8640

Published by AuthorHouse 12/08/2015

ISBN: 978-1-5049-6682-5 (sc)
ISBN: 978-1-5049-6689-4 (e)

Library of Congress Control Number: 2015920215

Print information available on the last page.

In memory of Michael (Mike) Ariano (1962-2010). He inspired and encouraged countless individuals before and after becoming an organ recipient, speech patient, and my friend.

A trip to take have I, o'er land and sea and sky;
through waves of doubt and mount's of cheer,
'til "Home Again," I'll cry.

CHAPTER 1

The duck family marched across the clearing and wobbled into the overgrowth near the lake. The approaching bikers intended no harm, but the birds had no way of perceiving that fact anymore than humans have the ability to see their future. Mrs. Duck nudged her ducklings faster, repressing her instinct to fly, refusing to desert them. Mr. Duck scurried with them to the edge of the grasses; and then, fluttering his wings in a flashy manner, abandoned them to their fate. The scene put Maren in touch with her feelings. She was being left behind with their children, giving up her speech-language pathology career, while her physician husband Paul would soon be flying off to exciting adventures all over the world with Pediatric Possibilities, the international medical mission agency her brother-in-law had helped develop.

"Finish throwing your stones, Danl," Maren called, reaching for Zoe's hand. "We have to go unpack more cartons." The children had already learned the way from the creek behind their property to the village park by the river, through the village to a small spring-fed lake. They had in just one week tramped out a foot path through the woods from the their unkempt backyard to the creek.

The siblings were unusually self-sufficient for seven and eight, but that was their limit. An outing to the village or the lake was to be a family event.

The siblings had matured quickly in the small cabin west of Denver, trying to care for their mother when she couldn't care for them. That was already only a distant memory for them, as they pushed their bikes over last fall's soggy, rotting leaves that lay in their new backyard. Maren made a mental note to arrange for landscapers. It was one more item added to her growing list of resettlement projects.

By the time Paul arrived, dinner was long past. The children were in bed; and Maren, muscles aching from the physical exertions of the cross-country move, was unpacking books. She stood inside the open French doors just off the entryway, in what had been a formal living room. She and Paul had employed a local carpenter to convert it into a library. They wanted something reminiscent of the one he had built in his Chicago house before they were married. Now, floor to ceiling shelving units and the small, curved walnut desk by the window needed to be stocked. The new couch would arrive tomorrow.

Danl and Zoe had helped Maren drag and tote boxes from room to room earlier in the day, after Grandmom and Granddad McCloud had left. They had entertained the children while Maren organized the kitchen. Paul's parents were impressed at how efficient the move had been, even though Maren was overwhelmed. In Colorado she had directed the children to use colorful markers to print room destinations on cartons, expecting the unpacking process would be easier if their belongings were immediately placed in the appropriate room. Unfortunately, the movers had arrived late and had deposited boxes in whatever room was convenient at the moment.

Paul had eaten a burger in the car on the drive home. He greeted his tired wife, rolled up or as was his custom rolled his shirt sleeves under, and began energetically slicing strapping tape and unloading boxes. Maren was grateful for the help, but couldn't let go of the disappointment that she hadn't heard from him all day. "I thought you would be home before the children's bedtime. They were watching out the front window for almost an hour before I made them turn in."

He began dealing books like cards onto shelves, but offered no excuses. "I know. I hated to miss seeing the little guys." She struggled to find the words to tell him how painful this transition was for her. "I realize that our lives will change drastically, but I didn't imagine this kind of schedule would become the norm before you even start the overseas trips."

"The norm? Maren, this is only our first week here, my first week of training." He took a breath and tried to be logical. "We're treading on all new ground here. I don't know why you're so upset. Tonight was unavoidable, or I would have been here." Next he added analytical comments to reiterate their situation. "We talked this all out before we left Colorado. I expect you will have to learn to be more patient and independent than you've been in the past." He meant *their* past.

"Patient. Independent." Her words were reactive. "If you remember, I was a wife, a mother, and a widow before I met you." She gave him the old leather-bound volume on Native American legends to place on his higher shelf in exchange for the collection of C.S. Lewis to be assigned to the lower shelf she was stocking. His mind was filled with excitement at the opportunity which had presented itself to him at a crucial time. Pediatric Possibilities was a non-profit organization conceptualized by several retired physicians and was fast becoming a well-known, international medical mission agency. In actuality it wasn't limited to the pediatric population, so they recruited physicians of various specialties. Calvin Dodd, Maren's brother-in-law had brought the proposal to Paul on numerous occasions, both before and after Paul and Maren were married. Refusing to re-evaluate his decision on the spot, he tried humor. "But life wasn't worth living without me, right?"

"How can you say that," was her humorless answer. "I raised two boys, got a graduate degree, had friends…"

"Whoa, whoa. Lighten up." But it was too late. He had inadvertently pushed the wrong buttons. Why couldn't he remember the lessons his sister Penny had tried to teach him, "Some things a woman has to be told; some things she needs to be shown." He still couldn't seem to get it right. Placing the stack of historic fiction he was holding on the floor next to an unopened carton, he walked carefully around them and wrapped his arms around her. She felt the power of his embrace take control of her immediately. The world seemed brighter as his strength warmed her. The muscle tension and fatigue that had grown to alarming proportions began to melt. Still, she wanted him to understand.

"Paul, giving up my work was one of the most difficult things I've ever done. I didn't even do that when Jack died. In Denver we had the perfect positions for each of us, and as a bonus we got to work together. I wanted to adopt the children as much as you did, and I willingly gave up the chance to be Program Director at the college. I just feel I'm losing my identity. I went through this parenting routine before with Matt and Nick, but back then I had no professional identity to relinquish. All I've worked to become professionally is slipping away."

She couldn't think about, let alone verbalize her fear of having him routinely fly overseas, with the world still reeling from the 9-11 attack. They had talked about that before signing with Possibilities. Back in March, Kabul had fallen; and the Red Cross already had established a presence in Afghanistan. The new government had welcomed several non-government organizations, NGOs as they were called, to a celebration of International Women's Day. They paid tribute to women who had played a crucial role in helping children survive. It had looked as if terrorists were fleeing. The world might be a little safer, but it was still a dangerous place. Boarding a plane still caused tension if not outright fear in the stomachs of most passengers.

"Part of our connectedness has been through our working together," she continued. "I miss that. I miss academic conversations and working with patients, being part of their lives, their healing." She stopped, out of breath. Each time they went over it she tried again to make him understand, tried again to dissolve her reservations about their abrupt decision.

"It will all work out," he assured her quietly, not really knowing what there was to work out. From his perspective everything had worked out beautifully. When he resigned the hospital position he had arranged to provide for them. Like many other Americans after 9-11, they felt the need to be closer to family. They had moved back to Illinois to give Maren and the children the support of Paul's parents and his sister's family. They had purchased an expansive, modern house on a sizeable wooded lot in the charming, peaceful village of Dexum. Prospects were good for a comfortable and exciting future, in spite of some disquieting world events.

He thought Maren should be grateful for the freedom from the demands of the work world.

Paul's private motivations and feelings were more mixed than he verbalized. He hadn't told Maren the whole story, only that he had been asked by the new hospital administration to resign. At some level he knew he was fulfilling a need to be more adventurous—for the first time in his life to not take the safe, sure path. True, circumstances had propelled him onto this path, circumstances Maren couldn't totally understand. To his way of thinking, Maren's life would continue as it had in Colorado, except he would travel more.

He wished she wouldn't keep bringing up the subject of getting a job. Her earning power as a speech-language pathologist was a fraction of his—well, not at Possibilities, but of his potential. When they had adopted Zoe and Danl, Maren had gladly cut down her hours at the clinic, with Paul's enthusiastic support. He had missed seeing her there, but they had all benefited from the new arrangement. Their children were not only healing from their traumatic early years, they had positively blossomed. As a father, Paul had been content in a more complete way than he had ever before known in his adult life. He expected that the habits they were creating now would continue to be satisfying for all of them. It would just take a little time.

He relegated some thought to the back of his mind, unsure exactly what it was, something about Maren's gifts and talents. "Maren, I love you. You have amazing gifts. You're just tired right now. Let's give this new life a chance to grow on us."

"Paul I admire and love you, but I may not be able to live up to your expectations." She spoke evenly, but with irritation creeping into her voice. She recognized it, but was too close to exhaustion to control it. Tears stung her eyes, threatening to overflow.

"What I expect is that you will be happy. We made these decisions together." His quiet voice trailed off as he noticed her tears. She rarely cried. When she did, he felt as if his heart would stop beating. "Maren, Maren, no… don't." He kissed her forehead, her eyes, her wet cheeks, felt the softness of her neck on his face, and then he put his lips on hers. They knocked over a stack of text books as they made their way out of the library and down the hall to the only bedroom on the main floor.

The late August sun rays trickled through dry, green leaves and seeped through the accordion pleated window shades, illuminating their bedroom. The clock radio turned on, not with music but with the traffic and weather report. Paul would leave for the city at five-forty-five, after a hurried meal with Maren. They enjoyed breakfast alone together whenever possible. Later, she had juice while the children ate, and then walked them to the corner. They had to be out of the house by seven forty to catch the school bus. The trip to Village High would be walkable, but for the elementary years the bus would deliver them almost door to door. Fortunately, they had made fast friends with Andrew and Trisha across the street and had adapted readily to the bus and school routine. Maren could have gone back to bed by eight o'clock.

She didn't go back to bed, but with only an empty house and more chores to face she found it difficult to be enthused about the day. It wasn't that she didn't like the house. It was a wonderful home in a quiet neighborhood, just a fifteen minute drive from the larger city of Albright. They had thought they would live west of Edgelawn where she had lived with Jack and the boys; and had spent considerable time looking for property, on the east side of Edgelawn, in the older city of Albright. Their realtor had insisted on showing them a house she had found for them south and west of Albright, along the river in the village of Dexum. The children thought the house reminded them in some ways of the home they were used to in Denver. They all appreciated the wooded lot in back that was limited by a creek. Trees had been cleared to position the house in front of the spruce, pine, oak, and maples, facing Crescent Avenue.

Now that the children were in school, Maren needed a routine of her own. She walked each morning, both for the exercise and to become more familiar with the village. Eventually, she would define a circular route that took her out of her neighborhood, along a shady road, and into the village, with return by way of the creek path. The sun warmed her shoulders as she turned toward the center of town. On the corner she saw the large, weathered log building that caught her eye each time she drove past. It was the Village Café. She and Paul had stopped there for coffee the day they had first seen the house. The building, said to be over one hundred fifty years old, had been used as a hotel and trading post in the days when the stage coach and the village mill operated. The mill and village had existed long before Albright came into being, but the railroad had connected to Albright, assuring its growth. Dexum remained forever a village but continued to outlast dour predictions of its demise. The inn hadn't once closed its doors, but it was no longer a hotel, just a popular restaurant with a coffee shop in the back that overlooked Timber Creek.

Maren and Paul had relatives and acquaintances in the larger area, but they knew no one in Dexum. Seeking company more than coffee, Maren went in. She sat alone in the dark oak arm chair staring out at trees that were just giving up their basic green wardrobe for more colorful dress. The energetic water in the creek threaded its way through fallen branches, reminding her of a special place in Colorado, near the McCloud family vacation home. She started to recall those romantic moments with Paul, but a waitress interrupted her thoughts. Maren asked for half regular half decaf coffee, but there was no decaf brewed. She mixed three creams in a cup of regular and sipped hot caffeine into her system. The coffee was smooth. No need to open the sweetener.

Her attention turned from the windows to the locals sitting at various tables, mostly men. Some folks were obviously just passing through town, maps or guidebooks nearby. Others, looking more like workers, were starting their day with coffee or breakfast. She was, she admitted reluctantly to herself, more lonely than she could remember being in her entire life. When Jack had died she had been distraught, but with the demands of two teenage sons and the rigors of graduate school, there had been no time for self-centered loneliness. She smiled, remembering Zoe and Danl and their joyful embracing of each new day. She was beginning to realize that she might well need them as much as they needed her.

"Morning." A smiling, red-haired man at the next table interrupted her thoughts.

"Good morning," she replied automatically, smiling back at him.

"You're the contemporary house on Crescent Avenue," he said.

She nodded, remembering that their house, a departure from the mostly traditional homes on Crescent Avenue, was referred to as the contemporary house. She wondered if she should recognize him. She had met a multitude of residents when registering the children at school, and met others when she had applied for a position in the district.

"I'm Greg Carson the vet in town," he explained, relieving some of her anxiety, "And you are a speech pathologist with two young children who will undoubtedly want a dog. Word travels fast here." He smiled, enjoying his advantage. He and his wife Dolores, one of the secretaries in the school administration office, had two boys at the middle school he informed her.

Dolores had told him all she knew about the McClouds, and that there were no positions open for licensed speech-language pathologists. The small district, she had told Greg, had just employed a speech therapist to fill the last available slot. Maren was actually entitled to the position, since the "therapist" was a Bachelor's level paraprofessional, not a master's level, licensed professional. Employing a paraprofessional when a qualified speech-language pathologist was available was illegal, but Dolores and Greg weren't aware of that. Maren had no way of knowing that she could have demanded the position, so she was forced to create a plan B.

Dr. Carson laid his newspaper on the table in front of him and sipped his coffee while continuing the conversation. He made it a point to tell her that his clinic was at the end of Lincoln Street. She got the feeling that he was really welcoming her to the community, not just fishing for new business.

Greg continued giving her a short history of the village. "There's a belief that the unpaved basement under this building was once part of the Underground Railroad. Secret passageways are said to have led slaves under the road and into the graveyard north and west of here at the end of Maple Grove and Crescent Avenue—near your place—where they were met and taken further north. I've heard that the owners Gene and Emma Caufield are going to reconstruct it and turn the Dexum Inn into a tourist attraction.

This part where we're sitting started as an outdoor porch, but eventually it was enclosed with windows and called the Dexum Inn Café. Now we call it the Village Café."

It was like an old fashioned porch she thought, looking around. The upper half of the wall was glass and provided an unobstructed view of the bend in the creek just downstream from the mill. It was a peaceful spot for coffee or a quick meal, quiet and private on the café side with a convenient entrance and small parking lot right on Main street.

She took another swallow of coffee, enjoying the lift it provided. She was comforted by the warm mug, the historic setting, and by the friendly voice of the red-haired veterinarian. He called the waitress Della and asked for his check. She could see him through the front window, walking down Main toward Lincoln Street. When Maren asked for her check, Della Mason told her Dr. Carson had already paid for her coffee.

Maren felt aloneness press in on her again as she continued her walk through the three blocks of "downtown." She saw a one story, red brick building just a block off Main Street. It was surrounded by shade trees. A large, brass sign read, "Stanton House." It appeared to be a nursing home or rehabilitation center. Curious and energized by the caffeine, she ventured inside. A large formal living room with upholstered furniture and tasteful draperies was a cheery greeting in itself, but a woman with a toothy smile and large heavy eye glasses provided a friendly, verbal welcome from behind a desk, "Hello, come in." As Maren crossed the room to introduce herself to Lynne the wiry receptionist, she commented on the low picture windows, low enough for residents in wheel chairs to enjoy the view of the park-like grounds. She noticed the wide-screen TV on one side of the carpeted room and a grand piano on the other, assuring residents and visitors of pleasant leisure activities.

Lynne was obviously proud of the facility. She enthusiastically informed Maren about the origin of Stanton House. It was named in honor of Hope Stanton the mother-in-law of a local doctor who had kept her in his home during her final years. "She had Alzheimer's," explained Lynne with her wound-up-tight voice. "They didn't call it that back then, but that's what it was." Lynne talked so fast, she gasped for air when she did pause. "Stanton House is a private facility that was designed like a stylish home. It used to be called a nursing home, but now of course it's an extended care facility. Its fifty years old, has five wings, and can accommodate up to ninety-seven patients. Rumor has it we'll be bought by one of the major healthcare consortiums soon, but I hope not."

When Lynne finally took a longer breath Maren jumped in to explain that she was a speech-language pathologist and would like to speak with the administrator or head of nursing. "Through the double doors." Lynne jerked her thumb over her shoulder, "but sign in first. Security, you know, since 9-11. Like some terrorist might want to blow up an extended care facility." Maren signed the little guest book, writing the time she was arriving in the appropriate space, and proceeded to the nurse's station where she found Noreen Anderson.

The head nurse's thick, dark hair was cut in a short, practical style that matched her efficient, but warm manner. The two felt drawn to each other immediately. Extended care facilities had difficulty finding SLPs and often used large contract agencies. Stanton House hadn't yet done so, and Noreen was pleased to learn that she and Maren lived in the same neighborhood. By the time Maren left, she had established herself as an on-call speech-language pathologist for the home. *It's a start,* Maren assured herself on her way out.

After the children had gone to bed that night, Maren shared the events of her day with Paul. He was relieved more than pleased that Maren was getting established. He acknowledged that she needed some interests outside the house. "That's great," he said with enthusiasm, but was obviously distracted by the thoughts of his own day in the city. He had been in training sessions with other physicians and nurses who were joining Pediatric Possibilities. "Maybe you could call the hospital and get on the auxiliary, too."

She bristled, wondering why he suggested the hospital auxiliary. He had mentioned it previously, and she had pointed out then that they could use her income at this point in their lives. Her time might be better spent being gainfully employed, rather than joining volunteer organizations, even very worthwhile organizations. "I know volunteers are an important part of the community," she stated cautiously, "but I have a wonderful profession; or at least I had one before we decided to move back here."

Paul noticed the edge to her voice and tried to placate her. "Remember what Cora accomplished as a volunteer." Before she had gotten sick, the children's birth mother had worked for Visiting Nurse Association. That was before her husband Larry had left them. When cancer prevented her from keeping a full work schedule, Cora had volunteered. At the end, VNA staff members had taken care of Cora. The reference gave Maren an idea, something to pursue as soon as possible.

CHAPTER 2

The Labor Day weekend was packed with family get-togethers and 9-11 memorial events. The country was grief-stricken all over again, watching the videos of the previous year—reliving the awful day of death and destruction. Bob and Gloria, Paul's parents drove out from the city. They came for a cookout on Saturday and brought Bob's sister, Paul's Aunt Elizabeth. As they had promised Paul and Maren, they were searching to buy property, a condo preferably, somewhere between their children's homes. Paul's sister Penny and her husband Jim were with his folks on Saturday, but arrived for more festivities on Monday. Family interaction was one of the reasons for moving back to the Midwest, and the adults reaped the benefits, watching Penny's girls Erin and Colleen befriend cousins Danl and Zoe. Maren's son Matt didn't make it from California, but his younger brother Nick and his wife Carrie came from Champaign for the entire weekend.

The weekend's events assured Paul and Maren of the correctness of their decisions. They had enjoyed being on their own in Colorado five years ago as newlyweds, but now their situation was different. Everyone's situation was different. They weren't the only couple sensing the fragility of life and making decisions to live closer to family.

It was the following Thursday before Maren called the Visiting Nurse Association in Albright. She spoke to several individuals before reaching Sue Williston the rehab director by phone. Sue told Maren the VNA always needed speech-language pathologists. She also assured Maren she could set her own schedule and accept or decline a patient assignment based on the diagnosis, the time she had available, or the travel distance required. It sounded like a perfect way to re-enter professional life, considering her home responsibilities. She arranged to stop by the VNA facility in Albright the next morning to sign paperwork and pick up the forms used for evaluation reports and treatment notes. Maren smiled as she reviewed her accomplishments. First, the residential facility, Stanton House. Now home visits... *I'm building my own private practice, piece by piece. Paul will be surprised to learn that he gave me the idea.*

The following morning Maren kept to her newly established custom, stopping at the Village Café for coffee. Crisp, cool air, and a sky dotted with puffy white clouds brightened everyone's mood. The barometer was high; the humidity low. Long ago she would have considered it a perfect day for flying—flying in a private plane with Jack before he died and later with their friend Steve. It was the kind of day that made you believe that all was right with the world. The hum of a passing airliner caught her attention, causing her to pause at the door. *The fun of air travel has been lost. All is not well in the world.* She wondered how Steve and her friend Bonni Dailey, who both flew commercial jets, were handling the stress of being pilots. Besides being routinely searched, she knew there must be additional, secret flight deck procedures. She had talked to Bonni only once since moving back to the area. Bonni had not been flying that day, but she told Maren that many female pilots and even more flight attendants were so traumatized they never returned to work after the air disasters. Whether they had been personally involved or not, their lives had been personally impacted.

The aroma of fresh baked goods and brewing coffee filled the air inside the café and cheered Maren. Greg Carson was paying his check at the counter. After exchanging greetings with him, she settled herself by the windows. Instead of studying the trees and creek, she observed the other customers in their morning routines. One couple seated away from the windows on the wall side were obviously painters, their spattered coveralls dry but colorful.

A tall, middle-aged man with wavy brown hair sat alone at a table on the far end of the windowed wall, a plate of steaming food and a glass of water in front of him, but no coffee. White shirt and tie, no jacket. *An engineering type* Maren imagined. *Must be heading to Albright or another suburb*, she guessed; since there were not many white collar jobs in Dexum. A foursome, three men and a woman, were in a booth, talking intently. The few words she overheard indicated the topic might be politics. A heavy-set man in a suit sat at the table next to Maren's. He was focused on an open notebook.

The noise of conversations and silverware against dishes was pleasantly muted by the flowered carpet and acoustic ceiling tiles. Della poured a cup of regular coffee for Maren and started the decaf to brew. While Maren carefully sipped, the heavy-set man drank refill after refill. The caffeine seemed not to bother her as it had in the past, but she did feel exceptionally outgoing after half a cup. "The coffee is smooth here," she said to the heavy-set man. He looked up and smiled, apparently not irritated by the interruption, and open to conversation. It was a full half hour before Maren excused herself, now acquainted with a local insurance agent. She was pleased that she was beginning to know the village culture.

Sue Williston was working on a grant proposal when Maren arrived for her appointment, but the rehab director happily set aside her financial project in order to meet with a much needed speech-language pathologist. "We are always looking for SLPS," she said. "Early Intervention is always looking too. Mind if I give a friend at an agency your number?" Maren was pleased to say yes, and asked for more information about how to enter the EI system. It would balance out the geriatric population at Stanton House. She thrived on variety. The VNA formal papers were quickly signed, and Sue immediately gave Maren two assignments. The first patient's diagnosis was severe traumatic brain injury, known as TBI. Sue gave Maren a brief history of the case. A nurse was always assigned to each patient, so VNA already knew quite a bit about Patient Mercer.

"Wendy Mercer is a forty-eight year old devoted wife and mother of two, who was in a head-on car crash twenty-two months ago. Wendy suffered severe traumatic brain injury. The daughter Marlo is the primary caregiver during the day while the husband works. The married son lives in Edgelawn, has a wife and son, doesn't come around much. Wendy can answer the phone and stay by herself briefly. She's been through a lot. The family has been through even more."

Maren appreciated Sue's reference to what the *family* had suffered. She had worked with TBI patients and, like everyone, had read their stories in newspapers and had seen some documentaries on TV. The patients featured often stated that they shouldn't have survived. It was reported that the man defied all odds to recover. The motorcycle rider who had been doing seventy miles per hour on a country road when he had spun out, successfully came out of a coma. He learned to hold his head up, chew, swallow, feed himself, speak, and walk.

The media always focused on the patient's struggle to achieve each of the physical goals. Few understood or commented on the complexities of the mental comeback, the cognitive milestones necessary for a TBI patient to achieve. Almost none wrote or talked about the goals which would never be reached, and how those issues impacted the patient's relatives and friends for life. The unseen issues, issues of responsibility, judgment, problem solving, and abstract thinking sometimes tore families apart.

After stopping at the Early Intervention Agency Sue had recommended, Maren sat in her blue van and made calls to schedule patients. While a phone rang she wondered if she should have discussed her employment with Paul. *Too late now,* she thought. In the pressure of the past few months she increasingly had the sensation that they were being pulled apart. She resented the things that pulled them apart. However, her resentment often focused on Paul, rather than the events. It had only been an uneasy feeling in the first weeks after leaving the St. Francis of the Hills University Speech and Audiology clinic. She had served as assistant director with the promise to move up to being director. Someone once had told her that the antidote to desire is resentment. She didn't want to cure her desire for Paul, but... *I have to take care of myself in order to take care of our marriage.*

"Hello." Marlo Mercer the nineteen- year old who did not get to start college as scheduled because of the accident, answered the phone. She suggested Maren call her dad at work. His name was

Brad and he would probably answer the phone himself. Brad did answer. The quiet, slow, monotone voice told Maren this man was weary and had been under a lot of stress over a long period of time. The smoldering embers of her recent discussions with Paul, discussions that if louder might have been termed arguments, cooled as she focused on Brad Mercer's story.

"She was driving our daughter to a college interview when it happened. Marlo wasn't as seriously injured, but she couldn't start school. I'm hoping next fall that will work out. You should know that Wendy has a G-tube, but she's been eating table food by mouth. She doesn't have any swallowing problems, anymore. I think they'll take the tube out in the next week or so.

"She does have a fixator on her leg. If you've not seen one before, it might look like a medieval torture device. Actually, that's practically true. Her right leg was nearly severed. It's in a wire cage that encircles her leg. Wires stick right through her leg. It's supposed to promote bone growth. You'll have to get used to it. It'll be there for a while longer. Most of her ribs were shattered. The ends of several fingers and part of her one ear were torn off. There were internal injuries—and the traumatic brain injury."

Maren didn't say, "um-hm," or ask a single question. Brad had repeated the history so often he was able to do it on cruise control. Like the victims in the media stories, Wendy had been sent to multiple hospitals and rehabilitation facilities during the past twenty-two months. Brad told Maren that Wendy could speak, but not clearly. "Uh, she also has trouble with memory. She can't remember her grandson's name," he lamented. "She used to keep him while our daughter-in-law Marcy took classes. Now she doesn't even hold him. But that's not the worst." He stopped, emotion momentarily choking his voice. "The worst thing is," he confided sadly, "she never expresses any feeling. It's like he's an object."

Maren made an appointment to meet Wendy the next morning. Brad wouldn't be there, but Marlo would let her in before going to her part-time job selling cosmetics at the Albright mall. Long after Maren completed the conversation she continued wondering if Brad was saying his wife didn't express any feeling for their grandson or if he really meant she didn't express feelings for him. Maren knew that many marriages didn't survive the devastating effects of a severe traumatic brain injury.

After making two other calls, she turned the ignition key and drove from the shade of a large Maple tree into the sunlight. Optimism about the future was beginning to creep into her thoughts. She might actually be able to maintain her professional skills without going too far from Dexum. She turned on the radio to a news and weather station. Everyone checked the news more frequently nowadays, and she was no exception. The newscaster was reporting that a car bomb had been detonated in downtown Kabul, Afghanistan, killing more than thirty Afghans. Afghan President Hamid Karzai was the target of an assassination attempt, prompting him to replace his Afghan bodyguards with U.S. special forces. There were floods in India, Nepal, and Bangladesh. Maren's stomach clenched. She wondered where Paul would be sent.

At seven that evening, insurance agent Vance Davidson walked heavily through the McCloud front door. Maren had talked to him at the Village Café' several times before asking him to provide the temporary insurance the McClouds would need. He reminded Maren of a bull dog—a square head, thick neck, powerful-looking arms, a stocky body, and short legs that attached to big, clumsy feet—all of which told you nothing of his gentle, caring nature. Maren led him through the French doors into the recently organized library and introduced him to Paul. She knew Vance had a considerable coffee habit from observing the number of refills he consumed at the Village Café, so a fresh pot was ready.

Paul and Maren had given up a good benefits package when they left the university and their COBRA policy was about to expire. One of the unexpected problems they had to face as a result of their decision to join Pediatric Possibilities was that they would have no health care package for the first year. Paul received added salary to compensate, and one of Maren's resettlement tasks had been to find an insurance agent. Vance came highly recommended by Della the waitress at Village Café. He settled himself into the oversized armchair, placed his materials on the matching ottoman, and patiently explained the terms of the insurance policies until Maren and Paul were both satisfied.

They watched him work, and both were impressed at how thorough and focused he was. A strand of coarse, dark hair fell out of place across his forehead, but he seemed not to notice. He continued working with some numbers, making notes. When he finally looked up, he gave them a broad smile. "Now if you'll both just sign here, we'll be finished." He handed them a pen and several documents. While Paul read and signed, Maren poured him another cup of coffee. "How long have you been in the insurance business?" He was middle aged. She assumed it was his life's work.

"Oh, going on four years now," he replied mildly. "I was a pastor until then."

"A Pastor! That's quite a change isn't it?"

"Well, it's taking care of folks in a different way. Sometimes I think I do more real pastoring without all the administrative

21

business of running a church. And the best part is," he added with another wide smile, "I get weekends off."

Vance and Laurie had raised four children in parsonages and only recently bought their first home in Dexum. Maren sensed a fatherly quality about the man. She could tell Paul was drawn to him, too. They didn't yet have a church, and thought he might know one to recommend. Paul's family was Catholic, his uncle a retired Maryknoll priest. Although Maren had been raised in the Catholic Church, she had joined an Episcopal church when she married Jack. She couldn't go back to Catholicism, but she couldn't ask Paul to abandon his church, either. They hadn't yet worked out the spiritual aspect of raising two children. "But you are still an ordained minister, aren't you?" He affirmed that he was and that he sometimes filled a pulpit on a Sunday morning. "In fact I'll be at First Methodist in the Village next Sunday. It's the oldest church in town... still has the original bell in the steeple. I'd be glad to see you there." They promised to visit the church, sometime.

"He can't be sixty years old," she said to Paul after Vance left. "I wonder why he retired from the ministry."

"You should have asked," Paul answered logically, smiling at his wife's intuition and curiosity. "But having failed to do the obvious, I am confident you will find out by other means." He put his arm around her and pulled her playfully onto his lap in the big arm chair, just as Danl came through the French doors. Danl stopped abruptly, embarrassed to be interrupting their snuggling. "Matt's on the phone," he said. "He wants to know when Homecoming Weekend will be."

Maren and Paul celebrated their anniversary each year—not necessarily on the exact date—but sometime in October, by hosting a gathering of as many family members as could attend for the entire weekend. Matt the older son made it a priority. His younger brother Nick had married his college sweetheart right after graduation, and neither of them would consider missing the celebration of one of the most significant days in their lives. Paul's sister Penny who had waited so long for Paul to marry, was thrilled that they could easily attend the Dexum gathering this year and that her daughters could grow up with cousins Zoe and Danl. Paul's parents enjoyed any opportunity to interact with their six grandchildren, but they were also active in numerous volunteer organizations. They needed to decide on a weekend, soon.

The last few years the celebration had been at the McCloud family home west of Denver where there were twice as many bedrooms as the house on Crescent Avenue. The good news this year was that Paul's parents, Aunt Elizabeth, and Penny and Jim's family lived close enough to come for just one day. Matt and Nick would need to arrange for longer visits. If Matt was already asking about the date, Maren and Paul needed to shift into high gear. At least the planning would give them something to focus on other than terrorism and Paul's departure day.

Paul flew to London the next day for more orientation and to meet members of the Board of Directors. He would be gone no longer than for an average medical conference, but still Maren felt deserted. She was comforted when her sister Ruth called from Maryland. Ruth's husband Calvin was a founding member of Possibilities. She gave Maren more information about what Paul's travel schedule would be like, and assured Maren the doctors were given ample time off. No one could say where Paul would be sent, possibly it would be with Calvin to Central America. "You'll get used to it Maren. They are perfectly safe. Soon you'll want to go with him." Maren was not convinced. She clung to every newscast, as if she could figure out their future from the bleak stories. Fortunately, her first home visit provided a much needed distraction.

Wendy Mercer seemed eager to tell Maren as many of the facts of the crash as she had been able to absorb from others telling her. "As I drove east at fifty-five miles an hour in our Chevy, the driver of a blue, panel truck was coming west toward the setting sun. He was in a hurry, going at least seventy. He accelerated to pass a car in front of him and crossed a double yellow line. I saw him coming, but he didn't see me. I braked as hard as I could and tried to get off the road. But he swerved too, and we hit head on." It was highly unlikely that Wendy actually remembered anything of the accident. Others had repeated the story so often she thought the memories were her own. Her speech was slow, but not slurred. No sign of the muscle in-coordination called dysarthria. The woman's recitation was intelligible, but as devoid of feelings as if she had been giving Maren a recipe.

Wendy's external beauty hadn't been touched really. Some tiny scars on her face belied the extent of her injuries. You had to know to look for the shortened fingers and misshapen ear that her blond hair loosely covered. She was thin. She had probably lost considerable weight during her recovery. Brad had been right about the fixator on her leg. Maren squirmed in discomfort just looking at the wires protruding through the woman's leg, but Wendy seemed oblivious. *Amazing what the human body can learn to endure.* "The metal of the car's hood folded almost to the steering wheel," Wendy was saying. "I saw the pictures later. My head broke the steering wheel and smashed into the dashboard…"

…*shattering the lives of the Mercer family,* thought Maren sadly. In such an injury she knew there is what is called a coup and counter-coup effect. Wendy's brain crashed into the front of her skull on impact, and then boomeranged to crash against the back of her skull. Unlike a stroke which usually affects a limited area of the brain that is briefly starved for oxygen, a traumatic brain injury sheers and tears tissue throughout the brain. Many cells die, taking with them knowledge, skills, memories, abilities, and sometimes personality. The swelling in Wendy's brain had been severe. Coma had been immediate and lengthy, guaranteeing an extensive rehabilitation process.

Maren allowed Wendy to continue talking about the collision and her family for several reasons. She was establishing rapport, making informal judgments about the woman's language skills and cognitive status; and she was curious. The small living room held only the couch Wendy was occupying, a coffee table where she rested her right leg with its heavy "cage" and two worn side chairs at opposite ends of the couch. Wendy's wheelchair sat in the corner of the room on the thin, drab area rug. This was not a wealthy family, and what resources they had were likely being drained due to rehabilitation expenses. Insurance wouldn't cover it all.

Maren went to the chair farthest from where she had been standing and sat down. She was watching to see if Wendy would turn left, toward her, or would continue looking to the right. Being unaware of one side of the body, a symptom called "neglect" was common in brain injured patients. Wendy did turn, after a short delay. It was a relief that there seemed to be no violent tendencies, although she may have had some of that earlier in her recovery. For all Wendy had suffered she was considered a high-functioning patient.

Maren administered a brain injury test to establish baseline functioning and help determine appropriate goals for her patient.

She found that Wendy had a visual cut of some kind. She saw parts of everything, but not the whole of anything. This primarily affected her attempts to read. She also needed new corrective lenses, but couldn't get out of the house for an eye exam.

Maren's evaluation revealed that the woman who had been the manager of the household and director of every facet of family life, now had weak problem solving skills and poor emotional comprehension. She needed cues to correctly sequence steps of a simple task like fixing a can of soup. She could dress herself without help, but that was only since spring. She would have significant trouble resuming her place in the life of her family any time soon. When Wendy began showing signs of fatigue during the mental tasks, Maren noticed she slipped into very concrete thinking. Wendy did know that "raining cats and dogs" actually meant very heavy rain, but she missed nuances of language and talked about family members without any affection. The evaluation confirmed what Brad had told her—Wendy had little capacity for emotion. Yet, she seemed happy. Maren assumed she was on anti-depressant medication.

Sitting in the van to wait out a rain shower, Maren called Paul's sister. After arranging a time for Penny to bring Colleen and Erin for a play date with Zoe and Danl, Maren broached the subject of "Homecoming Weekend."

"Nick and Carrie can get away any weekend, how about you and your parents?"

"We're all available any weekend except Halloween," Penny assured Maren. They arranged the anniversary celebration for the second weekend of October the eleventh through thirteenth, because Paul would be leaving the country—Haiti or India they thought—for four weeks right after that.

By the end of the week Maren had evaluated four patients for VNA and two for Early Intervention. Her neck and shoulders ached. Was it from tension, the damp weather, responsibility? She wasn't sure. *Paul, where are you.* She hadn't heard from him for several days. *I miss your fingers on my neck and back. I miss the sound of your voice, tripping over your big shoes in the hallway, and your wise-cracks.* Paul could always brighten her mood. He reminded her to take a break, lighten up, and laugh. He wasn't due home until Saturday, and she knew he might not be himself at first. He was likely to be tired, humorless, and pre-occupied until he recovered from jet lag and re-entered the quiet, relaxed atmosphere of Dexum.

After reading bedtime stories and praying with each of the children, Maren tucked them in bed. She realized that although the evening had been delightful, she had exhausted her day's supply of energy and patience. She had talked with the children during breakfast and played games with them after dinner. *Nothing like the exuberance of children to give one a smile,* she reflected. Maren had kept too busy during the day to be truly lonely, but tonight was more difficult. Supervising the children, working with patients, running the house, and maintaining communication with family and friends without Paul's presence was bound to take its toll. In her marriage to Jack it had been assumed she would be the primary care taker of the boys, but Jack was home every night. He kept the cabinets stocked, paid the bills, balanced the checkbook. He took charge of the boys only when Maren was overwhelmed. In contrast, Paul tried to truly co-parent when he was home. Maren now missed what she never had while raising her first two children. She was sure she should have more energy and good humor in Paul's absence and didn't think she could blame it on the stress of the move.

Why does everything seem so hard? Maybe I'm just getting old. She felt irritable, tense, and...decidedly vulnerable. She had tried to tell Paul about her feelings over the phone the night he had arrived in London, but he didn't get it. "You'll get through this," he had encouraged her, thinking she was having a rough time trying to make new friends in the small community. "Take a day off. Meet Bonni. Go shopping in Albright," he suggested; as if Bonni, now a captain flying jumbo jets, was readily available. Her old friends in Edgelawn had moved on with life when the McClouds had moved to Colorado. They all had full-time jobs and busy social lives. And they were couples.

In any case, there didn't seem to be enough time to get away. She was always doing something, and they were mostly things she enjoyed. She just needed a little more... a little more of what she wasn't sure... *sleep, maybe?* She just never felt quite satisfied. She put on some CD's, lit a fire in the fireplace, and made hot chocolate the old fashioned way, with cocoa powder. She sat with her slippered feet propped up in Paul's newly re-covered wing-back lounge chair. She recalled their dating days in the city, when she had been a graduate student and he was an otolaryngology intern. Their dates had been discreet, secretive in fact. That had made it all the more romantic. She had resisted falling in love with him. After all, she was a decade older than Paul. He had been so patient, so persistent, so sure they were meant to be together. She had admired him, idolized him.

She slurped the whipped cream from the top of her mug, stared into the flames, and found herself focusing on her encounter with Brad Mercer earlier in the day. The autumn rain had let up just as she had finished working with Wendy. An optometrist from Albright had made a home visit after Maren's initial recommendation. He had the glasses made in his office, and personally delivered them while Maren was there. Wendy had been a voracious reader prior to the injury. Maren was hopeful she could help Wendy experience emotional content through fiction and journaling. After the session, Maren had packed up her materials in the wheeled case she now carried to home visits and pulled it down the driveway.

She had been sliding the bag into the back of her van when Brad Mercer arrived. The case was heavy with evaluation instruments and therapy materials, and as she struggled with it she heard him behind her. "Hi there, are you moving in, or out?" She wasn't sure if he recognized her. She had recognized him, even though they had never met.

"You're the speech therapist," he had said, revealing that he did keep track of Wendy's appointments. He stared at her for a moment. "I feel like we've met."

"Not met, but I see you at the Village Café." He was the tall engineer type in a white shirt and tie who often started his day with a hot breakfast.

"You eat there?"

"I coffee there. I've seen you having breakfast, though. How do you have time…" She had stopped momentarily, choosing her next words carefully, not wanting to induce guilt over his solo breakfasts. "I'm amazed that you can be a stand-in mom, your wife's caregiver, the house manager, a dependable employee, and still find the time for a relaxed breakfast on weekdays."

Brad had put one foot on the brick planter that surrounded a lovely White Birch tree. Ignoring its occasional drips from the recent rain, he leaned toward her, letting his shoulders droop a bit and rested his arms on his bent knee. He was a tall, lean, quiet-spoken man, with a control to his voice that she had learned to associate with pent-up tension. Had she been the betting type, she would have put up considerable money that he had high blood pressure.

He had obviously wanted to wind down rather than rush inside the house. It had felt good to Maren too, standing by the dripping tree and breathing in the cool, rain-cleaned air, instead of hurrying into the stuffy van. She had expected him to ask how his wife was doing in therapy. Instead, he had engaged her in chit-chat, seemingly as hungry for conversation as she was. She had reminded him how important it is for the caregiver to take care of himself. That's when he admitted he had recently started medication for high blood pressure. It was still more common for women to be primary care-givers for children while caring for sick or aging relatives—to be the ones to hold down a full time job and even juggle a social life on the side. It seemed to be more difficult for a man. She wasn't tempted to criticize. Not many men or women had been through the devastation of living with the needs of a spouse who had sustained traumatic brain injury.

"The truth is the house is barely held together. There are a variety of caregivers, and I've taken so much time off work the past two years it's a wonder I have a job. I'll grant you being mother and father is a tall order, and I'm often overwhelmed. I just can't keep going unless I have some islands of peace." She had nodded her understanding.

"Is this your last visit for the day?" he had asked. It was. "It would be good to have a twilight round of golf." Was it an invitation? She didn't think so. She had not revealed that she used to play. Instead, she had looked silently to the sky, which had appeared to have yet more water to deposit on the landscape. "Golf is another one of my escapes," he had said with a sigh, looking up and acknowledging the dark clouds overhead with a wrinkled smile, "but not tonight." She had wondered when he had last played, and he had answered her unasked question. "It's been over two years since I had time for a game, so my peaceful island is breakfast at the Village Café two or three times a week." A drop of moisture had rolled off a leaf of the Birch and become trapped in the curve of his brown hair, but he hadn't noticed. They had chatted on, sharing stories about their children. A new rain shower had ended their break from obligations.

Maren sipped her hot chocolate now, realizing that what she didn't have enough of was male companionship. She hadn't told Brad anything about the fact that she played golf or anything about Paul. She hadn't shared that she was recently spending a lot of time alone or that she had needed the conversation with him as much as he seemed to need the chat with her. Her problems seemed puny next to his. He wasn't able to get outside his own concerns to inquire about her life. *Just as well,* she thought now. *I don't need that kind of complication in my life.*

Maren always made a conscious effort to share a bit of personal information with patients and their families, but she did not routinely trade stories. She was friendly, but she was there as a professional, not a neighbor. She asked herself now where *she* might find islands of peace. She lifted and dropped her shoulders releasing tension, rolled her head forward, and rubbed the back of her aching neck with her fingertips. She wondered where Paul was and if he ever felt vulnerable. She was stopped from her journey to self-pity by the ringing of her phone.

CHAPTER 3

Paul had spent the week in London and was feeling decidedly invulnerable. In fact he was charged with excitement. His day had been filled with meetings with doctors and administrators who were the nucleus of Pediatric Possibilities International. When he left the restaurant after a late dinner, the drizzle had stopped, and he had enjoyed walking under a starry sky back to his apartment. He understood now that he would be spending more time in London than he had initially realized. He had been told that the central headquarters for the agency would continue to be Washington, DC; but when Doctors Beverly Skelton and John Westlake assumed more leadership, things had changed. London would be the main office, with smaller offices in D.C. and Chicago.

John had explained over dinner that Bev brought major backers for the organization who weren't interested if there wasn't a central connection in England. Bev also had connections in India that would smooth the way for Paul's first assignment. Bev knew everyone, was excited about getting the project off the ground, and offered to go along to India in October to show Paul the ropes.

Soon there would be connections in other countries. Calvin and others from D.C. and John and Bev in Europe were already starting to establish the necessary networks. Things couldn't be going better, Paul told himself. Expansion was on the horizon. He wanted to share the news with Maren, but it was late. He leaned against the stone fence, enjoying the imagined fragrance of the fall flowers inside. It was a tiny garden, not far from his inn. Studying the night sky he tried to imagine the feel of Maren in his arms. He decided against making the call. The six hour time difference meant she was probably meeting the school bus. He'd be home on Saturday. That was soon enough. Once again something nagged at the back of his thoughts, but he couldn't quite frame it. He continued his walk to his flat and was sound asleep when Maren answered her phone.

"Mom, are the kids in bed? Can you talk?" It was Matt calling from California. Pushing the lounger back to a deeper recline, hoping for a warm conversation with her oldest son, she assured him it was a great time. "I have news. I have met, really re-met the most incredible woman. She majored in double E at UCLA. She's the daughter of a friend of Paul's Uncle Mike and Aunt Cloris. She used to hang out with Mike and Cloris and their kids. That's when I first met her, the last year I was in school out here. But in the past few years, while I was in Wisconsin, she really matured a lot. She surfs and sails, and she's taking lessons in deep sea diving. She's an award-winning markswoman, too. In her spare time she sings with a group at a coffee house near here. She never had to study. She's just naturally brilliant."

"Wow, that is amazing," Maren managed, scolding herself silently for taking an immediate dislike to the woman who had her oldest son's heart in her hands. "We'll have to meet her sometime. Does she have a name?"

"Her name is Sydney Webster, and I called to see if it's OK to bring her for Homecoming Weekend." Maren heard something or someone in the background and had the distinct impression that the object of Matt's adulation was right there with him. When Maren hesitated he went on. "I know we've always said Homecoming is just for family, but Nick will have Carrie there. Sydney is, well practically..."

Maren was now sure she heard a giggle. She interrupted before he finished saying what Sydney practically was. "Carrie is Nick's wife, Matt." Sensing that this might be a crucial decision, she immediately backpedaled. "Of course any close friend of yours is always welcome." She knew it had been lonely for Matt since Nick married. Instead of gaining a sister, he seemed to feel he had lost his brother. He often lamented that he and Nick didn't get to have any grand adventures after college. He thought Carrie was the reason. Once, he had told Maren he thought he would have to have a wife in order to reestablish his relationship with Nick. Maren believed the problem existed entirely in Matt's mind. Carrie had done nothing to jeopardize their relationship. Maren promised to get back to Matt, and they ended the call as they always did with, "I love you." She thought about calling Paul, but it was the wee hours of the morning in London. It could wait until Saturday.

In the morning, Maren decided to take a short walk between the time the school bus left and her regular stop for coffee. Crescent Avenue was a loop. It branched off Maple Grove Drive, hosted two dozen homes, and led right back onto Maple Grove. One end of Maple Grove led to the village. The other became a county road. She walked away from the village where there was no sidewalk, just the blacktop surface. She felt her calf muscles stretch to accommodate the substantial angle of the hill. Out of the corner of her eye she noticed a slight movement and turned to see a brown leaf flutter to the ground. *Just the dryness,* she told herself, but she knew fall was sneaking into Dexum. She usually enjoyed what she considered the most beautiful season of the year, but in her mind denying fall now delayed thoughts of winter. This year she was not looking forward to cold, dark, lonely days. Just ahead an elderly Cottonwood had dropped a small circle of brown leaves. *They're always the first to go,* she consoled herself. But when she looked up to search other trees she was confronted with more brown leaves awaiting a breeze strong enough to extricate them from their branches.

Peaceful though, she thought for probably the thousandth time since their move. *Dexum is so peaceful.* Suddenly, contradicting her thought, she sensed more than heard something rushing toward her; and immediately a large Chow dog with a panting, purple tongue bounded down a grassy hill and onto the road. Tail curled quietly, not wagging, it approached. She stood still with the backs of her hands turned out for him to sniff. "Hi there," she said as calmly as possible. She wasn't sure what he had in mind until he brushed his ample girth against her, demanding affection. She accommodated his desire by scratching behind his perky ears and on his furry chest. When she tried to resume her walk her new canine friend trotted along beside her.

"Chauncey, you get back in your yard," called a female voice. In the clearing of the trees and on a grassy hill some distance from the road, Maren noticed a white cottage with a red roof. Noreen Anderson the nurse from Stanton House was hurrying down the hill toward her. "Oh hi! Gosh I'm sorry about Chauncey. He's overly friendly." Maren assured her she welcomed the dog's attention.

Noreen attached a leash to Chauncey's collar while she talked. "I was planning to call you when I got to work. Doctor Wagner, one of the older family practice docs, ordered a bedside swallow evaluation for a very ill resident and there's also a twenty-one year old woman I'm getting an order for you to see. She had oral cancer and during her treatment was in an automobile accident." Maren agreed to stop later in the day. *It's so efficient to live in a village,* she decided. She retraced her steps to her driveway, actually smiling. Before backing the silver blue minivan out of the garage, she checked her voicemail. The Early Intervention Agency in Albright wanted to know if she could make some extra home visits for them the following week while another therapist was out of town.

Sue Williston had left a lengthy message saying she had another patient to add to Maren's caseload, but it wouldn't be through VNA. George Sapien was a middle aged man with what she referred to as a "complicated history." He was not homebound and didn't qualify for home health services, but his wife had called VNA for a recommendation of a therapist. Finances were not an issue. Sue wondered if Maren might be interested in taking on a private client. *What a good idea,* Maren thought as she returned the call.

Coffee time will be short today, she told herself as she parked in the Village Café lot. There was a longer list of patients than previously. Penny was arriving at four with the girls, and there was cooking and baking she had promised to do with the children, in preparation for Paul's return. Fortunately, Della had learned to expect Maren, so the decaf was ready. Brad Mercer had probably been there and gone, but the intense political foursome sat in their regular booth with some kind of papers spread between their plates and mugs. Two of the painters were there, too. Maren wondered if they were father and daughter or husband and wife. They both kept their caps on, so it was difficult to get a good read on their faces. *No time for people games Maren,* she told herself as she opened her notebook to plan her route and list activities for each patient.

Maren didn't take time for lunch, and it was after noon when she rang the doorbell of the Sapien's enormous two-story home. A tall thin man leaning on a three-legged cane answered the door. His equally lean wife Alice was right behind him. He lumbered awkwardly to a sturdy armchair and fell, more than sat, in it. His thick salt and pepper hair and trim mustache made him look distinguished, even after the stroke and various medical crises. He looked slightly confused, but nodded his head as if agreeing with what was being said. Alice recited his medical history. Her dark hair brushed her shoulders when she turned to give him a reassuring look. Bright red lipstick didn't look outdated on her. It emphasized her warm smile.

Maren heard a child's voice in the house and learned that one of the Sapien's married daughters, along with her husband and three-year old daughter, lived with them. She also discovered that Alice was one very well-informed and devoted wife. "George was a professional baseball player. When he retired he invested in the purchase of golf courses. He loves sports," Alice told Maren. "His stroke was an AVM," she went on, demonstrating her in-depth knowledge of her husband's medical issues. This abbreviation told Maren that his stroke had been the result of an arteriovenous malformation, a tangle of arteries and veins in his brain—an aberration he had carried since before he was born. It had ruptured when he was fifty years old. "He bought and sold golf courses all over the world and routinely gave motivational presentations to large groups of sports enthusiasts. He is a very well-known and popular man in athletic circles."

"What are you looking for at this time, speech, language, or swallowing therapy? Remember, language is what you say. Speech is the way you say it."

"Everything. We want everything. No one can understand much of what he says. Mostly we know because he gestures. I've been trying to help him; but I need a new perspective, someone to guide me. If it had just been the stroke it would have been bad enough, but he was on a ventilator for several weeks. He had a trach after that."

Maren made more written notes. Several weeks on a ventilator meant a lengthy recovery. She started through the evaluation process, with substantial help from Alice. "Does he speak English or is he trying to use another language," Maren asked while trying to make a judgment on his respiration for speech. *Mostly chest breathing*, she noted. His voice was deep in his throat. He seemed to be exerting effort, maybe pushing air against the recently healed stoma during speech attempts. His resonance sounded like the "before" in an ad for decongestants. Articulation was uncoordinated, slurred and imprecise, as she would expect to hear with dysarthria. Usually in such cases other deficits would surface once intelligibility improved. An old saying came to mind as she listened to him—*a light in the window, but no one is home.* She wondered if George was cognitively intact.

"Just English," Alice answered, not realizing that Maren was hoping he was trying to converse in another language. Then Alice added a very important fact. "He's been working on his computer lately, and he can type most anything." New hope pushed the old saying from Maren's thoughts. She listened to the couple, trying to get a feel for the trauma the Sapiens had suffered during the past year, while making decisions about how to begin the therapy process. Paul always said to address what meets the eye first, or in this case what met Maren's ear. His speech was degraded at every level of production—respiration, phonation, articulation, and resonance.

"Dysarthria," she repeated at Alice's request, while George listened intently. "Dysarthria is a speech disorder that results from an injury in the brain." Well-informed Alice expressed surprise that she had never heard this term before. She wanted to know all about the new diagnosis and the proposed therapy. She was eager to help him do whatever exercises Maren recommended.

When she was finished Maren walked heavily to her car, burdened by the reality of what Sue Williston had warned her was a complicated medical history. She turned back to look at the couple standing in their doorway, full of new hope. *They're like two individuals who have been to the gate of hell,* she thought. *Hopefully, now they're on their way back.* She drove toward the Mercer home on the other side of town, already planning therapy for George.

She knocked and rang the bell several times. Finally, Wendy called for to come in. Marlo had helped her dress and get to the couch, but had already left for work. Maren noticed bloodshot eyes and tear stains on Wendy's face. Something had obviously happened since Maren's previous visit. "I was in the hospital overnight," Wendy explained. They took out the G-tube and adjusted the fixator. *Pain, she's in considerable pain this afternoon.* Maren abandoned her plan to get Wendy into her wheelchair and up to the dining room table. It took only a few questions to understand that as soon as the pain began to resolve, the fixator was always adjusted. That caused increased pain. "It was infected twice," Wendy told her. "That was really awful." When Maren asked her for today's date, Wendy got the year wrong. Sadly, Maren realized her goals for today would have to be reduced. Pain could significantly restrict memory and concentration ability. None the less, Maren pulled the new notebook she had purchased out of her case and began showing Wendy how to organize her life.

They started with the Mercer family calendar that chronicled Wendy's appointments. This book was to be Wendy's personal schedule. It would give her ownership, responsibility, and hopefully control. Next, they made a page for family names. Pictures provided by Marlo were stacked on the table, thanks to a phone conversation with Brad. Maren encouraged Wendy to talk about Billy her only grandchild, but didn't get much response until Maren shared about her family.

"Paul and I met Danl and Zoe the first week we were in Denver. Their mom Cora brought them to the clinic with ear infections. Paul saw them and wanted to be sure speech development was at age level, so I saw them too. Their dad had already disappeared by the time we met them, and it was only a few weeks later that Cora's cancer was diagnosed. She came to the hospital for treatments, and we volunteered to watch the children when she needed help. They were not quite two and four. Zoe was still in diapers."

"Doesn't it seem like they're your grandchildren," Wendy asked flatly. She looked intently at the wallet photos Maren carried, unaware that she was insinuating Maren looked like the children's grandmother. "Not really," Maren answered, taking no offense. "Paul and I were newly married, and I wanted him to have children of his own." She didn't talk about her older sons or mention that she was no longer able to have children. Wendy didn't think to ask for details. Maren had been sure from the start that any man who wanted a pediatric practice needed to have children of his own. She didn't want him to regret marrying her and had thoughts of adoption in mind before they had said, "I do."

"They are cute. Billy is cute too, but…" Wendy winced in pain.

"It's hard to be cheerful and playful with a little one when you're hurting, isn't it?"

The hour went by quickly. Wendy did some word matching, a pre-reading exercise, and had warmed to the idea of grandchildren. Not as much progress as Maren had hoped would be achieved, but she was learning to make modest goals for home health patients.

The last home patient of the day did not answer the door. A call to the VNA office confirmed that the woman had gone to a medical appointment. Speech-language therapy in the field didn't seem to be as predictable as in other work settings. *Now I have time on my hands.* Her car steered its way to the Village Café where the coffee crowd had left and the dinner group had not yet arrived.

CHAPTER 4

Della greeted Maren with her always ready smile. "Decaf or are you ready for afternoon tea? We're famous for our brewed iced tea." There was only one other customer in the café, but he was at Maren's favorite table nursing a cup of coffee. "Come sit over here," Della said, "I'll join you for a glass." Maren was surprised but grateful for the invitation and sat at the table Della indicated, near the kitchen. "Hank's retired. He'll be here working his crossword puzzles and reading for an hour. I just gave him his own coffee pot and a stack of creams. He's happy as a clam."

Della brought two filled glasses and sat across from Maren, grateful for an opportunity to get better acquainted with Dexum's newest home owner. "I didn't mean to eavesdrop, but I did overhear you talking to Vance Davidson and Doctor Carson. How do you and your family like village life so far?"

"We all think it's great. It's just that Paul isn't here much. But that's why we moved back to Illinois, to be close to family when he's away." Before she realized it, Maren had explained about Pediatric Possibilities, her failed attempts to find work in the schools, and her present employment for VNA, Early Intervention, and Stanton House.

"And you have kids," Della said, encouraging Maren to continue.

"I was widowed and have two grown sons. Paul and I adopted Zoe and Danl. While we were in Denver my oldest son Matt finished his graduate degree in Biomedical Engineering and took a sales job for a prosthetics company in California. Paul's aunt lives there with her family, so I'm glad he's settled and has some relatives nearby." The shadow of Matt's new love would not be shared with strangers, not even strangers as friendly as Della Mason.

"Nick married his college sweetheart right after graduation. They're both in their last year of grad school now." Della said she had only one son, presently unmarried, and she was yearning for grandchildren. She poured more tea in their glasses and pressed Maren to talk about the youngest McClouds.

"Danl, spelled D-a-n-l will be nine in October, and Zoe is seven. We adopted them at their birth mom's request before she died. Their dad deserted them. Cora figured he left to escape responsibility and the reality that he wasn't prepared to support them. Cora and Larry fell madly, passionately in love one summer when she was teaching music in a summer program on the reservation in Wyoming. He was living there at the time. They moved into a cabin he built in the hills west of Denver and started a family. He insisted on giving the children names with only letters that were pronounced, since his spelling wasn't the best. He seemed to love the children, but had no idea how to be a husband and father. No role models I guess. He showed less interest in them as he became involved in activities back in Wyoming."

Maren and Paul suspected Larry had become addicted to alcohol or drugs, but she didn't reveal that. "Cora's part-time work turned into full time employment, and she never saw him again. Zoe was almost two and Danl nearly four when we moved to Denver. Cora took them to the hospital's free clinic where Paul volunteered. They had been sick quite a bit. Paul placed tubes in Zoe's ears and took out Danl's tonsils and adenoids. On a re-check visit Paul commented on Cora's deep voice. She sounded more hoarse each time he saw her. As Paul had feared, it was cancer. Cora had no one to care for the children during her treatments, so Paul brought them home during her first hospital stay. Many times when Cora was simply too tired to think about the children, I would take them home with me. In return Cora would invite us up to her cabin for a meal and a violin concert when she was able to play. She was very talented.

"The five of us had some good times together, but the cancer had sent seeds to her brain and liver. By the time she died she had legal papers drawn up for us to adopt the children. Larry was presumed dead after all efforts to find him failed, and I think Cora was relieved. Her only relative was her dad in Arizona. He was in an assisted living facility there and they had been estranged since Cora married. She knew the children would be well cared for with us and insisted that we legally change their names to McCloud. She wasn't aware of any relatives on Larry's side, but wanted to be sure nothing would ever threaten their security."

Maren stopped talking and took a swig of tea, reminiscing. The adoption had actually taken place before Cora died. For Danl and Zoe it was a pretty smooth transition, although she remembered once in the first few weeks at the dinner table Zoe had asked, "May I have my mommy, please, " as if she were asking for some food.

"Got any pictures?" Della asked. Maren pulled two snapshots from her wallet.

"Zoe's serious and looks more like Larry." Her Native American features were subtle; Danl seemed to have none. "Danl's a tow-headed, wiry ball of energy like his mom."

"How are they doing now with a new house and school?"

"Great. I was worried that the move would stir up old anxieties, but they've adapted very well." Maren and Paul were aware of the strong bond between the siblings. Maybe their traumatic early years created it. Maren felt each would always be a comfort to the other. "I haven't had a parent-teacher conference yet, but I understand they have great teachers who are married to each other—Lois and Richard Smith. Do you know them?"

Della assured Maren the Smiths were excellent teachers of outstanding character. "It's a good thing Danl has Richard this year. Next year he'll be principal at the grade school." Suddenly, Maren felt a twinge of guilt. She may have revealed more about her children's background than she should have. In the West many children had a Native American heritage. She now realized some individuals in the Midwest might have difficulty accepting their mixed culture. "Paul and I are open about the children's background, but some people, or even their classmates, might be narrow-minded or cruel. I hope you won't…."

"Don't worry, if anyone finds out I'll know you told them." She waved off Maren's money. "Consider the tea my welcome wagon gift." Maren felt relaxed and refreshed as she drove to Stanton House. *Della Mason is one unusual waitress. Next time we have a chance to talk I must find out more about her.*

Maren made a practice of leaving the van's radio set to her favorite news station. There was always some news of the War on Terror. It was almost a year since the anthrax attacks, but the day's news carried a related story. An epidemiologist at the Centers for Disease Control who had investigated the anthrax attacks last fall was being interviewed. "As first responders and animal disease experts, veterinarians are essential to the national Centers for Disease Control and Prevention's bioterrorism preparedness initiatives," the expert stated. Maren parked at Stanton House and got out of the van before the story was completed. *I can't wait to hear what Greg Carson has to say about this.* She hurried to the nurses' station.

"Have you seen your patient yet," the certified nurse's assistant asked.

"No, my note just says he's a sixty-three year old with resolving pneumonia and that he needs a bedside swallow evaluation prior to being sent to the hospital for a video swallow study. Can you tell me his name?"

"Harvey Eichelman, but the resolving part is questionable. You're going to need a lot of help getting him up." Maren glanced at the medical diagnosis in the chart, left the evaluation forms on the counter, and followed Terry the CNA to the end of the hall.

"Harvey," Terry shouted, "Wake up." Turning to Maren she stated that she would go to get more help to move him.

Now it was Maren's turn. "Harvey, wake up." The form beneath the sheet was curled, only his head visible. She looked at the grizzled, unshaven face, closed eyes, dry, cracked lips, and matted hair. *This isn't the pediatric clinic at St Francis of the Hills, Maren.*

For a moment she thought she had seen him someplace before. A scene flashed through her mind… a sidewalk, a doorway, an empty whiskey bottle, and a man in rumpled clothes sleeping, or rather passed out. It could have been Harvey or a brother in the bottle. She had been in San Antonio for a conference, walking to the convention center by herself. She had turned a corner, and there he was. She had hurried on, just like the Pharisee in the Good Samaritan story. Only today she couldn't hurry past. She was supposed to evaluate this man's swallow function. The referral note indicated she was expected to recommend Harvey be transported to the radiology department in the Albright Community Hospital for a video swallow study.

She pulled down the sheet to reveal a withered body, knees drawn up, and arms and hands that were useless appendages due to muscle contractures. She chided herself for her revulsion. *What could Doctor Wagner have been thinking? Here's a man whose diet already has been reduced to puree and thickened liquids. He's only eaten that on the few occasions when he was awake. There's no option left but to go to a G-tube. Surely he wouldn't order a G-tube to prolong the life of a basically unresponsive patient who, according to the chart, was in the last stages of alcohol induced dementia.* She had seen DNR by his name, specific instructions not to resuscitate him.

At the sink, Maren soaked a washcloth in cold water and returned to the bed. Terry entered and read Maren's facial expression. "The family left orders to place no feeding tube of any kind," she volunteered. Maren began to wipe Howard's face with the wash cloth while repeatedly calling his name. She was establishing that she had attempted to wake him. "I can't complete a bedside swallow evaluation, and I can't recommend a video fluoroscopic swallow study. He's just not a candidate." Terry nodded, relieved to have the new speech language pathologist agree with her appraisal of the situation.

"The family could use some support," Terry said over her shoulder as she left the room. Maren pulled the sheet up to Harvey's neck. *There is nothing I can do here. What caused his life to be so devoid of hope that he literally destroyed himself with alcohol.* Still, he had family who evidently cared enough to help him die peacefully; and they needed her recommendations.

She sat at the counter at the nurses' station and wrote on plain, lined note sheets; because the facility had no official forms for speech-language pathology services. "Assessment: Patient was not responsive and by report of the CNA is rarely awake. He is not a candidate for a swallow evaluation or a video swallow study at this time. Recommendations: Offer pureed food and honey thick liquids as tolerated. Hospice care would be helpful for patient and family. Please provide educational support/counseling for family members."

There was no tab in the chart neatly labeled "Speech Therapy" as she was used to in hospitals. She realized someone was reading over her shoulder and looked up to find Noreen. "Welcome to the end of the road," she said sadly. "Just file it under Miscellaneous. We all know to look there for special services like speech. Thanks for documenting the recommendations."

Maren began to gather her bag to leave, but Noreen reminded her there was another patient. "Go down to the day room at the end of B wing. I'll send Ronnie to you." Maren took her notebook and walked to a room that doubled as a family gathering area and staff meeting room. She went in alone, sat at the round oak table in the bright room, wrote the date on her note sheet, and looked around. One wall was covered with a mural of Boston ivy climbing a white lattice. Another wall was mostly windows, facing south. The multipurpose room had now become a speech-language therapy office.

Ronnie Cameron pushed through the weight of the self-closing wood door by leaning a shoulder into it. Her hands gripped a gray metal walker. The woman didn't look more than twenty. The sight of such a young woman hobbling across the room with a walker took Maren by surprise. "Hello," she said, and introduced herself. Ronnie seated herself on the ladder back chair across the table from Maren and started talking. "My name is Ronnie Cameron. If you're surprised I'm not a guy, I understand. My mom named me Veronica, but no one ever called me that. So, when I turned eighteen I had it legally changed. It confuses people sometimes."

She continued without any encouragement, perhaps out of nervousness. "I'm one of the few public aid patients Stanton House takes. Because of the cancer, half my tongue was removed. Oral cancer runs in my family. I have a G-tube and I haven't eaten a meal by mouth in over two years. I was finishing radiation when the car accident happened. That crushed my leg and damaged the G-tube. Dr. Kalevic in Albright told me there is no hope of my ever eating again, but for some reason he suggested I have a speech and swallowing evaluation. He said it was my last chance. *You* are my last chance."

Maren felt a weight settle on her chest. Logically, rationally, Maren knew that patients learned to accept their losses, and that meant giving up hope that they would return to some former state. They came to accept the new person they had become. With an older patient that was easier somehow. Hearing now that this twenty year- old had to face a sentence of "no hope," unless Maren could help her, made Maren determined to find some way to commit Ronnie's sentence to "time served."

"Doctor Kalevic is a good ENT doctor," Maren said, "but he's not a speech-language pathologist. I am wondering why you are pursuing this after two years."

"I want to go back to work at a church that hires me for child care and I can't with the smelly G-tube. The kids might bump into it or kick into me. It already leaks since the accident."

Ronnie was surprisingly easy to understand, considering the left side of her tongue was missing. There was something else though, a sweetness to her voice—an innocence in the way she told her story. It had all begun just after Ronnie had married.

"I was pregnant when they found the cancer. It spread really fast because of the hormones. The doctors said I had to lose the baby or it would kill me." She spoke calmly, giving the necessary details, without judgment or emotion.

"Were you a smoker?" Maren couldn't help but ask.

"No, no smoking or alcohol. My grandma had the same kind of cancer so..." Her lips had a slight twist when she spoke. Others might not even notice the compensatory postures she used to articulate speech sounds. They would be aware only of the sweet innocence, and that would distract most listeners from the slight slurring. Ronnie had trained herself to speak slowly, and that kept intelligibility high. She spoke quietly, without a trace of anger or frustration, as if describing someone else's tragic life.

"They did the surgery." She meant the abortion. "Along with the oral resection. I was eating after that. Then I had a lot of radiation. My neck is still hard here." She pulled her blue blouse collar down. "And my mouth still burns. I have all my reports here." She pulled a thick manila envelope from the large beaded leather bag that hung on her walker. Maren noticed a bottle of drinking water in it.

"Do you eat or drink anything?"

"I can take sips of water or coffee, and I munch cookies or crackers all day, just bits at a time. When I was in the accident my car was totaled, and my femur was crushed. I had to come here for care until I could walk." Ronnie told her she would be checking out of Stanton House in a few days and VNA would provide services at her apartment until she could drive again.

Maren had been looking through the various reports she had pulled from the well-worn envelope. She raised her head at the word "femur." The girl was not only calm, she was knowledgeable. Ronnie continued to relate her history… cancer, aborting her baby, the crushed vehicle, the surgeries on her leg, the pain, the damage to the G-tube, the medical appointments… Her losses were incredible, but she saved the most devastating for last. Her young husband had moved out.

The swallow evaluation was brief. While Ronnie used multiple swallows for both food and liquid, there were no signs of aspirating particles into her airway. Maren began to ask herself what kind of therapy, if any, she could provide. There was no history of pneumonia or choking. Ronnie was sure she had been on a soft diet following her initial surgery. Then came the heavy radiation. "Did you ever have a video-swallow study? I don't see a report of one in your papers."

"Yes, just before the G-tube was placed. They didn't see anything to explain my problem."

"Well, I'm not going to try any therapy until you have a new one. It's been two years. Things could have changed." Maren stuffed the papers back in the bag. Ronnie expanded the metal walker which she had folded, arranged the long double straps of the bag over her shoulder, and pulled herself to a standing position. She was ready to leave. Maren watched her struggle to the door and wondered what she could say that would be encouraging. She stepped behind her new patient, pulled the door open for her and said something she never said without knowing a patient better. "If you are a praying woman, I suggest you pray." Ronnie looked startled, but made no reply at all, not even good-bye. She focused on the mechanics of getting herself, the walker, and her large suede bag through the doorway.

Maren hadn't felt so overwhelmed with compassion since Cora was diagnosed with cancer. She finished her report, checked her watch, and hurried to the van. She turned the radio off for the ride home. Compassion for others had obliterated her self-centered fears.

A craft to choose or win of wing or wheel or fin.
I'll use the keys that Life provides.
The first of course is kin.

CHAPTER 5

The only traffic on Crescent Avenue was generated by the homeowners. Children crossed the street with caution, but not fear. This evening Maren supervised from the sidewalk, watching neighborhood children, including her own, who were riding bikes and scooters. Danl and Zoe were not allowed on Maple Grove Drive, so they turned around at the end of their street, by the small civil war era graveyard. Maren chatted with Will and Louise Botna, residents of the house to the north of the McCloud home. They both seemed like outgoing and friendly neighbors, but were rarely home.

"We have our own business," Will said. "Yes," Louise added, "it cut down on commute time when we moved it to the village. We still work way too many hours, so you may not see much of us." Just then Danl tried to turn his bike while traversing the bump that separated the sidewalk from the street, but he didn't quite make it. He tumbled into the street, his twisted bike beneath him. Maren excused herself and hurried toward him.

An elderly gentleman with thick white hair suddenly appeared and stooped to extricate Danl from his bike while Zoe watched silently from her trainer bike. Danl was bravely trying not to cry, but the skin was scrapped off both knees and one elbow. The handlebars were twisted out of alignment causing the bike to look injured. "Hey there young fella, you didn't break anything, did you?" Danl shook his head. "I haven't met you before. What's your name?" Danl wasn't able to find his voice. "His name's Danl," Zoe answered. "He's my brother and he's almost nine years old."

"Daniel, that's a fine, brave name."

"Just Danl," Zoe corrected. "Our dad didn't like extra letters."

"Oh, I see. And what is your name?" He asked as he put the bike on its wheels and worked to straighten the handlebars.

"I'm Zoe. I'm seven, and here comes my mom. Her name's Maren. We have two other brothers named Matt and Nick. What's your name? Do you have any kids?"

"I'm Peter Winslow, and yes, I do have a daughter named Meredith. She's grown up and moved away, I'm sorry to say."

As Maren approached, she heard Zoe's commentary about her family. "Hey Danl, you and your bike must have hit a bump. Are you okay?" He nodded his head and looked sadly at his bike. "Just my bike is bent. It doesn't turn very well." He managed to keep from blubbering in front of a stranger. Peter Winslow fidgeted a bit more with the bike wheel and handlebars, putting them right again. "There," he said, "I think it's going to be fine. Are you two allowed to have ice cream bars?" He looked at Maren for a cue. "I have some in my refrigerator and I can't eat them all by myself." He gestured to the house that stood next to the graveyard.

Now, all three were looking to Maren, their eyes pleading. She gave her consent, and they followed Peter into his house. He led the way to his kitchen where Danl's injuries were tended with a band aid, and they all enjoyed the treats. Maren noticed some kind of an addition to the back of the house, and Peter gave them another treat—a tour of his greenhouse. When they headed for home they carried a small potted red geranium. "It's not an ordinary geranium," Peter informed them. "It's a prairie plant, a perennial geranium. It will come up every year. Welcome to the neighborhood."

Danl and Zoe reminded Maren of the plan to bake goodies for Paul's homecoming, and with considerable supervision, they turned out five dozen large chocolate chip cookies. Bedtime arrived before clean-up could be accomplished, so Maren tucked them in and took care of the mess. She looked at the potted geranium next to the sink and smiled at their good fortune to have met yet another kind neighbor. *Dexum is such a friendly place.* Her thoughts drifted to morning when they would meet Paul at the airport. She was looking forward to being a whole family again for an entire week.

When Maren pulled up to the Arrivals station at O'Hare Zoe shrieked, "There he is. There he is. Yea, Dad's home." Danl still called Paul Doctor Paul; but Zoe, who remembered no other parents, never called him by name. Danl did call Maren Mom, mainly for Zoe's sake; but when Paul got to the van he was charged with excitement and joined Zoe's chorus. "There's Danl and my girls!" Paul climbed into the front passenger's seat, gave Maren a quick kiss, and turned to give each of his kids a hug. He ruffled their hair before urging them back into their seatbelts.

"What have you two been doing lately?" he asked, noticing Danl's band aid.

"He fell off his bike," Zoe tattled, "and a nice man fixed the wheel and handlebar."

"My bike doesn't turn very good," Danl explained. "We made some cookies for you." He wanted to change the subject.

"Your favorite kind," Zoe hinted. "Will you go for a bike ride with us? Will you swing us in the park? Can we have a cook-out?" Maren was pleased. *Re-entry might be smoother than I anticipated.*

In the morning Maren watched Paul pour himself a cup of the coffee she had brewed for herself. That was unusual. "Any caffeine in this or did you strain it all out?" He was referring to her habit of drinking half regular mixed with half decaf. "How about some of those cookies. I'll get my caffeine from the chocolate chips."

"For breakfast?" Maren was challenging, knowing the children would follow his lead.

"You made them to welcome me home, didn't you?" Maren rolled her eyes, knowing she was defeated, and handed him the cookie jar.

After eating and drinking two cups of the brew, Paul offered to help with kitchen duties; but Maren encouraged him to go outdoors with the children. She enjoyed seeing them respond to his magic. Jack had never really been playful with their boys. He was mostly a disciplinarian. While she loaded the dishwasher she watched them through the window. She noticed that beyond the grey deck that wrapped around the back of the house the old oaks, ashes, and maples were beautiful shades of red and yellow. Only the cottonwoods were nearly bare. The trees were so dense in the summer and fall it was impossible to see the homes on the other side of the creek, so the backyard was a sanctuary for birds, small animals, and the human inhabitants of the contemporary house on Crescent Drive. "Me first, me first," she heard. Paul swung each of them around and around until they all collapsed on the ground. The children jumped on top of Paul, yelping with joy.

Not such a bad idea to have a younger husband, she thought while stretching her back.

The weekend seemed to blow past like the leaves across the yard on a windy day. Saturday afternoon Penny, Jim, and the girls came for burgers on the grill. By evening Paul was fading. The adrenalin rush he had experienced from coming home finally gave way to jet lag. Maren read a professional journal while he turned in early. Sunday afternoon Bob and Gloria came to see their only son and his family. After an early dinner of pizza, ice cream and popcorn, they gave everyone hugs and thoughtfully left early.

Once the children were in bed, Maren started to fill Paul in on the events of the week; her work for VNA, Stanton House, and the Early Intervention Agency. His only comment about her employment was, "In Colorado you didn't have time for one position. Now that you have to be the rock of the family you've taken on three. What a woman." But the usual humor was missing from his voice. He was distracted. He was thinking he should tell her about London being the new base for Pediatric Possibilities and that he would likely be away much more than they had originally believed. Tonight might be the best time to work through her reaction and help her see that she would not be able to reassume her profession any time soon.

"Paul, are you listening?"

"Yes... no, not like I should. I've got training information I need to digest. I should be at the computer now.

"I wonder if the kids will even recognize you by the end of the year." She presented it as a problem for Zoe and Danl, but that was a cover for her sense of premonition, of increasing estrangement.

Before he could answer her, the phone's call tones cut their talk short. Matt wanted to talk to Paul, so Maren switched to speaker phone. After a perfunctory greeting, the topic quickly changed to Sydney. Paul looked quizzically at Maren. Since she hadn't yet shared the Sydney news, Paul was lost. They both listened while Matt elaborated on Sydney's wonderful qualities. "And she gave me a surprise last night, a set of Ping golf clubs were delivered to my door with a note that said she's hoping I'll accept the small..." He emphasized the word small. "token of her affection; because we would have one more thing to bond us together."

Paul's eyebrows raised, but he left it to Maren to answer. "Wow," was all she could manage before Matt continued. "Yeah, she's great. She's competing the second weekend of October, though. Could Homecoming possibly be on the third or fourth weekend?"

Maren looked to Paul for help, and his glib tongue saved the moment. "Hey Matt it sounds like you're doing great. We'd love to meet Cindy, but I'll be in India by then. Hard to celebrate an anniversary from there."

"It's Sydney, Paul. When her dad was stationed at Warren Air Base he got a short assignment that took him to Australia. She was conceived in Sydney, and they wanted to remember that time." This was more information than Maren needed; but he continued, unaware. "Her folks split up ten years ago, though. Her dad is career military. Her mom's from Germany, and she wanted to go back there. I sure would like you to meet her." They were certain he meant Sydney, not the girl's mom. "Her next preference would be Halloween. I really want to bring her."

Penny had already ruled out that weekend. Their only viable option, besides not having Matt attend the gathering, was the first weekend of October, only a week away. Maren felt pressure building, just thinking of how much effort would be required to pull that off. It was only Paul's humor that got them through the remainder of the conversation.

Maren was smoldering by the time they ended the call. "We're celebrating our anniversary on a date Sydney prefers."

"Well rock of the family, I hope you can pull this together in a week. I've got training in the city almost every day to get ready for India." He gave her a pat on the back and headed for the library to work on a presentation John had asked him to give on Monday morning. The London discussion completely slipped out of his mind.

Maren stayed up late making lists. She hoped Paul's Uncle Frank could make it on such short notice. For a fleeting moment she remembered how she had always considered Jack her rock. He had his shortcomings, but when the chips were down Jack was right there at the helm. When he had drowned she was forced to go on without his assuring presence. Now she was the rock. *How ironic. Life is full of surprises.*

Monday morning everyone scattered to their own work, Paul to the city, the children to school, and Maren to see ex-golf-pro George Sapien. Alice was anxious to work directly on words; but today they would start with respiration, breathing for speech. "Speech starts with a column of air," Maren said. "If you have a good foundation, you can build on it."

"I get it. It's like a good marriage," Alice said as she helped George lie down on their contemporary couch. His frame dwarfed the long leather cushions, and his feet hung over the wide armrest. Maren picked up a small book from the end table and placed it on his abdomen. "Just relax for a couple of minutes. Tell me more about George's work before he got sick." Maren was making conversation to distract them.

"He managed the golf courses and played quite a bit," Alice reported. "He also developed a series of motivational talks. He's a very intelligent and outgoing man. He just got a bad deal with the AVM rupturing. If it weren't for the wise investments he had made, George and I could have gone homeless after his illness. The bills are fierce, even with insurance."

Investments and a very smart, articulate wife, Maren thought. Apprehension collected in the pit of her stomach as she covertly monitored George's respiration. The book didn't move. There was hardly a sign of respiration. She tried to sound light, "Hey George, are you still with us? We can't see the book or any muscles moving. If you're breathing we should see something happening."

"I know," he answered in his dark monotone.

"I don't think he breathes right," Alice stated, as if Maren needed help figuring that out. "I used to see him breathe when he slept. Now there's nothing moving."

Maren pulled her chair next to him, and began explaining respiration. "Where are your lungs?" Most patients would point to their chest, but George knew that his ribs protected his lungs. He put his hand on his ribs—low, closer to his waist.

"Right. Now move your fingers across to your midline. There. That's your diaphragm muscle. When you expand your ribs and contract your diaphragm, air rushes in."

George didn't get it. There still seemed to be little or no movement. "I'm going to put my hand on your diaphragm muscle and press in. You push my hand out." She felt his muscles tighten as she pressed in. "Now let all your air out. Hooo," she demonstrated. "Now push your stomach out and let air come in." He was successful, but looked puzzled.

"I can't really feel it."

"You will George," encouraged Alice, before Maren could decide how to respond. Alice had been watching studiously. "We've been told to do breathing exercises before, but no directions other than, 'Take a deep breath.' Now that we understand what to do, we'll practice two or three times a day." No matter how much Maren would assign them in the following weeks they would do it and more. She was encouraged.

After writing specific instructions for the couple, Maren drove to a modest, yellow vinyl sided ranch home on the edge of Albright. There she met Joanne Harrison and her two and a half year old daughter Stephanie. This was an assignment from the Early Intervention Agency. One year old Eric was down for a nap, as Maren had suggested when she had called for the appointment. "Stephanie has never been one for napping," Joanne reported. "She's a good girl, always very quiet, but she's just not getting many words. There are others in our family who have had speech problems, and I know that makes it more likely that she'll have problems." Maren took notes while Joanne talked. Stephanie had never babbled—those baby syllables that sound like words and usually tumble out with melodic inflection. It sounds to listeners like a foreign language. Currently, Stephanie did have a few words that she used consistently; but Joanne was afraid she might be regressing.

When Maren tried to establish rapport with the dark haired girl, there were tears in her large round eyes. Her beauty reminded Maren of a Precious Moments doll. Joanne quickly handed her daughter a pink handled pacifier, and the crying ceased before the object was sucked into place. Maren suggested Joanne leave the room to get some of Stephanie's favorite toys and books. Before the mom returned, the pacifier had been coaxed away in exchange for a little blue train engine Maren had produced from her case. "Puh,

puh, puh," Maren modeled, instead of the more difficult Choo-choo sound. Stephanie tried to make the train sound. "Mmuh." In that instant, with that single sound, Maren knew that the future for this lovely child held years of speech therapy. With the simple, usually easy to produce sound, came nasal air emission. Air escaped through her nose on other sounds, too…puh, tuh, duh, and sss. Joanne come back in time to see Maren finish the testing.

With her mom's encouragement Stephanie pointed to the picture Maren requested on page after page in the book that was part of the language evaluation. The toddler seemed to have great comprehension. The expressive subtest didn't take nearly as long as the receptive portion. Not many pages were turned as they tried to elicit sounds and words. Stephanie mainly communicated using gestures. She did produce a few vowel-like sounds but hardly any consonant-like sounds. All the speech sounds were distorted, with air rushing out her nose. *That has to be uncomfortable. It's no wonder she prefers not to talk.* Joanne estimated that her daughter definitely had a vocabulary of no more than ten poorly articulated words.

Maren asked Joanne to hold the child on her lap, so she could shine her flashlight in and "count her teeth." The soft palate did elevate, but only slightly with voicing or pressure. Stephanie had very little response to Maren's gloved finger exploring as far back as her tonsils. She wiggled once, only slightly uncomfortable with pressure that should have been enough to gag her. That completed the evaluation. Maren felt substantial concern, almost fear. It was a fear that Joanne, although worried, would not fully understand for months to come.

Now that Stephanie was at ease with Maren she wanted her to play in her child sized kitchen. Between sips of imaginary tea from tiny cups, Maren managed to assure the worried mom that her daughter's speech problem was not anyone's fault. She reported that Stephanie's comprehension was well within normal limits at the seventy-fourth percentile while her expressive skills were at the first percentile, an extremely wide discrepancy. "Of one hundred children her age, ninety-nine would have better speech skills," Maren quietly explained. Tears began to slip from Joanne's eyes. "The cause might be a weakness or separation of muscles that control the soft palate. Another possibility is apraxia, an inability of the brain to program the speech muscles to form the sounds correctly." *Or it could be both,* Maren reminded herself.

Joanne could be brave no longer. She began to cry with muffled sobs. Quickly Maren re-assured her that therapy would make a huge difference, but they would also need to have Stephanie examined at a cranio-facial center in the city. Maren would help make the arrangements at the right time. "Meanwhile," Maren said, "let's wean her off the pacifier and teach her to drink from an open cup without a spout." When she left, Maren promised they would be seeing a lot more of each other. She assured Joanne that she would give her plenty of activities and exercises to do with Stephanie. As if aware of Maren's new importance in her life, Stephanie ran to give Maren a goodbye hug at the door.

After tuning the key in the ignition, Maren automatically hit the radio knob to the on position and heard again the news that was worrying the country. The Bush administration was pressuring Congress to pass a resolution giving the President the authority to use all means he determined appropriate to oust Saddam Hussein and disarm Iraq. The announcer reminded listeners that General Tommy Franks had presented detailed war plans to the President earlier in the month. "And from Israel," the newscaster continued, "another suicide bomber has killed five in Tel Aviv." As always, Maren wondered how the new efforts in the war on terror might affect her family.

CHAPTER 6

Paul had to stay late in the city to complete orientation training. The India trip was getting closer. At least he had been available to agree on menus and help make other decisions for Homecoming weekend. After an early dinner, Maren climbed the steep blacktop road that led to Noreen's driveway. This time Danl and Zoe skipped along ahead of her, collecting fallen acorns. Maren had decided that grocery shopping for the weekend crowd would best be accomplished on a solo sortie. Chauncey greeted them enthusiastically but silently and soaked up the affection they showered on him. Noreen had offered to "borrow" the McCloud children, her way of saying she would provide child care whenever needed. Her husband Randy had recently re-enlisted in the army, and Noreen who wanted to start a family was clearly not happy about their current living situation. Having the McCloud children there would be a comfort.

Noreen's homemade ginger cake with maple-flavored whipped cream was waiting for the children. Two pieces were already packed for Maren and Paul to enjoy later, when the children were settled for the night. Maren stayed long enough to see that

Noreen, Chauncey, and the cake were big hits with the children. They hardly noticed that she was leaving. Danl was throwing a ball for Chauncey, and Zoe was asking about the cello and violin she had spotted in the corner of the dining room.

The next few days passed in a blur of activities. When Maren wasn't supervising children or getting beds, food, and shuttle service arranged for the weekend she was making home visits. Although Paul was home every evening, he didn't devote much quality time to Maren, except at five a.m. for breakfast. Neither was willing to talk about any subject that might lead to an argument. That left a lot of silence. While he was preparing to leave Maren made her list for the day. *No time for Village Café this week*, she admitted to herself ruefully, wishing for some island of peace.

Paul had tried several times to explain to her more fully about the London office, but Maren seemed too preoccupied to listen. It was obvious, from her curt replies when he mentioned his work, that she was not happy. He felt sorry that she was getting the brunt of responsibility for their anniversary party. He wanted to make it up to her, but it was not his fault. *That's just the way life is sometimes*, he told himself. He needed to assuage his guilt as well as expunge any negative judgments against Matt and Sydney. *No use starting out with bad feelings toward Sydney*, he reflected. He grabbed the India materials he was supposed to have read and decided to take the train instead of driving.

Maren managed to check up on Ronnie Cameron in her new efficiency apartment as her first stop of the morning. The paper work transitioning her from Stanton House to VNA had gone smoothly. The young woman had exchanged the clumsy walker for a cane, and something else was new… a serene smile replaced her normally dispassionate expression. The video fluoroscopic swallow test had been done at the hospital, and Ronnie had received hopeful news. She had a stricture, a narrowing in her esophagus. She was excited that it was something that could be corrected. "It's probably the result of the radiation treatment I had. Now I just need to find a gastroenterologist who will accept my public aid card, and do the procedure to dilate my esophagus. Dr. Kalavik is having his nurse call around."

Ronnie had found hope where none had existed, thanks to Maren's recommendation. Maren told her she would ask VNA for a copy of the report from the evaluation. She would then determine if any therapy or compensatory techniques were recommended, either before or after the procedure. *Thank you God. It is a good day*, Maren decided as she got back in her van and drove to the Mercer home.

Wendy was feeling better and at Maren's suggestion they held their session in the kitchen. Wendy could now stand long enough to hobble a short distance, from chair to chair. The daily log Maren had set up for her had no new entries. "What have you been doing with yourself?" Maren asked with a friendly tone. The response wasn't what she would have hoped, but it was pretty typical of TBI patients once they were at home. "I watch TV, and there's always someone here. I mean a nurse or physical therapist or speech therapist." She didn't smile as she would have if she had realized that she was also referring to Maren.

They worked on Wendy's memory using kitchen utensils, cans, and boxes. Wendy had to listen and remember the directions Maren gave her. "Give me the half teaspoon, the measuring cup, and the baking soda." Wendy repeated the directions shakily, as if unsure; and then followed through correctly. "Is that right," She asked hopefully. "I want to do it right, so I can cook something."

Maren assured her she was doing well. The next directions would have four elements. "With a little more concentration you'll be ready to bake me a cake."

The TBI patients in Maren's experience were more accepting of exercises that were pragmatic, functional. Wendy previously had expressed a desire to cook dinner, and Maren was pleased that it was an activity they might be able to tackle together. It would have to be something simple, with only a few items to remember and few steps to sequence. Cooking on her own was still a long way off for Wendy. She needed to re-learn to sequence other activities correctly and read with comprehension and memory.

After some word matching exercises that required Wendy to match a word to a synonym or to the correct picture, Maren introduced exercises for sentence completion with one or two words. She gave Wendy pages to work on by herself and scheduled her next appointment on the wall calendar. Together they put it in Wendy's personal log book.

Maren was driving to her next appointment when her cell phone chimed. She pulled over to take the call. It was the school nurse. Danl appeared to have Pink Eye and would have to leave school immediately. A call to Paul's cell phone confirmed that he had turned it off during his meetings. She left a voice message asking him to phone a prescription to the pharmacy in Dexum, called her next patient to reschedule, picked Danl up from school, and made lunch for them. It was fun having Danl to herself. Zoe tended to talk for him when they were together. Maren enjoyed hearing about the fall choral concert the third graders would perform. "It's songs about American heroes, and I like Charles Lindbergh best, because he flew planes."

Danl wasn't really ill, but couldn't return to school until he'd been treated for the conjunctivitis. Maren now needed to find someone to stay with him for a couple of hours. *Who to ask... Noreen will be at work, Penny is tied to the girls' routine.* That left Paul's parents. Bob and Gloria were not sedentary grandparents. They very likely would have other commitments. She was asking them to drop everything and come immediately, which is exactly what they did.

By the end of the week all the preparations were completed, and good weather was promised for their celebration. Paul was just starting the grill when Matt and Sydney arrived, so he had the honor of being the first to meet her.

"Welcome aboard."

"I've heard so much about you and Maren. Congratulations on your anniversary. It must be awesome to be with the same person for such a long time." Paul looked quickly to Matt for a clue. Did she believe Paul to be Matt's biological father or did she consider six years to be a long time. Matt seemed unaware of the confusion, so Paul ignored the statement.

"I got the recorder Paul. Nick's bringing a guitar."

"That's great Matt. Thanks. You'd better introduce Sydney to the rest of the family."

Sydney was as gracious as a guest could possibly be. She found a complement to bestow on each person she met, offered to help with chores, and brought gifts for Matt's family—toys for the children, a slide pendant made of abalone shell for Maren, and for Paul an impressive watch that could simultaneously indicate the hour in three time zones. Try though she might, the blond Sydney could not get Danl to make up with her. Maybe he wanted to keep his big brother for himself. Zoe, on the other hand, was quite smitten with her. She couldn't take her eyes from the beautiful princess, and was practically speechless.

When Maren went to the front door to let Uncle Frank in, she noticed Sydney was on the living room floor helping Colleen, Erin and Zoe cut out the paper dolls she had given each of them. Danl's Lego set was unopened nearby.

The now retired priest gave Maren an enthusiastic hug. "I am so glad you could be here Frank. You know you're my favorite uncle."

"That's because you have no other uncles."

"That's not true. There's Cloris' husband Mike. Technically he's my uncle, too. You're my favorite because you married Paul and me." Cloris and Mike wouldn't attend Homecoming weekend. Although they had been at the wedding in Colorado, Paul's Aunt Cloris and Uncle Mike rarely left California for family events held in the Midwest. They were more likely to make the trip to the family house in Pine Bluff, Colorado for events held there.

"Are Ruth and Calvin here?" he inquired about Maren's sister and her husband.

"No, they should be leaving London about now on their way to meetings in D.C. Nick and Carrie are here. They came yesterday to help and made seven bean casserole and some monster brownies."

"Sounds perfect for my new diet," he said patting his ample stomach. "And Matt?"

"Yes, he's here. He brought a friend, Sydney Webster. Paul is at his post—the grill by the back deck." Maren gestured to Sydney and then to the door leading to the deck, without offering an introduction. Frank, left to take his choice, headed for the deck.

When Paul set the platter of meat on the kitchen island the clan, as Maren had always called Paul's family, gathered in a circle. Father Frank gave a blessing, not only for the meal but for the marriage and family. "Heavenly Father, these are blessings far greater than food," he said. "Here we are for each other and for You, combined, adopted, and extended—all part of your family through love, faith, commitment, trust, and respect. We thank you for keeping us in your care."

After the prayer, which Maren noticed was more gratitude than supplication, Paul's Aunt Elizabeth went to collect the stuffed mushrooms from the cooler she had left in Penny's minivan. Bob and Gloria opened their cooler and began serving a variety of beverages. Maren heard Sydney comment curtly, as she chose a soft drink, "I never use alcohol. It causes you to lose control."

After everyone had eaten their fill, Nick helped Danl and Zoe haul the bean bag toss game out of the garage. It was Sydney who quickly organized a tournament, efficiently assigning teammates to teams that would balance age and strength.

"She fits in to new groups very easily," Matt said, boasting about his girlfriend to Maren; and Maren had to agree. "Well, she's had a lot of practice. Her Dad's in the army, remember. She's lived all over the world. Now she just wants to settle down to one group in one place." Paul joined them.

"Sydney's very good at bean bag toss. Is that the competition she has next week?"

"Oh no. She's a finalist in the annual marksmanship competition. She'll probably come away with a couple of awards in rifles and pistols."

When it was too chilly to be outdoors, even for those gathered around the grill toasting marshmallows, the family moved indoors. They crowded into the large family room and spilled into the adjoining kitchen. Uncle Frank, quite pleased to be on the winning bean bag toss team, was describing how he made his last shot. Nick half listened while he gave small bells to Danl and Zoe. They rehearsed the signal he would give them, so they could get everyone's attention at the right moment. Then he handed Matt the acoustic guitar he had borrowed for the occasion. "Mom we have a little surprise for you," he announced. Maren looked around for Paul, thinking the children had come up with some gift for the two of them. She wanted him by her side.

Paul was making his way through the kitchen with a counter stool for Matt to perch on near the fireplace. He stood, looking across the room at Maren while Matt began quietly strumming the strains of a vaguely familiar tune. On that cue, Danl and Zoe rang the bells for quiet. "Maren I know when you agreed to marry me you thought we would always be together—and we will be. But this year offers us an opportunity to experience love from afar. I have already spent several evenings, just about this time of night, watching the stars in another time zone, thinking of you and hoping and praying that you were thinking of me." As Matt's playing increased in loudness Paul's talking turned into song.

> "And now the purple dusk of twilight time
> Steals across the meadows of my heart.
> High up in the sky the little stars climb,
> Always reminding me that we're apart."

He sang of the stardust in his heart, a garden wall where he had stood imagining holding her in his arms, and how he remembered their kisses. Tears of joy leaked from Maren's eyes and trickled across her cheeks. Gloria and Bob beamed. Father Frank said, "Amen," and Zoe and Danl began clapping. "Got it!" shouted

Nick to Matt over the ensuing din. He rushed off to the library with his laptop and digital recorder to burn a CD. Each family member hugged Paul and Maren, keeping them a room apart from one another. When Nick returned he handed Paul the CD case with a white bow taped to the top. Paul took it and made his way to Maren, never taking his eyes from hers. It was the look that always made Maren believe he could see into her soul. He handed the newly made CD to her. "So you won't forget," he said softly.

Maren dried her eyes and turned toward her family. Her sons, for whom Paul had become a role model, came and hugged her. Nick and Matt had returned more love and devotion to her than she could ever have hoped possible. Bob and Gloria smiled and joined the line waiting to hug the couple. They had unconditionally accepted her and had become her parents and grandparents for all four of the children. Uncle Frank was next. He supported Paul and Maren and their union without judgment, even though she had not embraced the church he loved.

Aunt Elizabeth was behind her brother Frank. She always gave advice to Maren as freely as if Maren had grown up under her tutelage the way Penny had. Penny and Jim came with outstretched arms. Penny and Jim were friends as well as in-laws. They provided nieces for Paul and Maren, playmate cousins for their young children. Nick's wife Carrie who had become a special friend and Maren's first daughter chatted with Penny, waiting her turn to give congratulations. Danl and Zoe both received and gave new life in this home. They observed carefully how the family expressed love to their parents. Sydney who was trying so hard to be accepted into the combined clan gave everyone within her reach a hug or handshake. Each person added a colorful thread, enriching the living tapestry of the McCloud family.

Maren was overwhelmed with joy and gratitude. "Thank you," she said repeatedly to everyone. She turned and hid her face against Paul's chest. Just when she had begun to think they were drifting apart he did or said or *sang* something that stirred feelings she couldn't quite label let alone express. "Thank you," was all she could manage to whisper.

CHAPTER 7

Paul completed his series of inoculations and flew to London after Homecoming weekend. From there he traveled with Bev Skelton to India for three weeks where flooding had been the worst and illnesses from contaminated drinking water was the primary health issue. There was a possibility they would stop in Haiti for a week before Thanksgiving. Paul told Maren that the people of African countries routinely suffered from contaminated drinking water. He thought they should have been dispatched to South Africa. His training with Possibilities had been extensive, and when he was home he often talked of areas she didn't even know existed. Their communication for the present was limited to email, fax and occasional phone calls.

Maren resumed her established routine, breakfast with the children, waiting with them for the school bus, and then walking. That hour of the morning was too early for most home patients, so she usually stopped at the Village Café. After that she would work through the lunch hour. Afternoons were short with a school bus to meet. Still, the children grounded her, provided levity at the end of the day, and were a constant source of personal fulfillment.

They were a special gift, neither birth children nor grandchildren. She never thought of them as a burden, but they did take as well as give energy.

A warm friendship with Della was developing, and through Della she was getting to know many of the villagers, except for the painters.

"No, I don't know anything about them. I think they're part of a big company that's building the strip mall on the edge of town. I can tell you that those official-looking folks that always sit at the big table are part of the Winston family. You do know, don't you, that our state representative Ross Winston is running for the U.S. Senate? Ross's wife Meredith is your neighbor Peter Winslow's daughter. She didn't even have to get new monogrammed towels when they got married." Maren smiled about the towels, but didn't have time or energy to care about Ross Winston's campaign-planning breakfast meetings.

She listened to the radio as she drove away from the Village Café. Everyone she knew monitored the news about Afghanistan, Iraq, and Pakistan as well as the threats on American soil. Noreen's husband had been deployed from his base in Germany to Afghanistan a month ago. He told her that more troops were needed and expected. Today's news confirmed Randy's early appraisal of the situation. The Afghan government did not have the means or power to deal with the underlying problems that caused security threats. They needed a well-trained, well-equipped, and regularly paid national police force. *Every American listening knows where that will come from, at least for the foreseeable future,* thought Maren. She felt sorry for Noreen.

Indian summer had so far been exquisitely beautiful, somehow magnifying Maren's aloneness. During the past two days, however blustery winds jolted the village community into real autumn. Temperatures dropped more than twenty degrees overnight and clouds settled over Dexum. Maren's mood plunged.

Her cell phone rang, demanding that she turn off the car radio and refocus. It was Sue Williston asking her to do an evaluation for Sylvia Villisca ASAP. "Sylvia and Guy Villisca are a charming, loving couple in their eighties. They're trying to graciously meet the challenges presented by a devastating stroke. I know she has aphasia. She just can't say what she wants to say, but she seems to understand pretty well. Our physical therapy team goes to the house three times a week. The PTs tell me they understand her easily when she does manage to get a few words out. I hope you can help her. They're kind of special to a lot of us in this area."

Maren called immediately. The phone rang more than five times. As she was about to hang up, Guy Villisca answered. His pleasant, baritone voice was evidence that Sue's description was accurate. He was more than gracious. She was able to schedule the evaluation visit for later that morning.

Her first stop was to see Stephanie. She was first on Maren's route several times a week. Maren had introduced activities that caused the child to be more aware of her ability to move her mouth and tongue, and control her breath. Initially, they drew faces with crayons and made silly faces showing tongues and teeth, using plastic magnets designed for therapy. That was followed by tongue movements and some blowing activities. At first Stephanie was not able to produce even one bubble in a quarter inch of liquid by blowing through a straw. She had to start by blowing soap bubbles through a wand and playing a toy harmonica and horn.

Now Stephanie's favorite activity was blowing through a straw to make bubbles in chocolate milk. If she could make bubbles without pinching her nose closed to prevent air escape, she was allowed to drink it. Joanne laughed and told Maren their house was where children were not only allowed, but encouraged, to blow bubbles in their milk. Sometimes, often in fact, Stephanie's muscles got mixed up and when she was supposed to be blowing she would suck the liquid up the straw. They knew it was not intentional because the same thing occurred when soapy water was used.

After each session Maren spent time with Joanne, educating her about the various activities and giving assignments to do each day until Maren returned. She made sure Joanne understood that the best blowing exercise was against the pressure of deeper and deeper liquid and for a longer time. They always counted the seconds. Joanne was an ideal mom, routinely doing exactly what Maren recommended.

On the floor together, Maren and Stephanie made animal sounds using the plastic figures from Stephanie's toy barn. In only a few visits Maren had elicited all the vowel sounds from the astute two year old while Joanne played with Eric on the other side of the room and kept one ear and eye on the speech session. "Ah…oh… eeee…uuu." Yes, they were slightly nasal, but they were acceptable. Usually parents saw no value in a child's production of vowels and syllables. They were only interested in real words, but sounds and syllables were the essential building blocks for words.

"Next I'd like to see if we can get her to make an /s/ sound. We want sounds that can be prolonged and that should come out her mouth, not her nose. It doesn't matter if it isn't perfect," Maren assured the eager mom. "Next time we'll make a puppet and give it a tongue." When Maren closed the door on her way out Joanne was smiling, but Stephanie was kicking the floor and crying because Maren was leaving.

Maren sat in the van parked at the curb, and called Dr. Bodey. Stephanie was almost ready for a team evaluation. Sue Williston would technically make the referral, but it was Maren's contact. He had been a colleague of Paul's when they worked in the city. She was thankful they hadn't lost all of their connections during their five year absence. Before Maren could drive away, Joanne opened the door and shouted excitedly, "She just blew a birthday party blowout. She made it unroll all the way to the end!"

As Maren drove north to the Villisca home in Albright, the predicted rain began as a cold mist. It had increased by the time she rang the doorbell. Guy led her to the warmth of their rustic living room to meet Sylvia. Mementoes from various islands decorated the mantel of a stone fireplace, and antique-looking books sat on rough-hewn, handmade shelves that flanked the fireplace. Guy did most of the talking, but Sylvia added "Yes" from time to time and nodded and smiled appropriately. *Good social skills.* Maren made a mental note.

Maren sat on a footstool directly in front of Sylvia to administer an oral motor examination. She asked Sylvia to puff air in her cheeks and swish it from side to side, "but don't lose any." Maren did not demonstrate, and Sylvia followed the verbal instructions without a repetition or a cue. Maren directed her to try to touch her nose with her tongue tip and then protrude her tongue and move it from side to side. Here Maren did demonstrate. Sylvia's tongue deviated considerably to the right during protrusion, indicating right-sided weakness. The stronger left side dominated. Sylvia pushed her tongue against a wooden tongue depressor that Maren held. Next, she pushed her tongue alternately against the inside of each cheek while Maren pressed her finger tips on Sylvia's cheeks to oppose it. "Hold your tongue to the roof of your mouth like this," said Maren, demonstrating a spoon in spoon posture with her hands. Sylvia could hold her tongue to her hard palate but only for a fraction of a second.

Now for the language. "What happened to you?" She was testing for an appropriate response. "Ah hah da twag." came the jargon. Maren knew by the way Sylvia looked away and shook her head in frustration that she realized the words weren't right. Guy quickly filled in the answer, "She meant, 'I had a stroke.' She does know," he told Maren. "She just can't say it." Maren smiled and nodded her head in sympathy. "I understand," she assured them both.

Maren pulled a diagnostic screening test form out of her satchel to begin assessing Sylvia's language disorder. She tested listening, reading comprehension and writing, as well as spoken expression. On the evaluation form provided by VNA Maren wrote "Severe aphasia with probable dysarthria." She explained to them that just as Sylvia's right arm and leg were weak the right side of her tongue was also weak. *There's a lot of work to be done here,* she told herself.

Maren was hoping conservatively for good intelligibility on automatic phrases and a few spontaneous phrases as attainable goals for Sylvia. Under prognosis she wrote, "Fair." When Guy asked what the testing meant, Maren was honest in saying Sylvia probably would not regain all her abilities, "but," she added tenderly, "only God knows a person's true potential."

That night seeing her happy, healthy children was the high point of Maren's day. Their days were spent in fluorescent school rooms where they did not notice the weather and were spared hearing most of the news. She tried to cheer herself with the thought that three weeks, half of Paul's projected time for this trip, had passed. He would miss Danl's birthday next week, but at least they would have Thanksgiving together.

Paul's cell phone had been mostly useless and email unreliable, but he had found a fax machine that he could use. In a high tech world their communication was presently relegated to the medium of Elizabethan times—written letters. Although speedily delivered by fax, it wasn't what they had hoped for. A note she received before dinner stated that he was just beginning his day. Nothing for the children this time. He was obviously in a rush.

"Maren, first just know that I think of you in some corner of my mind all the time, even—no, especially when I'm sleeping." He knew that wasn't quite accurate. Most days there was no corner of his mind that was not occupied. At night he was so tired from treating victims of the floods or earthquakes that had followed he fell onto his cot and slept, before he was fully aware of whether he had a pillow. When he did think about his family, he worried for their safety. Still, he wanted her to know how much he loved her and their family. He considered his words poetic license, not dishonesty. He did include enough details of his work to let her know that his ENT skills were not being wasted. He assured her that the group's leader Bev Skelton was always monitoring the wellbeing of the medical team. "We're well cared for. I should be home by the end of November. Be the Rock."

That must be a mistake. He was to be home for Thanksgiving, and that's still four weeks away. Maybe he thinks of Thanksgiving as the end of the month. Her shoulders slumped. If she was a rock, she was a sinking one. Nick and Carrie had called after dinner, already asking about the holiday. Carrie's mom had to work, so it was Maren's turn to have them for the weekend. Maren felt overwhelmed.

Since the first year of their marriage Maren and Paul had hosted the family Thanksgiving gathering. Paul's parents' place had been too small even then, and anyway Gloria and Bob were ready to give up such duties. Penny seemed to look to Maren and big brother Paul to take leadership, since that first year when Penny had been pregnant. It had been fun sharing the planning and cooking with Paul back then. Now it was questionable if he would even be present. She wanted to call him and complain, "You said six weeks. That would put you home *before* Thanksgiving. What's going on?" But she didn't, not then.

After getting the children tucked into bed, she called Matt. She was hoping to tack down some details, but their conversation did not go well. Sydney answered and seemed disinclined to take the phone to Matt. After as much chit-chat as Maren could manage she asked bluntly, "Is Matt there?"

"Yes, he's working on a computer project. Do you want me to interrupt him?"

"Well, yes, I would like to talk with him."

"Okay, I'll see if he can talk now."

Thankfully, Matt's voice came on the phone after a few moments. He seemed rushed or pressured. "Hi Mom, what's up?"

"I wanted to see how you are, and talk about Thanksgiving."

"Oh, uh, I don't know what we're doing, yet."

Maren suddenly realized he might want to go with Sydney to meet her family and perhaps Thanksgiving would be the time to do so.

"No, she doesn't spend much time with her dad. We might go hiking that weekend. My employment situation is unclear right now so… I was just doing a job search on line." Unclear wasn't exactly honest. He had been let go. The unclear part was where he would find another position.

This was the first inkling Maren had that his job might be in jeopardy. She heard Sydney's voice in the background, distracting him from hearing her offer to pay for plane fare, if that was the issue. She caught enough words to understand that Sydney was saying they should be thankful just to have been brought together and that they should celebrate alone. If Maren criticized Sydney's philosophy, Matt would surely feel justified in staying away. She clenched her teeth and encouraged him to bring Sydney along. Again she could hear the conference. When Matt came back to the phone he reported it was too early in their relationship to spend a holiday with parents. Evidently Homecoming weekend didn't qualify as a holiday.

Theirs is too deep a relationship to be separated, too new to meet relatives. Where does that leave us? Matt had told her at the Homecoming gathering that Sydney was ready to settle down in one place with one group of people. Evidently that didn't include Matt's parents. It did not leave much ground to be explored. It wasn't the words he had spoken that bothered Maren so much as the general tone of the whole conversation. He had ended the call without the usual assurances of love. It was not only questionable if Paul would be home, now it was doubtful that Matt would show up.

She began typing a fax. Non-controversial news first.

"Dear Paul, I went to the parent-teacher conferences this week. Richard and Lois Smith seem to be outstanding teachers and human beings. I'm sure their interest in Zoe and Danl is genuine. We talked well past the allotted time, and each assured me the children are doing well. They promised to watch for signs of stress during your absences.

"Your parents are moving into the condo they found this fall. If you don't hear from them for a few days they're just unpacking. I don't envy them getting resettled, but they seem to be happily looking forward to living midway between Penny's place and our house. Your dad is pleased to see more of their grandchildren and doesn't seem sad about giving up his boat. They are planning to take Zoe and Danl for an overnight during spring break. They will be here for Danl's birthday celebration, too."

Now for the more touchy issues, she thought. If she got her letter off by midnight, he might receive it when he stopped for lunch. She finished typing what she hoped was a stoic summary. *Rocks feel no pain,* she remembered as she guided her letter into the paper feed and pressed the numbers that would guide her message through the air waves. She was a human rock though, and she hoped Paul would understand her emotions. The Paul who sang to her at their anniversary party would know how she felt. She wasn't sure about Dr. McCloud in India. She needed more than a return fax. She needed some minor miracle that would allow her to hear Paul's voice—his perspective, his assurances.

She sent the letter off with the push of a button, swiveled the leather chair away from the pear shaped desk, and went to the kitchen to brew a cup of tea. Sitting at the counter, eyes closed, waiting for the cup to cool she was mentally back in Edgelawn with a cup of tea and an anatomy textbook in front of her. She had been studying for finals. Jack had died the summer before, and she was really dreading the holidays. Matt was so wise back then. He had put one hand over the text to get her attention. She had looked up, into his serious, young face. "Do you think you could teach me how to cook a turkey dinner?"

Matt had always helped her in the kitchen. She had told him that if he could cook he would never be lonely. It was Matt who had pulled her through those first holidays, insisting that he had a real desire to improve his culinary skills. She sipped a spoonful of tea to test the temperature and returned to the present. Maybe he wanted to use his cooking skills now to impress Sydney. He had come home at every opportunity that ill-fated first year of law school. Maybe he had missed some other chances and now needed to fill in the gaps. She forced herself to think of her patients. She needed to prepare several sessions for morning.

The day dawned bright and clear. The strong west winds sent the clouds scurrying. The sunshine brightened not only the landscape, but Maren's mood. She parked in the Mercer's driveway. During her last visit with Wendy, Maren had checked Wendy's appointment book. Her schedule for the week had been entered, but definitely not in Wendy's handwriting. "I asked Brad to write them for me. I don't write very well, you know." Part of the plan, of course, was to get Wendy to do some writing. *I'll have to come up with another plan,* Maren had decided. There was no lack of goals to work toward. Today Maren brought some pages to stimulate divergent and convergent thinking, making a list of items that belong in a category, and naming a category from a list given. *Kind of dull stuff,* Maren chided herself. *Maybe I can think of something more functional.*

Wendy called to Maren to let herself in. Marlo had already left for work, and Wendy was watching TV, waiting for the next therapist to arrive. She seemed genuinely happy to see Maren. That was new—an expression of happiness—an expression of any emotion. Maren led a chatty conversation about family and friends, until Wendy mentioned that she and Brad had an approaching anniversary. They had been married on Thanksgiving weekend twenty-three years ago. "Would you, uh, help me write a card for him?" She pulled a large flowery, commercial card from her speech notebook. Surprised, Maren immediately agreed. Whatever had sparked Wendy's interest she didn't know, but wanted to take advantage of the moment.

"Did Marlo get the card for you?" Maren noticed a slight stammer and jerky rhythm that she hadn't observed previously. It could be excitement, but it might mean neurogenic stuttering. She had filed the observation for future monitoring. "Oh no. That's not something you'd want your daughter to do. I asked Peggy a friend from church. Sh-she's known us for a long time." Maren understood the logic. It didn't seem appropriate for a child to pick out what was essentially a love letter for her mother to give to her father. Some parts of Wendy's brain were on track.

"We have a few visits before Thanksgiving. If you just want to add a sentence and sign your name it won't take long."

"I want to write a letter to put inside. I asked him why he married me. He said at first he just liked the way I looked. Now I can't do anything. He does everything." She stopped.

She has to be wondering what's binding him to her through all of this, Maren thought while silently nodding her head to encourage Wendy to continue. "I want to thank him for making a commitment. He said he made a commitment." Maren wasn't sure Wendy understood the nuances of the word commitment, but she didn't stop the unexpected surge of conversation. "And for helping me and I want to write a prayer for him."

Maren was momentarily taken aback—a prayer. Why, she wondered hadn't Wendy asked for help from her church friend Peggy. *Does she feel how much I care for her? That would be very encouraging.* But Wendy brought her back to reality with, "I'd be too… you know… to ask someone like Peggy." It was that her disability would be exposed. She would be humiliated with a friend, but not with a therapist.

They started the letter, which in the course of the following weeks would expand to almost three pages. Wendy would dictate, ask questions about phrasing, words, synonyms, and shades of meanings. She was beginning to direct her own therapy. Maren felt like she was along for the ride and was contented, honored in fact, to be the facilitator of this amazing woman's recovery process.

Some days, therapy seemed to be so fruitful. It was like being the director of a magnificent screenplay in which right and good always won out. She knew to savor those times, for there were sessions when nothing seemed productive. She knew the explanation… therapy was having an effect even when it wasn't immediately apparent. It didn't make those times any less distressing, but when she reminded herself it encouraged her.

As Maren drove into the Villisca's driveway, she prayed that the magic, the grace of this day would be sufficient for them. Guy ushered her in and back to the rustic family room at the back of the house. She felt such love in this home, as in most of the others she visited. "We were just reading some poems," Guy told her; as if that was the most natural way to pass the time. "These are some of our favorites." He showed her one of the collections. Maren had encouraged him to try some parallel reading with Sylvia, reading together out loud, to see if Sylvia would automatically say some of the words. She had left some phrases to complete and some fill-in- the- blank exercises. She was hoping by today Sylvia might answer, "pepper," when Guy read, "Salt and…" or say "down," when he prompted by saying "up and…" The poems he was showing her were two and three pages long. *I should have been more specific with my directions.* Maren was concerned the man would expect too much and they would both become discouraged.

"We used to sit on our porch and read these together," he said in his rich, baritone voice.

"I'd love to hear some." Not knowing what would happen next, she sat in the deep, soft arm chair across the coffee table from the couple on the couch, ready to console them if it didn't go well. He lifted the old tome and chose "Vagabond's House" by Don Blanding "West of the sunset stands my house, there… and east of the dawn;…"

Sylvia's face brightened. She seemed to be following along, nodding her head, and making sounds now and again, perhaps remembering travels from long ago. Guy read like a professional, not the sing-song way novices read poetry. His voice was, even at his age, wonderfully mellow and resonant—full of love for the poem and his wife. Sylvia's eyes began to twinkle. "For I am a vagabond."

While they continued, Maren looked with new interest at the memorabilia and awards displayed around the room. She vaguely remembered the name Villisca, but couldn't place where she had heard it. Then a statuette of a music director on the corner cabinet triggered a memory and then expanded it like the click of a computer mouse enlarges a thumbnail image. Guy had been a very popular band director years ago. Before he retired he and the band had a regular, late night radio program. It—or re-runs of it—had been on the air when Matt was small. Guy would often read poetry between numbers.

"…Have…house…. may…way…books…" Sylvia was actually saying some of the words. Guy's band had traveled extensively, and Sylvia must have been right there with him, acquiring items here and there for their dream home. The poem was describing the house, Maren realized. Her throat tightened. She fought back the tears. *They had obviously been so very close, sharing so much of life, enjoying…* She had to stop her train of thought before tears began to roll. The devoted pair might not have much more time together, and they were aware of that.

The magic of the day did hold for them. Guy thanked her profusely when she left, as if Maren had caused some miracle. Guy and Sylvia and possibly some guardian angel, if one believed in angels, had done it. She knew she would never have assigned such a lengthy task as the reading. Before leaving, she had provided some ideas for how Guy could get Sylvia to speak more by slowing down, repeating rather than moving into a different poem each time, and pointing to the words. They practiced with her, but she wasn't sure Guy would follow through. They seemed to have an agenda of their own.

Maps be carefully planned; can't
draw the way in sand.
God's word, the key to my true North,
will be kept close at hand.

CHAPTER 8

Maren sat in the van and returned a call to Sue Williston who told her no gastroenterologist would accept Ronnie Cameron's public aid card. It was a sad fact of life that many healthcare providers either had limits on how many public aid patients they would accept per month, or simply stated they had reached their limit, when in fact they accepted none at all.

"Now that we know what procedure she needs to eliminate her dependence on the G-tube, we can't find a physician who cares enough about the young woman to help her. In twenty years of social work, not many cases have touched me like this one. I've been working with her for three years, and this is the first time I've seen a spark of hope in the girl. We're grateful for your help on this one. One thing that bothers me though, why didn't the earlier video swallow study find the stricture?"

"I can't be sure, but in some facilities the protocol is to focus no lower than the top of the esophagus. The stricture is below that point, so it would have been missed. I have some contacts. I'll see what I can do about finding a GI doc." Maren hung up feeling as low as she had been high on learning that Ronnie's problem could be resolved. She didn't want to believe that no one would help such a worthy young woman.

She forgot to turn on the radio as she moved on to see George Sapien. George staggered more than walked to the door with Alice just behind him. They moved to the dining room table to work. "Today," Maren began, "I want to take a giant leap forward in George's rehabilitation. In dysarthria the problem isn't muscle weakness. It's coordination. The problem is the muscles miss their intended target for many of the speech sounds. You were making those sounds for such a long time before your stroke you didn't even have to think about it. Now you're going to re-learn to make each of the speech sounds. The good news is there are only a certain number of speech sounds in our language. The not-so-good news is you will not likely be able to articulate those sounds as quickly and as consistently as you used to."

"We're just looking for progress here," Alice said, "We're not after perfection."

"That's exactly the attitude you need to have. The main goal is to be able to communicate." As cheerful as she sounded, Maren wasn't sure the main goal was actually attainable for George. She kept her doubts to herself and proceeded to introduce tongue tip exercises and the tongue tip speech sounds /t/ d/ n/, and /l/. She would save /s/, the most finely coordinated speech sound, for another day.

He held his mouth open and tried to hold the tip of his tongue to his upper lip. Maren counted, "One, two... oops try again. One, two, three..." His tongue shook with weakness that may have occurred from disuse. It bulged too far forward from the poor control, the dysarthria. Alice went to get a mirror and held it for him. Next he held his tongue tip to his upper incisors, right at the midline of the center teeth.

Maren pulled on a latex glove and asked George to open his mouth. She pressed the tip of her index finger firmly against the alveolar ridge, the bumpy area behind his upper teeth. "That is your next target for the tip of your tongue. Touch and hold your tongue there without touching your teeth." He did fairly well, but with obvious effort. Maren continued talking while he repeated the exercises. "That spot behind your teeth is the target for /t/ d/ n/, and /l/. Put your tongue tip there. Say, 'tuh… duh… nno… la,'" she directed.

Maren left lists of words that started with tongue tip sounds. As always she gave them a list of written exercises. The exercises were not to strengthen his muscles, but to allow him to use whatever control he was able to develop and to use it as efficiently as possible. Alice would read the words to him, and he would watch himself in the mirror. If his tongue strayed off target, Alice was to call it to his attention. And so the week passed for Maren, as she forced herself to focus on the problems of others, problems she knew how to solve.

Maren had walked within a stone's throw of the old white structure many times. This morning she took Danl and Zoe along with her, but they didn't stop to throw stones in the creek. They followed the sounds emanating from the steeple. She was sure it was a bell, a real bell, not an electronic chime. Perhaps that's what called her—its permanence. She felt drawn to it. She had nothing against groups that worshiped in auditoriums; but lately she had been feeling the need to again be part of an established community of believers, something traditional.

Only one thing made her nervous. Paul's parents, sensing her loneliness during their phone conversations had insisted on spending Sunday in Dexum, to celebrate Danl's birthday. They had attended Saturday night mass, arrived at the house very early Sunday morning, and Gloria insisted on going along to the little white church in the village. Vance had called it First Church. He said it had been at the same location for over one hundred years. Maren opened the glass door of the entryway, a modern addition off the parking lot at the rear of the structure. To her surprise Noreen Anderson, the volunteer greeter for the morning, stood next to Vance Davidson just inside. "It's a sign," Noreen told her later.

Maybe it was a sign. The morning did turn out to be a good experience for everyone. Gloria, never one to pass judgment on her daughter-in-law or anyone else, sang the hymns and praise songs she knew and actually took notes during the sermon. Vance was continuing to fill in for the pastor who was on a sabbatical of some kind.

Vance was a teaching preacher. He quoted liberally from various scriptures, both old and new and explained each in simple terms, using the same conversational tone of voice he used at the Village Café. He was on the third of a five-part series called "The Keys to Happiness." Today he emphasized the importance of God's word, not the still, quiet voice each believer has access to; although he acknowledged the importance of that. This morning he was talking about the words of the Holy Bible. "Staying in the habit of reading scripture for even fifteen minutes a day," he said, "can make a tremendous difference in life."

His talk challenged Maren. She had never read the Bible, just listened as it was read in the various churches she had attended. She decided to talk to her sister about it. Ruth and her husband had participated in a fairly substantial Bible study before Calvin had joined Pediatric Possibilities. Ruth always credited that experience with changing their lives.

The rest of the day passed pleasantly with the help and good humor of Bob and Gloria. They always seemed to know when Maren was at a low point and found a way to lend a hand without being intrusive. When she and Paul were dating, they had accepted Maren and her two grown sons as a part of the family. They had taken Matt and Nick "under their wings," as they called it, during Maren's surgery. That was shortly before she and Paul were married. Bob and Gloria were there with real joy to celebrate their son's wedding and with willing hands to help pack and unpack during the move to Denver and more recently back again. They accepted and loved their two adopted grandchildren with the same impartial enthusiasm that they showered on Penny's two girls. Maren had no complaints about her in-laws. They had different points of view on some things, but there was no doubt that they loved her and she loved them.

It was already November. Maren was counting down the days until Paul would return. She checked every morning for a fax from him, and was grateful to find one on Monday. It was already Monday evening in India where the low temperatures were more than twenty degrees warmer than the highs in Dexum. "Maren, I'm glad Mom and Dad are there to help you while I'm away. I'm being cared for and supported here, so you don't need to add me to your list of concerns. Matt's behavior must be hard for you to understand. He is a grown man though, and like all of us male types, he has to sort out his own life, find his own path. By the way, our group is finishing early here. Other NGO teams are replacing us. We're shipping out to a new location soon. I'll call you from the airport to let you know the details."

That was it, the whole text of the fax. *Odd to not name the destination—like it was a secret.* She sent her pre-typed letter by return fax, not adding any hint of her disappointment at receiving such a short note. He seemed very far away, not really in touch with her or with the family issues. She left the disappointing note on the desk. It was time to get the children moving.

Maren's daytime hours were usually full. VNA called regularly asking her to take on more and more patients. And there was always a waiting list of children to be evaluated for Early Intervention. Her work hours assured her she was more than a mother, as important as she believed that to be. She had more to offer, and had a need for diversity in her life. She made sure she didn't over commit herself. She needed to have enough energy for family.

Her stomach told her it was lunch time. She ignored the rumbles and drove to the Sapien mansion. She was scheduled to do a swallowing evaluation for George, and at lunch was the best time to do it. His speech therapy had been going well, but his voice was often gurgly. He reported a constant feeling of mucous in his throat. He would swallow, but couldn't get rid of it. Before sending him for another video swallow study or beginning any swallowing therapy, she wanted to watch him eat a meal. She relied heavily on Alice's reports, but needed to see for herself if he choked or showed other more subtle signs of aspiration.

She declined Alice's offer to provide lunch for her, took out her stethoscope, placed the tips securely in her ears, and positioned the diaphragm snugly against George's neck. She listened while he took sips of water and drank consecutively. Click-swish. Timely. No spillage before the swallow. No sounds of residue with the water. She listened as he took bites of his sandwich and spoonfuls of pudding. No problems.

She put the stethoscope away but continued to watch and listen with trained and experienced eyes and ears. As the meal progressed, she did notice that he cleared his throat a few times. She waited until he had finished and listened again with the stethoscope, although she didn't really need it. She could hear the slight gurgle when he said, "Ah." Some liquid or material had accumulated.

"He's been this way a long time," Alice reminded Maren. "He doesn't get pneumonia, so doctors say he's not aspirating. It's just so uncomfortable and sounds weird."

Maren explained that he could aspirate minute amounts and not develop aspiration pneumonia as long as he remained physically active. "Even if he doesn't regularly aspirate, he could be at risk for aspirating, especially if he's tired or ill."

She outlined their options. First she wanted them to have another video swallow study, often called a cookie swallow test. After that—depending on the results—they could try exercises and techniques, such as prolonged swallows to try to eliminate the residue. "Or there is a new therapy using small amounts of electrical stimulation that may be helpful. There isn't much research to support it, but there are encouraging clinical reports. If you do the electrical therapy, it should be at a facility that can initially monitor his swallows with video fluoroscopy."

Since she had skipped lunch, she decided a snack and coffee at the Village Café would help hold her over until dinner. Della held the carafe with regular coffee in her right hand and the one with decaf in her left. She waited for Maren to indicate how much caffeine she wanted. Maren looked tired, not her usual cheerful self; so Della assumed she would be pouring from both. While Della enjoyed serving the public and getting to know each customer, she particularly enjoyed Maren McCloud. She admired the work Maren did and the way she combined it—balanced it—with a complicated family life.

After watching George's lunch, Maren had stopped at Stanton House; and now couldn't fit another visit in before the children would be home. She was open to conversation. Della asked how things were going for the McCloud family. "My day is so short," she lamented. *It's the nights that are really long,* she realized. It wasn't a busy time in the café; so Della lingered, eager to chat. Soon she was sharing stories about her grown son Ray and her husband Terry. Maren began to open up about her concerns for Matt. She needed a safe place to vent about Sydney.

"I know two young people exploring a new relationship want to be together all the time, but something seems not right. I just can't put my finger on it. As nearly as I can tell they didn't exactly argue, but it sounded like a kind of power struggle under the surface. Sydney who claims to want to fit into a family, seems to be trying to keep him entirely to herself—through guilt if necessary. She may not have verbalized it or even realized it, but in effect she told him, 'If you were really a good friend you would stay in California with me. If you really loved me you would want to be with me exclusively.'"

"Oh, I'm sure she is quite aware of what she's doing. And if you approach the subject with Matt, he'll get defensive and feel justified in staying away." Della seemed to have natural insight.

"Exactly! I've never felt so estranged from one of my sons, not even when Nick was involved with a cult. But that's a story for another day."

Maren thought about her comfort level with Della. *I know waitresses are wonderful, kind women; but she is a remarkable person.*

Della seemed quite knowledgeable about many topics, including medical issues. They chatted for a while about the increasing concern that a war with Iraq seemed closer. Della asked if that was a concern for Maren and Paul. "Oh, I don't see how that would change Paul's work. They go where there are national disasters and ongoing poverty." Della thought a war would be considered a disaster and the people of Iraq were certainly constrained by poverty. Instead of pursuing the topic, she diplomatically brought their conversation back to local happenings. She outlined the plans for the underground railroad reconstruction under the Dexum Inn and out to the cemetery, Next, she brought up local politics.

"You heard the election results, didn't you? Ross Winston won the U.S. Senate seat. I suppose this restaurant will be famous, if he keeps coming here. He's very popular. People are speculating that he's moving up, maybe vice president or even president some day." Maren wasn't really interested in politics. She selfishly hoped that having a senator around wouldn't change the pleasant, quiet atmosphere of the café or the village.

"You know politics," Della said with a laugh, "You can depend on change, scandal, intrigue, and outright goofiness." Della managed to tame every unsettling topic with her humor. Today, she wanted to learn more about Maren's work. Maren gave general information about the huge variety of patients a speech pathologist sees. Della was fascinated and curious. "How can you focus on your patients with all the other problems demanding your attention?"

"It gives my mind some relief from what otherwise would be incessant fretting over family issues. The home visits give me some structure and a purpose that I need. It really touches my heart to see how dedicated the families are and how grateful they are for the smallest kindness. I'm seeing mostly adult patients now, and that is a challenge since I worked with children for the past five years."

"Would you like to see more children?" She looked as if she had a plan.

"Sure. In some ways working with children is more hopeful than therapy with adults."

"I'll see what I can do," Della said, as if she had some special power to arrange things.

John Westlake met Paul at Heathrow and took him to breakfast. As they drove he told Paul there was a new international effort to rebuild a major highway, in Afghanistan. "A human rights watch group issued a lengthy report on Afghanistan this week that calls for the expansion of the International Security Assistance Force beyond Kabul. It also calls for the US to exert its influence and adopt a peacekeeping role in the region. That means medical assistance as well as security forces and rebuilding efforts.

"They tell us the highway is expected to cost two hundred fifty million dollars, two thirds of it pledged by the United States, Japan and Saudi Arabia. It's a seven hundred fifty mile route that will run from Kabul through Kandahar and then to Herat, one of the areas that has been most heavily criticized by the watch group."

"And the highway would create a path for medical groups based in the secure areas like Kabul to travel to more needy areas?" Paul was guessing that John and Bev were positioning Possibilities to be one of those groups.

John cleared his throat. "Yes, well this morning the so-called secure Kabul reported at least four students of Kabul University were killed and dozens injured as students clashed with police in violent demonstrations. Students were protesting a lack of food and electricity in their dormitory."

"Have you initiated any discussions with officials there," Paul wanted to know.

"Actually, Pediatric Possibilities was approached by the military, pretty high up, from what Calvin said, to help in secured areas only. Bev flew out to D.C. for meetings right after getting back from India. We agreed we will not allow groups to be positioned in a mobile unit out in the field in a war zone. We will accept support from the military, but we will not risk losing our non-government status. We are looking now for a real hospital to work in or we'll not go."

"We'll be treating casualties of the war, soldiers?" Paul was concerned that his role was being changed. He wasn't trained to work in a war zone.

"Troops are immediately airlifted out to German hospitals," John assured him, "so the Possibilities crews will be there primarily to treat Afghan residents. The military assured Calvin that conditions will be better than what you just experienced in India."

Paul had been sleeping on a cot in a tent and slogging through mud to treat victims of floods and mud slides for weeks, but now had a bigger problem than that—how to tell Maren the latest news. He knew instinctively that an assignment in Afghanistan would not be a ten day stint. Neither he nor Maren could have imagined this over a year ago when they had made their decision, not that he really had any choice. When the child he had treated in the ER had died, the new administration had needed a scapegoat; and Paul was it. He still hadn't told Maren the whole truth.

Paul respected Calvin, Bev, and John, but in his judgment his team needed a break before starting a new assignment, a mission that almost certainly would be dangerous and very likely be long term. Fortunately, they agreed with Paul's assessment. He would fly home a full week before Thanksgiving. He would break the news to her then, not by phone.

As soon as he was outdoors, Paul turned on his cell phone and punched in Maren's number. "Hallo from London," He greeted her with a phony British accent and cheer that matched. Phony or not, it was the tonic, if not the miracle, Maren desperately needed. She had just parked in their driveway when his call came. She began briefing him on the latest developments. Nothing interrupted their conversation. Even the school bus cooperated by being unusually late.

"If I criticize or complain, Matt will feel justified in staying away," she finished.

"You raised him to value family, and he's always been especially close to you. I'm sure he will come to his senses in time. Listen, I've got to go. My ride is here. We're going to be here overnight, my last night in the inn with the garden where I dream of you. My flight leaves at five a.m. tomorrow. I'll be in Haiti briefly before coming home."

Paul was grateful to be updated on family news, even if it wasn't all positive. He realized what Sydney's behavior meant, and he didn't like it either. Mostly, he didn't like people or events that hurt Maren. As soon as he was in his room he called Matt. "Hi Paul," Matt answered eagerly. Since Danl and Zoe had joined the family, Matt and Nick usually called him Dad in front of the kids, never Danl's choice of "Dr. Paul." Mostly, it was just "Paul." He carried the authority of a doctor, if not a birth father, and his quiet firmness translated somehow into a parental authority.

"Your mom told me there's some doubt about you joining us for Thanksgiving." Matt sputtered a few words, without making much of an answer. "Have you made a permanent commitment to Sydney," he asked with male bluntness.

"Well no, but we have been pretty close." He left Paul to wonder exactly how close.

"Then you need to be with your family for the holiday. That comes first. Bring her or encourage her to spend time with her family. Flights will be full. Don't let it go until it's too late." Paul rarely made demands on the boys. When he felt strongly enough to confront them on an issue, they usually listened. This time Matt didn't answer, so Paul hit the topic once more. "I know you'll make wise decisions for both of you." Matt promised that he would certainly try to do that and asked about Paul's experiences in India. They finished their conversation not with "I love you," but what had become their traditional, "I'm glad we're family."

Paul turned on the TV in his room to watch international news and wind down. There was criticism of President Bush for insufficient humanitarian aid to Afghanistan. "There are European and Japanese aid workers in Kabul," the commentator said, "while American GIs are largely confined to a military base north of the city." From what John Westlake had told Paul, there would soon be visible signs that the Afghan people would not be forgotten.

Paul knew he would be monitoring the news from Afghanistan more closely. The very next morning's news carried the story of two Afghan children who were killed when they picked up an unexploded mortar in the eastern part of the city. Another child had a hand blown off when he picked up a butterfly mine. The U.S. State Department strongly warned U.S. citizens against travel to Afghanistan. Items of concern were military operations, landmines, banditry, and armed rivalry among political and tribal groups. Paul wondered how he could assure Maren of his safety. He wouldn't lie to her. His conscience accused him, and he answered back, *I didn't exactly lie; I just didn't tell the whole truth.* With an uneasy feeling he gathered his belongings and rushed out to catch his ride.

While Maren unloaded groceries, she reflected on how unsettled she still felt. Her conversation with Della relieved some anxiety. Talking with Paul had been comforting. But she needed a chat with her sister. Pocketing her cell phone, she positioned the hands-free earpiece and began putting dinner together while she talked with Ruth.

"When Paul signed on with Possibilities, I thought our husbands might work more closely together. Do you think their paths might cross any time soon?"

"Calvin has been mostly in the DC office," Ruth said. She realized that meant his travels would be more administrative than treatment oriented in the future, but she didn't say that. "He's been coordinating efforts for new locations. He told me to keep an eye on Afghanistan, but won't say any more until some arrangements are finalized. So, keep an eye on the news, Maren."

"Sure. I have the radio on all the time." Maren wasn't interested in talking about the Middle East. Her heart and mind focused on the events closer to home. "I want to talk to you about Matt." Maren brought Ruth up to date on all the family news, including Matt's mad crush on Sydney Webster.

"I feel like I'm too far away from the situation to help you. I think you should find out more about this girl. Would Cloris be of any help? Didn't Sydney live with Cloris and Mike at one time?"

It was a great idea. When Maren finished talking with Cloris later that night, she had a much clearer picture of what was going on. She could hardly wait to share the information with Paul when she met his plane, in just one more week. Totally forgetting Ruth's comments about Afghanistan, Maren called Danl and Zoe for dinner.

CHAPTER 9

Only a few days more, Maren told herself as she climbed in her van. She checked for voice mail messages, and retrieved one from Sue. The presenting diagnosis was traumatic brain injury. "John Spencer is in his late thirties and should be discharged from a VA hospital this week. He sustained a brain injury in an explosion in Afghanistan. He was just in the wrong place at the wrong time. As compensation he did get a medical discharge. He was able to talk in the hospital in Germany and then stopped by the time he checked into the VA hospital here. I think his wife Julie works at the school your kids attend. Isn't it Wayland Elementary? They have two kids, a four year old girl and a nine year old boy. Nice family. His wife said he's a commercial pilot and was a part time coach. He was in the reserves though—got called up. Get him scheduled as soon as you can, will you?"

Maren called immediately and left a message, asking to schedule the evaluation visit the next day. She needed to see Stephanie, Sylvia, and Wendy and stop at Stanton House before meeting the school bus in the afternoon. Tonight she would research the complications that might occur in TBI, other than the always possible seizures and CVAs.

She listened to the news broadcast as she drove. Boxer Muhammad Ali was in Kabul as a U.N. Messenger of Peace. He was scheduled to visit a boxing club, a girls' school, and President Karzai. Ali was bringing attention to the world regarding Afghanistan's humanitarian needs. The U.S. Treasury Secretary Paul O'Neill also had been in Kabul to demonstrate commitment to rebuilding Afghanistan. A five-star hotel was under consideration, he said, but didn't name the investors. "Afghanistan will not be forgotten," he assured the new government there. "The United States is committed to be here for the long term." *Sounds like things are going pretty well there.* It didn't occur to her that meant humanitarian aid companies would be moving into the area, or that the aid might include Pediatric Possibilities or Paul.

Maren found plenty of information about the complications of traumatic brain injury. There were numerous sequelae that could occur, including seizures, tremor, infection, and hemorrhage. Some of the drugs administered to prevent problems could themselves be toxic to the brain. One source listed ataxia, a gross in-coordination of muscle movements. She was familiar with ataxic dysarthria, the speech disorder that caused listeners to judge the patient as being under the influence of alcohol. This was especially true if the person's gait was affected. Such patients often walked and talked as if they were drunk. She was eager to meet John Spencer to see how his speech differed from George Sapien's slow, drugged sound. She was eager to help a veteran and his family in this next chapter of their journey.

The next morning she parked in the driveway of the Spencer's tri-level home on the west side of Dexum. They lived close to one of the schools where Julie worked as a physical therapist. She was the sole bread winner now and would be working today. The doorbell rang loudly and Maren waited a long few minutes before pushing the button again. Finally, a tall, muscular man wearing a sweat suit and a baseball cap opened the door. He was leaning heavily on a walker, but managed to turn the door handle and marginally open the door. It was up to Maren to open the storm door and push the inner door wide enough to enter with her wheeled bag.

"Hi," John said with a flat, overly loud voice. An older man with a pleasant expression stood behind John. "I'm John's dad Ed." Maren introduced herself and asked if there was a table where they could work. Nodding, but without a word John shuffled to the dining room. The back of an armchair was pushed against the wall. John let go of the walker and fell back into it. Obviously the chair was positioned there to keep him from scooting backwards or tipping over when he sat down.

Maren took off her coat and hung it over the back of a matching ladder back chair. No one had spoken since Ed had introduced himself. John's eyes wrinkled as he studied her. He kept the baseball cap firmly in place. A Cub's tee shirt that matched his hat completed his outfit. If he looked like a sports enthusiast, it was because he had been into sports, particularly baseball, all his life . "Ma…wy…ha…to…wou…to…day. Ma da ofa to hea."

The robotic clicking voice took approximately one second per syllable. "Your wife had to work. Your day for something?" She was guessing at his meaning. *This doesn't sound to me like ataxic dysarthria, but maybe he learned this style to compensate, to attain more control. I'm certainly not an expert like the guys who wrote the textbook.*

John's dad interpreted for her. "He told you that his wife had to work today, and I offered to help."

John sat quietly while his dad gave her a medical history. "When he arrived at the hospital in Germany they treated internal injuries and did surgery on his legs first. Then, to relieve swelling, the skull surgery." Maren had read in the VNA report that a section of skull had been cut away. The bone was stored "on ice" to be replaced later. That was not uncommon. She had worked with such patients before. "Has the skull piece been re-attached," she asked.

"Yes, but that's why the baseball cap. He likes to keep the site covered, even though the bone has been successfully restored. He could speak after that, but no one could understand him very well. He sustained burn injuries to his legs in the explosion, too. Fortunately, medics were able to save both of them. For a while, he stopped speaking altogether. There was a speech therapist working with him. She reported the same thing. The doctors ruled out stroke and seizures. They believe the brain swelling caused damage before they relieved it, while they were attending to his other injuries. Now he speaks, but..." Ed stopped and looked sadly at his son.

"How... lah... to... taw...uh... no...ma..." the clicking, monotone voice said.

"He's asking how long until you'll have him talking normally, again," Ed translated.

Maren had seen a number of patients with traumatic brain injury. She had been expecting cognitive impairments, but John seemed to be understanding and using language well. She wondered about his gait, the way he walked. And she wondered what, if any counseling the couple had received. *They are not going to be happy with me,* Maren realized. *I'll have to tell them he's never going to talk like he used to.* "Have you got a list of his medications?" she asked while formulating exactly how to answer the question. *Why didn't they explain this at the veterans' hospital—or maybe they tried and the family just wasn't ready to hear it.*

Ed produced a list of over a dozen medications—an antibiotic, anti-inflammatory, anti reflux, anti-anxiety, anti-depressant, as well as pills to lower blood pressure, and counteract the side effects of other pills. She stopped. In the few minutes she had been evaluating John she already knew he was depressed, in spite of the medication. She folded the list, put it on the table, and began in a business like way directing him to perform the basic oral-motor tasks. He was not able to puff air into his cheeks, but he could purse and retract his lips evenly and equally. Tongue movement was slow but even, no deviation. When he said "ah" Maren pointed her flashlight and watched the soft palate move with excess force, each "ah" was a gag. She watched, listened, and timed speaking tasks.

It took him eighteen seconds to say "puh" sixteen times. "Tuh" and "kuh" were about the same. He become less precise toward the end of the sequence. Alternating syllables seemed more effortful but about the same rate—"Puh-tuh" repeated twelve times took twenty four seconds. Maren noted that productions were performed with an extremely slow rate but with precise regularity. On each attempt some air escaped through his nose. And yet she heard "men" with no nasal sound at the end of the word. He pronounced it "meh." Air leaking out his nose during speech was probably due to slowness of his soft palate to open and close. *Not so good considering how slow his speech is currently. I can't ask him to slow down.* She recorded a speech sample on her digital recorder as he described an action picture and read the standard Rainbow Passage. That one hundred word paragraph contained each speech sound in the English language. She recorded a couple sentences of his spontaneous speech too. Intelligibility was better than George Sapien's at his initial evaluation. She had hopes that with repeated listening she could understand more of his spontaneous speech.

By the time they finished the recordings, Maren heard the back door open. It was John's wife Julie. She had arranged for a substitute to cover her students, so she could come home to meet John's new therapist. Unfortunately, the sub had arrived late. Julie's voice was quiet and calm. *I'll bet she's a good therapist,* Maren guessed, remembering that Julie was a physical therapist.

She was a stocky, short woman with long, curly, blond hair. She had braided it away from her face, revealing some gray roots. Days and nights of sitting in hospitals had taken their toll on her. There were dark circles under her eyes. John's illness would obviously have worn her down during the last few months, and Maren now knew first- hand something of the stress of having a husband overseas.

After introductions, Maren explained that she was starting to take some measurements that would help her understand more about how John produced speech. "The first thing you need for talking is air," she said, removing a length of flexible plastic tubing about the diameter of a narrow soda straw from a plastic bag. She filled a plastic glass with water, but not for drinking. It was marked with a laundry marker in metric increments. "This will show me how much air pressure hits his vocal cords when he speaks. It will establish a baseline, so we can measure progress."

She let him practice saying some syllables and phrases while she held the tubing in his lips. "Don't help me," she said. "Don't try to hold the tube in your lips, or bite it." Every speech task she asked him to say started with /p/. "Papa, papa, papa. Pass the pie. Put it away. Pa-pa-pa-pa-pa. Pop up a paper." Because she had heard air escaping from his nose during speech, she used a clip to hold his nose closed.

After he practiced, she held the other end of the tubing in the water, five centimeters deep. She directed him to repeat the sounds and phrases, again. Each time bubbles were produced she placed the end of the tube deeper in the water. The air flow of his speech was still causing a bubble when the end of the tubing was at the twelve centimeter mark. She knew her method was crude, not a computerized measurement for a research scientist; but it gave her valuable, objective, information.

"Most speakers would be around four or five centimeters of water pressure," she told them. "Eight or ten centimeters of water pressure makes for a pretty loud voice in a quiet room." *You're telling them what they already know*, she chided herself. "The question is, can we find a way to help him gain enough control to reduce that." She knew some experts said there was no way to change the speech pattern, once the brain had been damaged, but she had seen individuals learn to better use the control they did have. Before leaving, she would make sure there were no illusions about his speech returning to normal.

"Your work with John is really important to us," Julie said. "Jared is nine and Justine is only four. They understand him better than they did at first, but it's pretty frustrating for all of us." Maren took a long, slow breath. John's dad noticed that she looked away as she considered the mammoth task ahead. He realized that her hesitation was not a good sign. Maren believed that a cognitively intact, intelligent patient such as John might be able to exert some control once informed; but she didn't know how much and certainly couldn't make promises. "We'll do our best," was all she said.

"How much of what John says do you understand?"

"Oh, maybe half. More if I know what he's talking about. The biggest problem is when we can't understand him, he just gets louder." She wanted there to be no doubt what the family needed from therapy.

"Yes, we can work on that," Maren said. "We'll work on vowel sounds, too. I hear 'rinning' for 'running' and 'luck' for 'look.'" *Yes, distract her. Get her thinking about some things that can be changed.* It was obvious that Julie hadn't figured out the reasons for the poor intelligibility. "There's no melody to his speech, if you notice. Every sound and syllable has the same stress, same pitch." *Too much information.* Maren stopped verbalizing her analysis.

She asked him to say "ah" and hold the sound as long as he could—seven seconds. Normal was close to twenty for a healthy adult, but it was more control than the one second per syllable he currently used. She put the end of the tubing in the tall bottle of water, and directed him to blow bubbles as long and as evenly as he could, once again clipping his nose closed. "This will give me an idea how much air support he has for ongoing speech." She carefully held the other end of the tubing in five centimeters of water—thirteen seconds. She held it in ten centimeters of water— eight seconds. She tried it at fifteen centimeters of water—ten seconds. He had quickly realized that he needed to be careful or the water would bubble over the top of the plastic jug. He made adjustments, so he wouldn't make a mess and could make bubbles over a longer period of time. That was a very positive sign.

Maren hadn't been carrying tubing and containers when she had evaluated George Sapien. She was glad she had added them to her bag of materials right after that. "He's obviously strong enough for speech," she reported. "What I'm trying to find out is if he can learn better control. A good speaker takes a breath every four to five seconds. John currently takes a breath for each syllable he says, one each second. The measures I just took tell me he can do better than that." They were both educators and were listening attentively, interested in learning everything they could about the new word that described his speech disorder, *dysarthria*. While she spoke Maren wrote, "Severe Dysarthria," on her evaluation form. "I'll visit here twice a week, but he needs to work on his own or with someone else every day."

"Well," answered Julie skeptically, "We have a four year old daughter and a nine-year old boy, and I have to work full time. We'll do the best we can." John looked down, as if he were ashamed. Maren wrote "Prognosis: Good for improvement. Good family support. Good cognitive status."

Finally, it was Thursday. Maren met Paul at the airport where they could only enjoy a brief hug before being waved to move out of the pickup area. They drove to his parents new condo for a visit on the way home. Bob and Gloria were ecstatic to see them. "Penny and Jim helped us unpack. We've moved lots of times; so we really have it down to a science," Bob had talked non-stop as he gave them a tour of their new home. Maren felt more than a little guilt that she hadn't been there to help. Thankfully, there were no signs from Bob or Gloria that they had expected or needed more help.

Gloria poured coffee for herself, Bob, and Maren and gave Paul a glass of ice with a can of cola. "With caffeine," she stated, surveying the bags under her son's eyes. They had already listened to a brief version of the India trip. Gloria was the only one who realized that he was careful not to mention the next destination. Paul thought Maren might need some time to deal with the implications of shipping her husband off to Afghanistan before discussing it with the rest of the family. Intentionally, he shifted the conversation to Matt and Sydney, and Maren reported what she had learned.

"Cloris said Sydney is an attractive and extremely talented young woman with a beautiful voice. Her mother and father had vacationed in Australia, planning to fulfill their dreams by moving there one day. When he re-upped with the army and Sydney was born, things changed. Just before Sydney started high school her mom left—moved back to Germany. Sydney got through high school without much guidance, and went to UCLA for college and graduate school. She then seemed to attach herself to one family after another. She can be very charming and was invited to stay in various homes for extended lengths of time. She's never spent more than a few weeks in dorms and never had a place of her own.

"Cloris was originally very impressed with Sydney. She stayed with them between semesters, but that stretched into many rent-free months. Schmoozing, that's what Mike called it. She has a way of schmoozing with each person, giving gifts and compliments to each—to excess. Cloris made her sound very beguiling. She and Mike became concerned that their sons might fall under her spell. Every time Cloris started to ask her to move she either had some tragedy in her life that would make them feel guilty or managed to do something spectacular for one of their boys, like arrange a job interview. Cloris said she's a master manipulator, and when they finally did ask her to move she pouted as if they were ungrateful for all she had done for them."

"Where did she go after that," Bob asked.

"The last time they saw her she mentioned having bumped into Matt. She said she would be living in his area for a while, but was lining up more permanent accommodations."

"Maybe she's just looking for a family to join," suggested Bob.

"You're too kind," Gloria said, "I'd say she's more of an anaconda, squeezing the life out of one victim after another to maintain a lifestyle she enjoys."

"You're thinking of python, dear," Bob said; but they all got the idea.

Maren was shocked at her mother-in-law's lack of sympathy. She felt obliged to attempt neutrality. "She is talented."

"That's the truth," Gloria insisted, "She's got her talented tentacles around Matt already."

"Gloria, snakes don't have tentacles," stated Bob wanting to keep the metaphor straight.

"If that's the case," said Maren, ignoring the science lesson, why not accept our invitation?"

"Because," answered Paul, looking more grim than usual, "She's already been thrown out by one branch of the clan. She may need to keep him isolated from his family and emotionally dependent on her in order to maintain her meal ticket."

"Doesn't her dad support her?" That was Bob' question. Where were the parents, grandparents? "Matt said she doesn't see much of her dad and hasn't seen her mom more than once or twice since the divorce." The conversation moved to a discussion of Thanksgiving arrangements.

Back home Paul unpacked and rested while Maren made calls. Ronnie Cameron was running out of time. Her sister's wedding was coming up; and according to Sue, her exceedingly generous landlord was coming to the end of his ability to wait for rent. Ronnie needed her life back, and soon. Maren knew several GI doctors from her days of working at St. John's Hospital. She was persistent in her attempts to help Ronnie and reached one doctor as he was beginning surgery. In each case, after explaining the girl's plight she failed to find anyone to do the dilation procedure. Paul found her staring at the phone, the yellow pages open on the computer screen. "Can I help?"

"Maybe," she said, looking up at him with a new idea. "Maybe you can."

CHAPTER 10

Maren stopped at the Village Pharmacy on her way to see Sylvia Villisca. Chris Evans the owner and pharmacist noticed the name on her credit card and smiled. "Are you the traveling speech therapist I've been hearing about?" Maren was reminded almost daily that news spreads quickly in a small town. Still, she wondered how the pharmacist had heard about her.

"Della Mason told me she knows you. I've been wanting to get some private therapy for my son Cole, but I didn't know how to find someone. I know our insurance will cover it. He has neurofibromatosis. He's doing pretty well in school, but not making much speech progress. Would you consider working with him?"

Maren was somewhat reluctant. She would have to review the disorder. That part was easy. What was more challenging in her mind was that she had never filed an insurance claim for a patient in her life. Some business office had always done that. *Another new adventure. I'll find someone to help me learn the process.* "I'd love to work with your son," she assured Chris, with more confidence than she felt. "Let's start right after Thanksgiving."

Cole Evans attended the middle school, and the Evans family's busy schedule wouldn't permit more than one session a week. They would usually only have Monday afternoon available. Chris convinced Maren to do the evaluation the day after Thanksgiving while they were not on the school schedule.

Maren had planned her visits to spend maximum time at home with Paul and prepare the Thanksgiving feast, but Friday after the holiday now looked pretty busy. At least the beginning of Thanksgiving week was light. Today she only had therapy with Sylvia.

She parked in front of the "Vagabond House," as she now thought of the Villisca's home. Guy had told her their daughter Beth would be visiting for the holiday, and it was Beth who answered the door. She was wearing a food spattered apron and held a wooden spoon. "Come in, come in," she said cheerily. "I'm so glad to meet you. Mom and Dad talk about you all the time. Mom so looks forward to your visits. We're in the kitchen making cranberry relish."

"Sounds good," said Maren. Guy was nowhere to be seen. *I hope I can get some therapy accomplished.* She followed Beth to the kitchen where Sylvia was sitting at the table supervising the preparations.

"Hi, hi. Come," she managed on her own.

"I've never made cranberry relish with a food processor."

"Oh, we make a big batch—two in fact—one with the orange rind in and one without the rind, just the fruit. Here, taste them both and see which one you like best."

The warmth of love in the home was as comforting as sunshine on an early spring day. Maren judged the batch with the orange peel as the winner. "Just a little more zip, don't you think so,

Sylvia?" She was trying to get a modicum of therapy accomplished, even though one had to make allowances for visiting daughters and Thanksgiving preparations. "Zziff," answered Sylvia, as close to saying, "Zip" as she could. And there, spreading across her face, was the first real smile Maren had ever seen from her patient.

The three women actually had a fun hour together. An outsider would have thought Maren was a long time friend of the family. Sylvia was saying more words and phrases than Maren had expected to elicit. *Ah, the power of human interaction,* she mused as she left.

On Tuesday Maren had no patients, but her mind was on young Ronnie Cameron. It had taken a few days to make the arrangements, but once Paul said he was willing to do the dilation procedure for Ronnie—provided the stricture wasn't too far down the esophagus—he had found a friend in the city who had scheduled her for Tuesday during his OR time. The friend was to assist Paul. Just in time for Thanksgiving Ronnie Cameron could be free of the stricture that was blockading her life. Maren alternated between Thanksgiving preparations and silently praying for Ronnie, until she got the call. "I'll be having Thanksgiving dinner," Ronnie reported triumphantly. "And the G-tube is gone." Paul's GI friend had removed it while Paul dilated the esophagus. Ronnie asked Maren to make one more visit, even though she didn't really need it. "I have something I want to give you."

Before Maren could turn around, the phone chimed again. It was Matt. He told Maren he had a business trip on the east coast right after Thanksgiving weekend. "I decided I might as well make the trip a'two for the price of one." He meant he would be home for Thanksgiving, and Sydney would not be with him.

The next morning Paul helped with breakfast and getting the children off to school. He asked Maren if she would mind having company on her walk. She had already been planning her day, but realized that habit patterns formed during Paul's absences would have to be adjusted when he was home. She knew she should be glad for his company, but it felt like another demand on her time. Even so, it wasn't long before she began talking about Matt. Paul tried to be patient with her, as she talked her way through the situation one more time.

"Why do you think he keeps seeing her," he finally asked.

"I think she's built him up with praise and made him indebted to her with gifts. She can be quite charming."

"And she is very attractive," he added. "What kind of gifts, besides the golf clubs?"

"A tennis racquet, new bowling ball, clothes, books, a very nice watch…"

"What, no Lamborghini?"

"If she could come up with the cash down payment she would have. With each gift she tells him how special he is, how wonderfully amazing their relationship is, and how happy he makes her. He can't seem to see through it."

"Well," Paul said, trying to console her, "when a man is in love his brains tend to fail him."

"In love." She stopped on the path and repeated his words. Paul turned toward her. There was enough morning light to see the distress in her green eyes. "Maren," he said gently, "He's been seeing her for three months now. He's not putting up with her behavior just because he enjoys the gifts."

"Oh… I hadn't thought of it in those terms." Maren thought of love as selfless, a lifetime commitment, not a temporary euphoria.

Grateful, but stunned to have his viewpoint, she decided to explore it further. "Paul, how would you feel if you were in Matt's place? What would you do if you wanted some distance?"

"I'd like to say I'd confront the issues, clear the air, set some ground rules," he said.

"But?"

"But, when I felt pressured I'd probably become increasingly busy and unavailable until she complained."

"You mean try to wean her."

"At first."

"And if she kept pressuring you?"

"I'd confront her then... I know, what if she continued to put demands on the relationship. I'd see that as an unhealthy sign and do whatever it took to get out."

They had finished the circuit and went in the house. Usually she got in the van and went to the Village Café after her walk, but not this morning. Paul had been as patient as his nature would allow. He removed his shoes and grabbed her hand firmly. "Come with me wife," he said softly, "We have some catching up to take care of."

After they made love, Paul had a strong sense of how his dishonesty had become a barrier between them. He had to constantly monitor his words. It was constantly in the back of his mind. He had thought it would go away as the chance of her finding out grew less, but the feeling of separation just seemed to increase over time. Withholding one piece of information had led to bending the truth; and that had led to several mixed messages, statements that she might see as outright lies. He wanted the barrier to dissolve. He wanted to be totally honest with her the way it had been in the beginning. He pulled her into his arms.

"There is no good time for what I'm going to say, Maren. I just hope you can understand." He decided to tell her the most recent decision by Possibilities first, before she heard it on a newscast. He planned to follow up with the rest. Holding her tightly against his chest, he began.

"Afghanistan!" She pulled back and repeated the word. She hadn't thought of that as a possibility. She had been afraid of losing their closeness, but hadn't really considered that Paul might lose his life. She was grateful for his arms around her now. Neither of them moved. She closed her eyes, trying to absorb what this would mean for them. For the first time she had to consider the possibility that Paul, eleven years younger, might die before she did. Paul pulled back and said her name. When she opened her eyes, he could see that her peace and security had dissolve. He kissed her head, and assured her that everything would be fine. If only he could be assured. Maren was the best thing that had ever happened in his life. Sure, he had enjoyed a good, if somewhat lonely bachelorhood, before meeting her. And he continued to believe that they were meant to be together, destined even. He had believed that since that fear-filled night during the medical mission he had taken to Burundi. It was when the team had been surrounded by insurgents who were not supposed to be in the area that he had felt the need to be with her.

He had felt attracted to her at the hospital, but she was a new widow then with two teen aged sons. She was definitely not the package he had in mind for a wife. She was trying to get through graduate school, definitely not interested in dating. He had admired and respected her, but wanted to maintain the same professional distance he managed with everyone at the hospital. He couldn't though, not after Burundi. He had actually felt an intrusive thought that night, a directive to be with Maren. He could still taste that moment when he first knew. It had taken some doing, though to convince her that they could become life partners. Now, it had all worked out. Yes, he believed they were destined to be together. And for a year in Chicago and five in Colorado they had been constant companions at work and at home, until he was fired. It had taken a war in Africa to bring them together. Now a war in the Middle East would keep them apart. The word "Afghanistan" had brought their talk to a stop, and left each swirling in private emotions. It didn't seem right to hit her with another, even worse issue. His full confession would have to wait a while longer.

Wednesday night while Paul made the late airport run to get Matt, Maren relaxed with a book and watched the late news on TV. It was mostly soft news, during which she fell asleep on the couch.

She dreamed that a beautiful, beguiling creature blinded her with its poison spray, and then squeezed her until she thought she would suffocate. A bell of some sort seemed to send the creature into a frenzy. She awoke to the sound of the phone ringing. She kicked the afghan off. *When will I learn not to use heavy blankets? I wish a bell would frighten Sydney away.* The call was Uncle Frank from the Maryknoll headquarters in Ossining, New York to say he was snowed in. The plows would clear the roads within twenty-four hours, too late for the family Thanksgiving.

Thanksgiving Day dawned bright and cold. Maren slipped out of the bedroom early to put the turkey in the oven. Paul and Matt had returned from the airport within minutes of Frank's call. They had been too tired for any significant conversation and had gone straight to bed. Danl and Zoe heard her in the kitchen and insisted on helping stir the pumpkin pies and put whole wheat bread to bake in the bread maker. It was everyone for him or herself for breakfast. Paul got up in time to take charge of the stuffing, leaving Maren free to do and hot vegetables. The children had tired of cooking as soon as the pie and bread were baking. They went to build a castle with their Legos. Predictably, Matt slept late.

Nick and Carrie arrived early and brought salads, both green and cranberry gelatin. Bob and Gloria brought wine and shrimp, in addition to Zoe's favorite, pecan pie. Elizabeth rode with them and brought her specialty, stuffed mushrooms. Penny, Jim, and the girls provided a huge vegetable tray with two kinds of dip and munchies for later in the evening.

By mid afternoon, everyone joined hands around the table and began the traditional circle of thanks. "Lord, I thank you for the growth of our clan." Maren had never heard Bob use her label for the family before. Gloria was thankful that they had been given the ingredients, the key ingredients she said with a mysterious smile, for a happy life. Nick and Carrie each affirmed that they were grateful for the other and a good family. Matt was thankful for homecomings. Paul for the opportunity to serve the children of the world. Maren gave thanks for the extra season of life God had granted her with Paul. Penny and Jim thanked God for health and family. Erin for cousins. Colleen for pie with real whipped cream. Danl was grateful for Legos and the stars and planets. Zoe was last. "Thank you God that Daddy can help other children around the world, like he helped Danl and me." Maren's eyes were misty as Paul finished, "And all of God's children said…" They all loudly exclaimed, "Amen."

Everyone had more than their fill of turkey and side dishes, so pie was put on hold until the kitchen was restored to order. The leftovers were divided into food bags and marked with names to be taken home. "Nothing better than Thanksgiving leftovers the next day," said Gloria. She was pleased that Maren and Paul continued the tradition she and Bob had started, sending home a portion for each to enjoy the next day.

"I'd like to help," said Paul moving away from the dining room, "but Matt asked me to take a walk."

"Huh?" said Matt, unaware that a McCloud tradition was passing from one generation to the next. For years Bob and Paul would take a walk or at least spend some private time together after family dinners. Maren and Gloria observed the changing of the guard, as Bob called it. He had opted to play games with the four children, thus signaling that Paul was now the dad. "This is my new tradition," Bob proclaimed as Danl led him to the basement play area where an electric train and Lego village had been set up.

A dusting of fine, white flakes sifted through the air. Paul and Matt retraced recently made tracks on the front walk, footprints that led from the cars where their guests had recently parked and carried their contributions to the feast. They turned south toward the old graveyard. Paul's large shoes obliterated a single set of smaller indentations, but they didn't notice.

Paul was thinking about starting a serious discussion with his step son when Matt suddenly stopped and stared toward the old graveyard. A black Ford Explorer that had been parked, backed into the cemetery's entrance, had pulled out so quickly they couldn't see the driver. Matt had a heavy feeling that wasn't caused by the over abundant meal. He couldn't quite make out the license number, but he was positive it was not an Illinois plate.

Paul looked from Matt to the car, and as his eyes scanned the distance he now observed that the small set of footprints they had been following from the house ended where the tire tracks began.

"Someone you know?" asked Paul innocently.

"Uh, no—It's a… Sydney drives a Ford SUV like that."

On Friday the sun beat back the threat of winter. Maren had patients to see, and Paul was glad to stay with Danl and Zoe. Rather than take advantage of an opportunity to sleep late Matt offered to take his mom out for breakfast. He wanted to confess to her that he had lost his job and that his business trip was actually an interview in Boston. Of course they went to the Village Café. "I thought Sydney would be pleased about the job interview. You know she doesn't make any money to rave about and just keeps charging anything she wants or thinks she needs."

Maren passed up the opportunity to take a poke at Sydney's character. "She wasn't happy about the possibility of you moving?"

"We didn't get that far. She just didn't want me to go for the interview unless she could go along, and neither of us could come up with the ticket price for the day before Thanksgiving."

"Well, hello neighbor." Will and Louise Botna had come in. After introductions, Will explained that they were going to have breakfast before taking their daughter to the city for the day. Maren was disappointed to end her private conversation with Matt, but graciously invited their neighbors to join them.

Will was full of questions and quickly drew Matt into an animated conversation about his education and hopes for the future. "We're looking for a sales representative for this area," Louise said. "We develop and manufacture specialized medical parts for the kidney dialysis process. In fact Will has quite a number of patents."

Maren was surprised. When the couple had mentioned that their business kept them very busy she had assumed they owned a restaurant or small store, not a biomedical manufacturing company. As vice president of Botna enterprises Louise was in charge of hiring and had a sixth sense for recognizing talent. When she heard the details of Matt's background, she saw an opportunity. "If you're going to be around on Tuesday or Wednesday, why don't you come talk to us." She handed Matt her business card. Now it was Matt who had a lot of questions. Maren listened with growing hope while finishing her crepes. She signaled for the check, and explained that she had home visits to make. It looked like Matt and the Botnas would have enough in common to keep the conversation going without her presence.

She patted Matt's shoulder. "You can walk home, can't you? If I go now, I'll get home sooner. Thanks for getting up to have breakfast with me." As she moved around the table she stumbled on Louise's handbag spilling the contents, including some kind of electronic device, smaller than a computer but larger than a cell phone.

"Oh, I'm sorry," Maren said, starting to scoop up the items. She held a small electronic apparatus in one hand and the purse in the other.

"Always good to have a book to read if you have to wait someplace," Louise explained about the device.

"Especially the Good Book," Will added. "That little gadget was a gift from our oldest niece. She gave it to me because I travel so much. I mainly have music and the Bible on it. Compact, isn't it? It's amazing what a difference it makes in your life to read the word of God as little as ten minutes a day."

"Yes," Maren agreed absently, continuing to collect items from the floor. She recognized that Will had just said the very words Vance Davidson had spoken the day she had visited the old village church. She was also aware she still hadn't done anything about it. She handed the device to Louise. "Small for having a whole Bible, isn't it?"

"Not only the Bible, but whatever version you want and also in several languages. We do business internationally, so occasionally that is useful." Maren hadn't known Will traveled to other countries, but she did know what she was getting Paul for Christmas.

She said goodbye again, paid their bill at the counter, and walked through the door into the bright sunlight. As she opened the van's door, a reflection or movement across the street caught her attention. A thin figure with long blond hair swinging below a military type camouflage cap jerked open the door of a dark SUV of some kind. The woman entered the car, started the engine and began driving before she could have had time to fasten her seat belt. Maren stood and stared. For an instant she thought about pursuing the vehicle, because the driver looked for all the world like Sydney Webster.

Maren's first stop was to see Ronnie. A young man answered the door and introduced himself only as Aiden. Maren quickly put the pieces together. Reconciliation was in the air. Ronnie's future was looking brighter. There would be a role in Ronnie's sister's wedding, a job, and perhaps in the not too distant future a pregnancy. Ronnie came into the room holding an envelope in one hand and something round in the other. "I wanted to give you a thank you card for helping me and…uh, something I made." She handed Maren a white envelope. The gift in her hand was a necklace. It was a strung with beads in such a way that it held the image of an angel. "I made hundreds of them and sold them to raise money for the American Cancer Society. You're one of my angels. I think angels are human sometimes, so we can see them. Sometimes they are spirit, and we just experience what they do for us. The day you told me to pray was a sign to me that everything would be okay."

The gesture touched Maren's heart, softening her expression. She felt humbled. Ronnie could have used some income for herself, but gave away what little she had to help others. Maren wasn't at all sure she would have been as gracious in coping with all the misfortune that Ronnie had faced in her young life. She certainly didn't have the faith that Ronnie had, even now.

She drove west of Edgelawn to the Mercer home. Maren hadn't seen Wendy for over a week due to another short hospitalization. She was eager to find out how her husband had enjoyed the anniversary card and thank you letter they had labored over for such a long time. The hospitalization had come at a bad time. They hadn't quite finished the letter.

She knocked on the door and turned the handle. It had been unlocked so she could enter. Wendy was on the phone, and Maren could tell from the conversation she was talking to Brad. "I have to go now. A nice lady is here." Wendy couldn't remember Maren's name from visit to visit or that she was a speech pathologist. *If a family member would go over her notebook with her it might help.* Unfortunately, each member of this family had maxed out on the stress of being Wendy's helper long ago. No one but the professionals had much left to give.

On Maren's last visit she had made a notation that Wendy was resistant to any kind of language exercise that she sensed was an exercise. Only functional activities seemed to motivate her. The letter to Brad was fortuitous. It kept Wendy searching for words and nuances of words for a few weeks. Now she needed to find a way of continuing with pragmatic activities.

"Let's start making some menus," suggested Maren. Wendy was eager to cook, but reluctant to do the preparation necessary. She confused a grocery list with a recipe, but insisted if it weren't for her leg she would be doing the shopping and cooking. *Unrealistic assessment of her own abilities,* noted Maren again. Patiently, she worked through the tasks with Wendy. She asked if Wendy wanted to read aloud the letter she had written Brad, but for some reason that was off limits. Wendy reported only that Brad was very impressed with the letter. It took some probing to get the problem. "I don't think he believes I wrote it," she said. "He thinks you wrote it."

Maren promised to talk to Brad about the letter and cued Wendy through some easy reading material, nothing very interesting. Some fiction would be better. She would see if Marlo or Brad could stop at the library to get a few books Wendy might have read in the past. Next, Maren placed some pages of words and phrases to be matched with pictures in her exercise folder. Finally, they went through Wendy's notebook and talked about the appointments and activities for the week. Maren sighed as she let herself out. *We're still in the beginning phases of her therapy.*

She switched on the radio as she drove away, listening to the announcer go over the latest news. It was mainly about the hunt for al-Qaeda members and Taliban fighters. The U.N. Security Council had voted unanimously to extend the International Security Assistance Force in Afghanistan until December of 2003. Germany and the Netherlands would take over command of the four thousand eight hundred man force that was stationed in Kabul, at least for the next six months. As an aside, the announcer stated that about nine thousand U.S. troops were currently in Afghanistan. There was no mention of terrorist attacks so far during the holiday weekend, although city hospitals were warned to be on alert. Knowing Paul would shortly be working in Afghanistan, Maren wondered how the news might impact her family in a personal way.

Some friends must come aboard
to laugh or wield a sword.
Companionship's key number three.
We'll weave a three-strand cord.

CHAPTER 11

The Thanksgiving Day snow had already melted under a warm autumn sun. As Matt left the café he felt the south wind ruffle his hair. Seeing the barber shop across the street he decided a haircut was a good idea. He was feeling pretty cheerful as he crossed the wide street. After all, he had a job interview. Not one interview, two. He had to walk around ladders extending from a white paneled truck parked at the curb. That's where he collided with a tall woman who was wearing paint-spattered coveralls. Her cap fell off, revealing shoulder length dark brown hair. Matt chased the wind-driven cap across the sidewalk, trapped it with his foot, brushed off dried leaf particles, and returned it to her.

"Guess I shouldn't have stepped on it," he said in apology.

"Not a problem. Thanks," she said stuffing the cap in a pocket. Her hands looked strong, but feminine. He noticed no paint spatters, and no rings. Their eyes met briefly and he was aware of her thick lashes and dark eyes. No mascara needed, he thought. In fact, no make-up needed. Before he could say anything more, she turned, got into the truck, and drove off.

After his haircut, Matt went straight back to the house and changed his flight plans. He called Sydney's cell phone to let her know about his new arrival time, so she could meet his flight. He wouldn't tell her that he had an appointment to meet Louise Botna the following Tuesday morning, just that he would be spending an extra night in Dexum. She answered on the first ring.

"What about our Monday night plans? You were going to have the interview and fly straight home."

"What Monday night plans?" He didn't recall that they had any special plans.

"We always have dinner at Westby's in the mall."

It was true that for two or three Mondays in a row they had gone out to eat, but he didn't consider it a tradition. In the back of his mind he thought it was a bit rigid. He had thought of Sydney as a free spirit. This was a new trait. "Maybe we could have our Monday night dinner on Wednesday night," he said trying to cheer her. It didn't work.

Sydney clicked off her phone. She was not happy. Exactly what she feared seemed to be happening, but she hadn't argued further with Matt. She did scowl as she drove her Explorer into a service station and used a credit card to tank up. She had a long drive ahead of her and would have plenty of time to think of a way to counteract this turn of events. She wasn't about to be a scorned by this family a second time.

The breakfast meeting with Matt and the Botna's left Maren feeling hopeful for the future, especially Matt's future. She mentally reviewed the information she had read about the speech and language problems associated with the little known disorder Neurofibromatosis. Chris Evans had told her that Cole's diagnosis was Neurofibromatosis type one, or NF1. She knew it to be a genetic disorder of the nervous system. There was a long list of various symptoms used in making the diagnosis. Her attention had been drawn to a paragraph describing weakness of facial muscles and the growth of soft, fleshy tumors on the skin and occasionally in the brain or on cranial nerves. Fifty percent of people with NF1 also had learning disabilities, her online medical source had stated.

She found Chris Evan's big, old two-story house without difficulty. "I thought all the houses on this side of the village were bungalows. It was easy to spot your place." Chris' shiny, dark auburn hair fell across his forehead, pointing to a few freckles splashed across his nose. He had Irish ancestors for sure. The fourteen year old boy who stood timidly behind his dad was obviously his dad's son, same coloring, same freckle pattern.

Chris told her that Cole had two brothers and a sister who more nearly resembled their mom. Both Chris and his wife Tanya had been college athletes, according to Della. They played basketball at state, and expected their children to do the same. That wouldn't happen for Cole, unless it was Special Olympics. There were unidentified bright objects, UBOs, in his brain and fibrous benign tumors at various places in his body. The tumors tended to form along nerves.

The symptoms of the syndrome that most concerned Maren were delayed speech and language. No one knew why. It was just part of the syndrome. Cole's language disorder had originally been mistaken for autism, but he wasn't autistic. He now extended one limp hand for Maren to shake. His knees and feet angled in, similar to a child with cerebral palsy. His voice, barely audible, emanated from a stiff smile. He seemed to be trying to hide his orthodontic bands. Most kids find the teens a challenging time of life, Maren thought, but most don't have to cope with neurological disorders. Maren couldn't understand anything he said. He lowered his eyelids and looked sideways at his dad, expecting Chris to speak for him.

"What grade is he?"

"He's in ninth. His language is below age level, but he doesn't have a diagnosis to explain that. He doesn't speak often, and when he does no one can hear him or understand him. Loudness really isn't a problem when he's home with family, just with others."

"Can he blow bubbles through a straw?"

"I think so."

"Let's find out."

Chris had an empty half gallon milk jug. Maren had the plastic tubing. She cut it and pushed one end to the bottom of the jug half-filled with water and dish soap. She set the jug in the kitchen sink and directed him to blow. He expended his breath all at once. Poof. It wasn't enough to make soap bubbles appear in the water. He blew repeatedly, puff, puff, puff, little short blasts, no more than two or three seconds in length. He wasn't able to make bubbles with the end of the tubing at the bottom of the jug. *Poor force. Poor control.*

Maren asked him to name pictures from her articulation book. He demonstrated confusion of phonemes. He slurred both consonants and vowels in conversation. *Here is another example of dysarthria, but it's mixed with something else. Maybe central auditory processing disorder or select mutism. Possibly both. Doesn't matter. He has a medical diagnosis of neurofibromatosis.* At least she had some ideas for therapy. "I think Cole has a lot of potential." Chris nodded, guarding his emotions. He stuffed the spark of hope down, like a tissue in a pocket, thinking it should not be allowed to show. "Oh-kay," was all he said.

It was almost midnight on Saturday before Paul and Maren found time for a private talk in the dinette over coffee and pie. They had found private time in the last few days, but not for conversation. They had discovered that being apart caused potent physical reunions. Early in their relationship Paul's nearness had caused Maren to be immersed by sensations she had rarely if ever felt in her first marriage. To some extent that continued now, six years into the marriage—especially after absences, but in a more comfortable way. It was a miracle, she decided that what she most enjoyed seemed to be what he most enjoyed. With these memories running through her mind, she had to force herself to return to the reality that Paul seemed very quiet, never a good sign for Paul.

"Maren, there's something I've been wanting to talk to you about." She hoped it wasn't about giving up her work. She had already severely limited her hours so that he wouldn't feel she was spreading herself too thin.

It seemed a lifetime ago that he had held the baby's life in his hands and lost it. The pediatrician had not shown up, so Paul had been named the attending physician. He had to start someplace. "Do you remember how abruptly I was let go by the hospital in Colorado?"

"Yes, when the new administration cut the staff."

"But if you noticed, I was the only physician who was let go."

"John Whitson left, too."

"He was an intern. His term was up." This was going to be more difficult than he had thought. "He was an intern, Maren," he repeated. "I resigned to prevent an investigation and possible lawsuit in the death of a patient, an infant." He had Maren's full attention now.

"The case was complicated, and the pediatrician on call didn't show up. Well, when he showed up it was too late; and with the luxury of time to think, he had other ideas about how things should have been handled. In retrospect, I should have left the child to the ER staff; but I intervened. I tried to help."

"I don't remember hearing about this before."

"No, I never told you about it."

"And the parents blamed you?" She knew Paul couldn't have been to blame. She didn't see a problem and hadn't a clue why he was bringing up the incident now.

"The baby had an allergic reaction to some medication I ordered. It was listed in his medical record, but I didn't feel there was time to look for and read records. I didn't take the time. Adverse reactions are always a possibility, but are rare. The records were in his pediatrician's office three miles from the hospital. It might not have been fatal if a lower dosage had been given. The point is I administered a drug the patient was allergic to. At the time the child needed immediate intervention. The parents were never told that I was there. They were in the ER waiting room. ER talked to them." His look was begging Maren to see the grim reality of what had happened, and that he had been trying to help. "There was a deal Maren. I could stay and make all the facts known, including the late arrival of the pediatrician. But if the parents sued, the hospital would have sacrificed me, saying I wasn't called and shouldn't have been in the ER. The pediatrician—with hours, days, even months to think about which drug and what dosage—might have testified against me... to save himself... would likely have testified against me. Then they would have fired me outright. My license and reputation were at stake. I was afraid, Maren. Every doctor in the country lives with that fear."

"Why didn't you tell me this before?" It was her first reaction. He had kept a major incident a secret from her, for a long time.

"I didn't want you to be put through that, to be married to a doctor who had lost his license."

"Paul, you know I…"

"No wait, that's not all of it." He wanted to be totally honest with her. He had been a liar for too long. He had even lied to himself. Now he needed to be brutally honest with himself and with her. "I didn't want to be disgraced in your eyes. It was pure pride. I wanted to be the doctor on a mission, the one you fell in love with. The worst part is I told myself you wouldn't be able to understand the complexities of the case, so it was best to not tell you any of it. It's true there was a closed door agreement. They promised no public statements would be made, as long as I resigned. The new company needed to cut staff. My reputation would remain untarnished if I didn't talk. I needed to be able to support you and the kids. It all seemed to work out. If I talked about the case, they could publish whatever version of the incident they decided to publish. But my silence shouldn't have included you. There shouldn't be secrets between us. I have suffered so much because of this."

"You suffered." She was beginning to understand the repercussions of his decisions. "So you didn't give me a chance to understand or believe you, or to be part of the decisions, decisions that affected all of us."

"That's right." He was glad to accept his guilt. He was hoping now there would be quick forgiveness.

"And you took the Pediatric Possibilities position to keep your secret, to escape."

That's where his thinking got fuzzy, and he was not used to that. He used to be so clear headed, before he started lying. "I think it started out that way Maren, but when I got involved I began to understand what drives Calvin and John and Bev. I began to feel what they feel. Now it's more like I was called to Possibilities."

Maren wasn't ready to hear that. She was still trying to process all the facets of his confession, and it had been a very busy week. She was tired and hurt that Paul hadn't trusted her enough to confide in her—that he had lied to her. "It's unbelievable that you didn't trust me. When we worked together there was no issue we couldn't discuss. Since I became a stay at home mom, you don't respect me. Only *you* could make decisions for the family. Only *you* could earn a living for the family, for us. Now because of your unilateral decisions I'm left alone in a new city trying to hang on to my professional competence. I'm essentially a single mom to two uprooted children; and you hide oversees to protect your reputation. I wondered why the sudden passion for Pediatric Possibilities. Calvin couldn't talk you into joining, although he tried for five years. Then one day you came home and had decided. You had done everything but sign the contract. You basically expected me to rubber stamp it." Her voice was getting louder. She stopped.

"It was just that you would have no way of knowing for sure— judging whether or not I was justified in what I did, given the circumstances."

"I think you are the one who wasn't sure you had done the right thing. Otherwise, it would have been easy to tell me the facts. Why did it have to be Possibilities? After 9-11 we were already talking about moving back, to be closer to your folks. Why not get on with a practice here? I've never gotten a good answer to that."

"Maren, with the political upheaval and down economy my options were limited. Maybe I could have worked, but not in ENT.

Specialists in private practices were seeing a huge drop in referrals. Pediatric Possibilities seemed like a great alternative."

"But you didn't even try. You dumped the family responsibilities on me and expected me to give up my profession, without even making a few calls." She was seeing it all at its worst and wanted every question answered.

"I was convinced no group would accept me, even if I had fabulous references, something my former employer was not likely to give."

"And now you are going off to a war zone, with your new buddies to escape reality, to satisfy your lust for excitement." In her hurt and anger she was descending into the pit of sarcasm."

"That's not fair."

"Fair? Is it fair for me to be left alone wondering if you're the next casualty? Paul, you're not in the military. Pediatric Possibilities is supposed to provide medical care to individuals caught in natural disasters. You did not sign up to remain stationed or embedded with troops in war zones. Can't you just refuse this location and go to the next one?" Her next comment was substantial. "You could resign Paul. We didn't join this organization to be in a war. Even if you work only part time here we'd be fine with my income. I'm asked to see more patients every day."

"Maren, even though I had mixed motives for joining, I gave my word I would stay at least a year. Maybe after a year something else will open up. Pediatric Possibilities will be my previous employer; and they will give glowing references, if I wait to resign until the end of the probationary year. You know I am not the kind of person who doesn't keep my word. You wouldn't want me to renege on a promise, would you?" He remembered then that when he had asked her to marry him he had gone down on one knee—a kitchen towel over his shoulder—and promised her if she married him she would never regret it. He hoped he would also be able to keep that promise.

Now she felt defeated. As hurt and angry as she was, she knew another broken promise wouldn't make right what he had done to her, to their marriage. Frustration, and anger boiled up, bile in her gut. Before she could answer she needed to count to ten, numerous times. "I need to be alone for a while, Paul." She turned and walked out of the room. He started to follow her. "Please, just go back to the kitchen, and leave me alone." Feeling miserable, he turned and walked back toward the kitchen. He hoped the worst was behind him, but he still hadn't told her about the new headquarters being in London instead of the states. Matt had left the TV running when he went to bed, so Paul hurried across the living room to turn it off before Maren could hear it. The newscaster was reporting that a total of fifty-three attacks had taken place against U.S. forces in Afghanistan in November—up from forty-nine in September and fifty-one in October. The tally of incidents, included mines, direct fire, mortar and rocket attacks.

Paul heard it, but Maren did not. She had gone straight to their bedroom and closed the door. *He was the one who told me our marriage was meant to be. He was always so sure. How could he have changed so much? He's gone so much I don't even know him anymore.* She thought she would soak her pillow with tears, but was so exhausted sleep overcame her emotions before Paul came in.

CHAPTER 12

Bob and Gloria McCloud spent Sunday night in Dexum, so they could take Paul to the airport early Monday morning, allowing Maren to get the children off to school and see the new patient at Stanton House Assisted Living Apartments.

Maren was relieved and grateful for their presence. "I really hate the airport run," she told them, but beyond that it masked the fact that she wasn't talking to Paul. They didn't seem to mind doing the favor, and if they detected a cool atmosphere between their son and his wife, they assumed it was due to Paul's departure. "That's why we gave up our condo and boat. We want to spend time with our children and grandchildren. We're grateful that you need us." Maren did wake early to tell Paul goodbye and see them off. He still hadn't told her about the new headquarters.

Matt's interview Monday morning went well. He liked the city of Boston and the staff he met. He thought they liked him, too. As he had expected though, they made it clear that they were looking for someone with a Ph.D. He doubted he'd get the position; even though he had started on course work toward a doctoral degree and promised to complete it, if hired. The bigger problem was that universities tended to move very slowly and he needed a job rather quickly. He caught a noon flight back; and Granddad Bob McCloud, the only grandfather Matt had ever known, picked him up at the airport. "Hey Matt. I heard United Air Lines is headed for bankruptcy. I'm glad your flights didn't get canceled."

"No flights were canceled, but it was a no frills trip—no food service." Bob got the message. They stopped at a restaurant in the new strip mall on the edge of Dexum. It was full, even though it was long past the lunch hour. "Probably a lot of folks hanging out for the free wi-fi," Bob supposed aloud, trying to impress Matt with how savvy he was.

Just then Matt caught sight of a wi-fi user he had seen before, the dark-haired painter. She wasn't dressed in coveralls though. Her tall, thin frame was outlined under a snug black sweater and black slacks. "Hey, did you give up your painting job?" She looked up from her laptop, startled, and something more than startled. Was she pleased or annoyed? He couldn't quite decipher the look.

"Oh, I... uh... I'm only a part time painter."

"Taking classes?" He guessed, judging by the books and a notebook on the seat beside her that she was a student.

"Yee-aah." She smiled, actually a full smile, at him. "It seems like a good investment for the future."

"I'm visiting Dexum. My folks live here. Uh, did you say your name is Carol?" His ploy worked.

"I didn't say Matt, but it's Laurel."

Bob had moved ahead, grabbed a table and was motioning to Matt. Reluctantly, Matt wished Laurel good luck on her studies, ending their conversation with, "See you around." *At least I got her name this time,* he told himself. He would probably find out more about her at the Village Café. His mom said the waitress there knew everyone in town. He suddenly realized that she had called him by name, and wondered how she had gotten it—maybe from the waitress at the Village Café.

Maren stopped for a comforting cup of coffee and equally comforting chat with Della before her stop at Stanton House and then a line-up of patient's before ending the day at the Evans' home.

Della already knew Maren had evaluated Cole. When she found out Maren was nervous about filling out insurance claim forms, she offered to help. "My sister bills insurance where she works. I'll get her to teach me. By the way, there have been a couple of robberies in the village. Keep your doors locked." Maren wondered if there was anything Della didn't know or have a contact who could find out. *What a resource, she is. She's better than a private secretary.* Della was also becoming a good friend.

By the time Maren was on her way out the door she was already thinking about her next patient. Carl and Barbara Voris lived in the new assisted living wing at Stanton House. He had no previous history of stroke or illness, but was having trouble swallowing. The elderly couple had no relatives nearby, so had taken a two-room apartment there to assure space in the rehab center or skilled nursing wing if they required it later. They had the option of cooking with their microwave oven and crock pot, or going to the dining room for their meals. The crowded apartment had a small refrigerator sitting on the counter. A twelve inch TV just fit on top of that. Maren had stopped at the kitchen in the rehab center to get some food for the evaluation—a quarter of a ham salad sandwich, a container of applesauce, and some potato chips.

They crowded around the table for two while Maren watched him perform the tasks of the oral-motor exam. He could move his lips appropriately, and protrude, retract, elevate and move his tongue laterally. He could circle his lips with his tongue clockwise and counter clockwise, without hesitation. She watched and listened as he ate almost all the food and chugged half a glass of water. She was wondering why the doctor had ordered a swallowing evaluation. He had no trouble whatsoever, yet the referral stated that Carl choked or coughed at almost every meal.

"Does he choke in the dining room, too?"

"Hmm, now that you ask, I don't think so."

"No, I don't think I ever choke in the dining room," he confirmed.

"I wonder what makes the difference."

"I can't say. I just sit right here where I am now and watch TV while I eat. Next thing I know I'm choking on something. I don't want to get a G-tube." He looked nervous.

Maren observed his posture change when he looked up at the TV. His head tipped back. "I think your problem has a simple solution, and you won't need a G-tube. Let's check out my theory." She turned on the TV. Sure enough, when he tipped his head back to look up at the screen he coughed on the first bite. That posture allowed bites or sips to fall into his airway. When she left they were already calling their son to bring a TV rack to stand on the floor, so Carl could safely see his shows while eating.

After completing the documentation for the day's VNA patients, Maren stopped at the Radio Shack in the new strip mall and bought a sound pressure level meter to use with Cole Evans. She wasn't worried about Danl and Zoe, because Noreen had readily agreed to watch them after school one afternoon a week. She told Maren she had wanted children since the first year she and Randy were married. He was career army though, and didn't believe it was possible to have a stable family with him away so much. Noreen would gladly work an early shift at Stanton House in order to have children in her home.

Cole Evans answered the door. Maren could hear him no better than at the evaluation, yet Chris insisted he could be quite loud around the house. Maren had asked them to blow bubbles in fifteen to twenty centimeters of water until he could do it for twenty seconds. He had been three seconds the first time he had tried it. They all went to the kitchen for the activity. Maren set a tall beverage bottle filled with water in the bottom of the stainless steel sink, hoping the placement alone would encourage him to blow water over the top of the container. She listened to the bubbles and watched the second hand on the Evan's wall clock. Eleven seconds. "Very good," she said with enthusiasm. He didn't blow bubbles over the top of the bottle, but he had definitely improved. She let him rest and then had him try it again.

"He's inconsistent," Chris reported, "but he has really gained more control."

"This should translate directly to speech performance," Maren said. "You don't really need twenty centimeters for speech. Eight to ten should do it. I always over train, though. I want speech to seem easy for him." *Still, Chris is saying he can be loud. I've never heard it. I wonder if that means on a single word or for prolonged speech.*

While she continued to monitor Cole's efforts, she took the new sound pressure level meter from her bag. She stopped the blowing exercise and praised him for his efforts. He smiled his dreamy smile and waited for the next activity. Maren demonstrated how the "loudness meter" worked. With the dial at sixty decibels she held the microphone near her mouth. "It should register at least sixty five," she said loudly; and pressed the Data Hold button.

She turned the device around to show them that it read seventy-one dB.

"Can you make it do that?"

"Yeah," he said softly.

The loudness meter said "Low."

"Try again."

"Yeah." This time it was sixty-two.

"Better. Can you buy one of these? Cole could check everyone in the house as well as use it during his speech practice."

"Just tell me where to get it," Chris answered.

Chauncey bounded to the door to greet Maren. Zoe and Danl were right behind.

"Mom, Mom, Miss Noreen let me play her violin," said Zoe. "She said she can teach me. Is that okay?"

"I play cello and sometimes violin with the Edgelawn Community Symphony. I'd be happy to get her started," Noreen said. "I'm really amazed how quickly she picked up the fingering."

"She actually has her own violin," said Maren with a smile. "She may not remember, but her mom played violin and left her instrument for the children." *Life in a village can be quite cosmopolitan. Here is a little girl whose Native American father deserted her; her very talented German descendant mom died; her adoptive dad is in Afghanistan; and a woman from Thailand wants to teach her to play her mom's Japanese made violin.*

"Danl, how about you? Do you want to play the violin, too?"

"Could I play with Chauncey, instead?" Maren sighed. They would have to deal with Danl's music education in some other way.

Relief and joy flooded through Maren as she drove home. The Monday child care arrangement would be beneficial to all. She could work with Cole, and thanks to Della would soon be able to bill insurance. Danl would have a pet in the neighborhood. Zoe would get music lessons. And Maren would have more opportunities to deepen her growing friendship with Noreen.

She got dinner while listening to Matt's recounting of his interview. As soon as she got a few minutes to herself she went to the computer to see if there was any email from Paul. She could never predict when he might be on line. It was not only the time change, it was the odd working hours. Ah, there was a short message. His group had arrived and they were getting settled in their new quarters. Unfortunately, the hospital they had planned to use in Kabul was another victim of the Taliban. It had been destroyed during their reign, and now radiation contamination from the destruction of the radiology department rendered the hospital completely unusable.

Maren decided it was better than no news at all. *Maybe if they can't get a hospital to work in, they won't stay in Kabul after all.* She remembered what Noreen had told her when she picked up the children. Randy believed the emphasis was changing from Afghanistan to Iraq. The news today seemed to confirm that. There had been nothing about Afghanistan. The President had signed the National Authorization Defense Act, and he made another strong statement that Iraq must provide a full and accurate declaration of its weapons of mass destruction or face the consequences.

The next morning Maren sipped decaf coffee and waited for Matt to return from his interview at Botna Enterprises. She marveled again at the resources available in the village of Dexum. Not three miles from their home was an international biomedical supplies company, and the owners lived right next door. Their facility was in a new industrial center tucked behind the elementary school. At noon Maren would drive Matt to Bob and Gloria's condo. The grandparents would take him on to the airport. Maren hoped this morning's conference would be more promising than the east coast interview.

Louise Botna spoke with Matt for only thirty minutes before asking how soon he could start. She hired by personality and character. He would make a great sales rep for their products in a five or six state region, but he had a lot to learn about dialysis systems and their other products. He would need to spend at least a week working with Will and her at the office before going on the road. When he told her he needed two weeks to finish some business in California, Louise told him she could email some reading material to him, but because of copyrights she preferred to wait until he was back in Dexum for the more detailed information.

Matt's thoughts meandered as he walked the narrow sidewalks to meet his mom at the Village Café. He was excited about working for the Botnas. It felt more right than anything he had done, except his decision to drop out of law school. If Sydney wanted to take over his apartment when he moved, he could help pay the rent until she got a job. He was sure his mom and Paul wouldn't mind having him at the house until he got back on his feet. He knew they had bought the large house to have sufficient room for family. If Sydney didn't want to move into his place, well maybe she could… He opened the restaurant door and came face to face with Laurel.

"Hey. Are you following me, or am I following you?" She was giving Matt such a captivating smile that he stammered when he answered. He told her he was meeting his mom for coffee. She kidded him about that. "Come on, there's no one in there old enough to be your mother." He pointed out his mom's van as proof, license number SLP N 4 to indicate her profession and number of her children. He offered to buy Laurel a cup of coffee in two weeks, when he got back to town. She agreed, if it was a latte. Since they didn't make lattes at the Village Café, it would be an official date out of the village.

As he joined his mom at her favorite table, his thoughts briefly returned to Sydney. He wasn't sure what she could or would decide to do. He was surprised that it didn't make as much difference to him as it had a week ago. It didn't even occur to him to ask her to come to Dexum with him. Maybe having some distance would clarify their relationship, he decided. Like Paul had said at Homecoming in October, it could be an opportunity for them to experience love at a distance.

Maren had watched Matt hold the door open, allowing the lady painter to pass in front of him. She noticed their smiles and eye contact. A glimmer of hope was born. *I'm not the only one making new friends in Dexum.*

After Maren dropped Matt at Bob and Gloria's, she started her home visits. Stephanie ran to the door to greet her. Joanne was almost as eager. Maren had talked with the professionals who had evaluated Stephanie the previous week at Circle Campus, and Joanne could hardly wait to hear what they recommended.

"Joanne, they basically said that Stephanie is making progress in therapy; and we shouldn't mess with success. Just keep on with therapy."

"Oh... okay. We can do that. We've been blowing lots of bubbles and not much air comes out her nose anymore."

Today's therapy games included "painting" lines on a mirror by saying "sss" through a soda straw. Stephanie tried to keep her teeth closed to do it. She was so successful Maren got her to add vowels to the sound, with a little pause between the /s/ and the vowel. "SSS…ah. SSS…oh. SSS…ee. SSS…aw." When she left, Maren asked Stephanie to say, "SSS ee you," instead of, "Bye-Bye." *She's not just making progress; she's making great progress,* Maren thought. Her young patient could produce at least ten different speech sounds, and Joanne had compiled a list of over one hundred recognizable words Stephanie used on a regular basis. It was enough to set Maren humming as she loaded her therapy suitcase into her van. She turned on the FM music station that played Christmas music during the holidays. It reminded her to put some of her CDs in the car. *Nothing like Christmas music to keep one cheered.*

CHAPTER 13

Almost two weeks passed in a tornado of activity. Things seemed to be going pretty well on both continents, except for a smallpox scare that turned out to be nothing more than a scare. It was Friday the thirteenth when U.S. intelligence reported a belief that the virus, long ago eradicated in America, had been kept alive by hostile regimes in laboratories. It's potential use in war was frightening. Government officials were considering having the entire military vaccinated. Paul had never been inoculated. Maren wondered if there was enough vaccine to cover those working for NGOs. Her fear for Paul's safety made her realize that as angry as she was at him, she still loved him.

Paul's situation, although he was living and treating patients in a tent in a war zone, was better in some ways than when he had been in India. He didn't have to slog through mud to treat patients. They came to him. Pediatric Possibilities had agreed to move temporarily into tents, courtesy of the US military, until a clinic of some sort could be built. He did have access to email, so he could send and receive messages every day. That was a significant improvement for both Maren and Paul.

The dormitory tents were larger and better equipped than in India, and the group was assured they soon would work in a hospital. The military had promised protection, including moving the medical team to an aircraft carrier if it became necessary. There was also talk that the non-military medical group's living accommodations would soon be in an actual hotel.

The first few days after the team's arrival, the city of Kabul was quiet; but they were warned that gunfire, land mine explosions, and roadside bombing would likely resume. Paul occasionally came in contact with military physicians and nurses and began to feel a kinship with them. Although he had no rank, it gave him a new feeling of connection with his ex-navy dad and ex-army uncle Father Frank.

The information Bev and John had been given proved to be true. There were plenty of pediatric cases as well as adult head and neck injuries. The human suffering was enormous. Unlike what he had encountered in India, this was human induced suffering. Paul increasingly admired his military colleagues. They seemed to function as if living the way they did was normal. He wondered if he would adapt, and they assured him that he would. What he privately wondered was if he would measure up. They couldn't promise that. Once again, he questioned his motivation; and his conscience was giving him no clear assurance.

His thoughts turned to his family less often than when he was in England, because his team was constantly busy learning the culture as well as treating illness and injury. It assuaged his guilt at leaving Maren alone with two young children when she assured him that she didn't feel alone in the way she had when Jack died. She didn't have Paul's companionship or constant presence, but she had to admit he still remained an integral part of their lives.

She had an active, healthy family support system nearby, and she and the children were making some really good friends in Dexum.

Fall was definitely at its end in Dexum. The gloomy, chilly days signaled the inception of winter. She was grateful to have patients that demanded her attention during the day. It would be easy to become as gloomy as the weather. Noreen an experienced army wife had coached her, "Don't hang on every news report while your husband is away. Turn off the TV. Keep busy. Be constructive." It was good advice, but easier said than done. She did avoid the TV newscasts and tried to wean herself from her use of the van's radio.

Maren turned away from the computer and saw the school bus through the French panes of the dining room window. It had just turned onto Crescent Avenue. She noticed a moving van backing into the driveway of one of the houses down the street. A fancy black truck of some kind was parked at the curb. She walked through the entryway and into their library to get a better line of vision. *Oh, it's across from Peter Winslow's house.* She had heard that the small ranch house had been rented. *And there's Peter.* He was coming up the sidewalk with a frisky, black dog on a leash. *When did he get a dog?* Danl and Zoe would be delighted to have a four footed friend living just down the street, even closer than Noreen's Chauncey.

She was putting on her coat when the phone rang. Caller ID displayed Matt's number. Awfully early in California for Matt to be calling. Something must be bothering him.

"Hi Mom. My car is packed and I'm ready to start driving." He stopped. It was a day earlier than planned.

"Okay, great. We'll be glad to see you." She didn't know whether or not to ask the reason for the early departure.

"Yeah, things have been kind of strange here." He stopped again.

"Strange? What do you mean?"

"Ever since I got back I think Sydney has been following me. I mean it seems like that. Maybe it's just a coincidence. I went out to the hardware store, and when I came out she was sitting in her car in the parking lot. The next day I stopped at a sandwich shop for lunch. She walked in right after I sat down. Last night I was loading some things in the car and saw her standing a half block away at the street light, just watching me."

Maren couldn't help asking, "Is she going to take over your lease?"

"No, she said she doesn't have that kind of money. She got kind of huffy about it, even though I offered to help pay the rent for a few months. I found a grad student from the university that was glad to get it."

Maren restrained herself from further questions. She didn't want to ask if Sydney would be coming to Dexum. The word *stalker* crept out of her subconscious and into her consciousness thoughts. That word, or a seed of it, had dropped into the fertile soil of her imagination the day she thought she saw Sydney across from the café. *Just a couple more days and Matt will be free of her, safe in Dexum.*

Greg Carson was having coffee this morning and motioned Maren over. She hadn't seen him in weeks. "You've got a new black lab in your neighborhood, but not in your house," the vet said, smiling. He loved to be on top of village news. Being the only vet in town he had been asked to check the black Lab over.

"Black lab? I saw it, but I thought it was a small dog." Greg was just the person to tell her all the details. The dog was only three months old. Meredith Winslow Winston, Peter Winslow's daughter was concerned about trying to take their new puppy to Washington, D.C. with them. Ross Winston had told Greg the real issue was she didn't like her dad being alone. "They decided to get another pet in D.C. and leave Baker with Grandpa. Poor Pete—I don't think he's really keen on having a dog to take care of. Mark my words, he'll find a way to pass that dog on to someone else. I'll give him your name when the time comes."

"Greg! I never said we were looking for a dog."

"But you should. How can you raise children without a dog?"

"I've already done it once. We had a cat. I saw no need for a dog. I know that a vet who favors dogs would have a hard time understanding that."

"I like cats alright. It's just that I know dog lovers when I see 'em. You and the kids need a dog."

Maren laughed at his good humored persistence and promised to let him know when, as he put it, the time was right.

When Greg left, Della came over with the insurance papers for Maren. Della had all but filled out the documents that would allow Maren to become a provider for Chris Evan's insurance company. Della sat down and showed Maren how to fill out a claim form. Maren thanked her. "I wouldn't have known where to begin."

"It was not a big deal. Do you think you can help Cole?"

That was a question yet to be answered, thought Maren; and turned the conversation to the latest news. According to Della the news in Dexum was disturbing.

"There have been two more robberies, the first out by the new strip mall; but one was right in the village. I've heard that some of the homes were second floor condos. Wouldn't you think someone lazy enough to be a thief would choose only ground-level targets? He'd have to carry a ladder around. Kind of obvious." Maren had lived in larger cities, so she didn't get overly concerned. She knew that one of the sad facts of the Christmas season was that there was always an increase in the number of thefts.

As Maren was paying her bill, the painters came in. *Don't they ever work early,* she wondered. *Isn't that strip mall finished, yet?* The lady painter smiled and nodded at Maren as if they were neighbors. Maren returned the silent greeting, observing that the young woman's good looks were not obscured by her overalls.

After drinking only one cup of coffee, Maren began her visits. George Sapien had a complaint, but Alice voiced it. "George wants to work alone, do his speech assignments, on his own." Maren could tell there had been some friction or at least frustration between the two over speech exercises. It was a frequently encountered and entirely normal part of the recovery process. He was trying to regain some fragment of independence. Until recently Maren had depended on Alice to speak for George, or at least to interpret. Since they had worked on breathing and /t, d, n,/ and /l/words, Maren found she more often spoke directly to George. "Sure," she answered. "But I think it's still a good idea to do some work together." *Even when he uses the mirror, he doesn't always realize when the midpoint of his tongue extends past his front teeth.* When the tip and middle of his tongue protruded that far, it took too many milliseconds to retract it for /ch, j, sh, k, g,/ and /r/. Those sounds were badly slurred.

They reviewed exercises and Maren impressed on George that he would have to be very observant when working alone. "His voice is so low," complained Alice. "His voice was never that low before." He seemed to be still trying to push his voice out the trach site, although the trach tube had been gone for months. "He learned new techniques for speaking when there was an opening in his neck. Now he needs to unlearn those technique." Maren decided resonant voice therapy might be just the thing for him. His voice sounded so de-nasal that she wondered if he had allergies. He had been cleared by an ENT doctor; so next session they would start working on voice and resonance in addition to breathing and articulation. *I'll have to make it very clear which exercises he can do alone and which assignments they need to do together. I don't want to be responsible for a divorce here.*

Wendy was scheduled to have her last leg-stretching procedure right after Christmas. That meant she would soon have less pain, but it would also signal the end of her home health care. She wouldn't be able to drive a car herself, but she would be able to more easily get in and out of the family vehicle. She would no longer qualify for VNA care, and while Maren was happy for the physical progress she was not satisfied with what had been accomplished in speech therapy.

She knocked and walked in, as had become her routine. Wendy had made modest progress with pre-reading activities. She usually completed the worksheets Maren left for her, but now it was time to jump to a new level. Maren wanted to raise the level of performance to assure that Wendy would qualify for outpatient therapy. She had missed many appointments, mostly due to medical reasons. Sometimes the family simply forgot Maren was scheduled, and she would find Wendy still in bed. Today Wendy was up, and Maren helped her hobble to the kitchen table.

She's not going to make progress fast enough to justify keeping her in therapy unless she starts reading and writing. Maren was sure

Wendy would like one of the stories she had brought along. One was about a woman becoming a grandmother. One was a woman's journey of faith. Another was the story of a family's struggle for survival after a tornado demolished their home. She hoped the stories would facilitate work on language, reading, and emotions.

They began by reviewing the pages Wendy had prepared for her. The first was a grocery list. The second page had several lists—items in categories. She had named three methods of travel, five fruits, eight items of clothing, and nine furniture items.

"I just looked around each room I was in to get those," she said proudly.

"Looks great," Maren praised, although disappointed that there weren't more items listed. "I brought some stories today. Take a look. See if there's something that might interest you." Maren had called Brad and Marlo to ask about Wendy's reading preferences. The pre-morbid Wendy, the Wendy before the accident, would be excited to read all of them, her daughter had assured Maren. Wendy chose the tornado story and for the first few sentences seemed to be doing well. She stopped. "I remembered you told me how important reading is. I've been practicing. I hope I do well today." Then she continued to stare straight ahead. Her face suddenly lost what bit of expression usually registered. She was a mask with a static, crackling sound, like a kid imitating a machine gun, emanating from her throat, "a-a-a-a-a-a-a-a-a." Her facial muscles twitched. Her arms twitched.

What's wrong? Oh… Seizure, seizure! Wendy's head fell forward onto the table. Maren grabbed her to keep her from tumbling off the chair. Her mind raced. She had read about seizures and worked with patients who had seizures. But never had she been the only professional present during a seizure. TBI patients were always at risk, though. That's why they were medicated, to prevent this from occurring. *Keep the patient from biting her tongue. Prevent falling. Prevent injury. Call for help.* All were great ideas, but not all were attainable at the same time. *How long—how many seconds were going past. Someone would ask… a few seconds, a minute, more than a minute?*

Maren fought the panic that threatened to drown her thought process. There was no one to take over if she fell apart. *Be the rock.* And then Wendy went limp. Maren nearly went limp with her. *Phone. Find the phone. Find Brad's number.* She propped Wendy against the kitchen wall. Brad didn't answer. She dialed nine-one-one and then Brad again. He answered on the first ring. By the time she told him what had happened, the doorbell was ringing. *Must be the EMTs.* They came in like the house was on fire—fast and serious. Wendy opened her eyes. She was confused, embarrassed, tired, and disappointed to realize that, in spite of the medication she took, she continued to have seizures.

Maren was not convinced she had done all the right things. She worried that she might have put Wendy under too much performance pressure. She drove to a nearby park and called Sue Williston at VNA.

"You did the right thing," Sue told her. "Brad will probably tell you not to call emergency if it happens again. There's really nothing anyone can do, and families resent the expense and what the patient is put through. The EMTs just check her over and clear you of any liability though, so you did the right thing. She'll be tired. Give her some time off. I'll notify her doctor that she needs a higher dose of her meds. Now, head for your next visit. Leave it behind."

Matt had spent three nights on the road. He had stopped to visit friends in Wyoming, but was supposed to be home by dinnertime today. Maren put the ingredients for stew into the slow cooker while Danl and Zoe were eating cereal. She slipped out of the kitchen to see if Paul had sent email—nothing this morning. She shut down the computer and started gathering her patient files and materials for the day. From the library window she noticed a man in a black leather jacket leaving Kraft's house across the street. *Kind of early for a salesman.* While Maren watched, Sally squeezed under Carolyn's arm and started toward the school bus stop. "Finish eating kids. The bus will be here soon," Maren called over her shoulder. She opened the closet door to reach for her coat, but the doorbell rang.

When she opened the door she couldn't see much through the blinding morning sun. There was a black jacket, but not much of the visitor's face. He handed her a card and introduced himself as Marc Vincent, free lance writer for Beyond Our Past Magazine. "I've been assigned to the Midwest for the next three months or so to research Civil War sites and memorabilia. I rented the ranch house across from the old cemetery. I just want to get to know my neighbors and be part of the community as long as the assignment lasts. It's bad enough moving around the world without having to live in hotels all the time."

As he talked Maren thought she smelled smoke. At first she assumed her new neighbor must be a cigarette, or worse yet a cigar smoker. About the time it registered that the odor was from inside her house, Zoe screamed. "Danl, it's on fire!" Danl yelled, "Mom, the towel is stuck..." The shriek of the smoke alarm drowned out the rest of his words.

Marc Vincent raced past Maren and beat her to her own kitchen. He surveyed the situation in an instant, grabbed Danl from the chair where he stood—before he could touch the toaster again—set the boy down, yanked the smoking appliance from the wall plug with his gloves as hot pads, and headed for the deck door in the dinette. Maren was by his side by that time, turning the bolt and opening the back door for him. Why Danl had poked a dishtowel into the toaster wasn't clear, but if there had been fire it had gone out quickly. Mostly there was an abundance of smoke from the damp towel still stuck in the toaster.

Seeing they were in danger only of being deafened by the smoke alarm, Maren opened the window over the sink, snatched her largest cutting board, and fanned the air near the alarm until the noise stopped. Zoe had followed the stranger onto the deck in case he needed her advice about where to place the offensive appliance. When they returned she was giggling and chatting with him as if she had known him all her life. Danl interrupted. "I'm sorry the toaster caught on fire Mom. I just put a frozen waffle in for Zoe, but when I tried to pop it up it wouldn't budge. You always tell me not to stick a fork or knife in to get them out, so I thought I could reach it with my fingers. I didn't want to burn my fingers though…"

"So he tried using the towel to get it," Zoe said, "but it's okay, 'cause I don't feel hungry anymore."

Maren introduced their new neighbor to the children and thanked him for his help. "You're certainly a neighbor worth having."

"I feel like I'm part of the community already." He smiled somewhat stiffly.

"I'm sure we missed the school bus by now, so I need to drive the children to school. Otherwise I'd invite you to stay for coffee. How about coming over tomorrow morning, say fifteen minutes earlier. Please bring your wife. We'll all get acquainted."

Marc looked at her intently for a moment longer than it should have taken to accept a casual invitation. His face didn't reveal much about him. *Not much inflection in his voice.* If she had been evaluating him, she would have checked the box for "Flat affect," a symptom of brain injury.

What is that look? It can't take that long to accept or refuse a cup of coffee.

"It's been a long time since I had breakfast with a seven and nine year old. There's no Mrs. Vincent though."

"I didn't really have breakfast in mind," Maren corrected with a laugh, "just coffee and a fresh roll from the Village Café. So if you still want to come…"

"And bring your light saber," Zoe said, "So we can slay the toaster dragon again."

Maren was surprised to see his face wrinkle into a really warm smile. "Oh, I will. And coffee and a roll would be fine. If Danl was just a little taller he could have dragged that ornery toaster out by himself, but then I'd have missed an opportunity to get to know all of you." As swiftly as the smile occurred it slid away, leaving that same well-rehearsed, neutral expression. Unexpectedly, Marc Vincent had been thrust into the comfortable domesticity of the McCloud home. Comfortable domesticity was not where his job usually led him.

CHAPTER 14

John let her in, and it was obvious he was alone... no wife or father to interpret. *I hope I can understand him well enough to accomplish something.* "John, I want to start working on breath control today. The easiest way to demonstrate the technique is for you to lie down on a couch and let me put a book on your stomach. Can you do that?" The bigger question would be could he get up again. And if he couldn't, was she strong enough to help him without having him fall.

While Maren had difficulty understanding John, he had no problem comprehending what she said. He leaned heavily on his walker, reminding Maren of his leg injuries, and made his way to the couch in the family room. He fell more than sat on the couch and pulled and pushed himself around until he was stretched out, with his head elevated on the armrest. Watching him move drove home the point to Maren that his balance was off. It wasn't just weakness from the leg injuries.

"Where are your lungs?" As she expected he placed his hands on his chest, near his neck. Patients usually believed that, probably because that's where a physician would first place a stethoscope to listen. "Where are your ribs?" he lowered his hands appropriately. "That's right. Those ribs are there to protect your lungs. Now if you put your fingers under your lowest rib and kind of walk them to the middle you will find your diaphragm muscle." He followed her directions.

"I'm placing this book on that area and I just want you to watch it while you breathe." They both watched the book. Unlike George Sapien, John caught on right away and seemed to have more feeling and control. She moved the book slightly and asked him to hold the book up with his rib muscles and abdominals. He complied. She asked him to say, "whoo" while holding the book up. He was able to prolong the sound for three seconds. Maren was elated and congratulated him on a job well done. She was hopeful that within a week he would use much improved articulation, which would result in greater intelligibility.

He didn't have as much difficulty righting himself as she had feared, although standing was challenging. The soft couch didn't give him much of a foundation from which to launch himself. She noticed the increasing strength he had developed in his arms in just a few weeks. When she commented on his strength, he said, "Ah woo wi puh suh nuh tai nuh." She could not decipher what he was trying to convey, and he wasn't able to control his hands and fingers to write it. "Good," she nodded after his third attempt, hoping that was an appropriate response. Just in case it wasn't she added, "Good first session John." She instructed him to practice three to six times a day, short sessions. If George Sapien had made such impressive progress when originally he couldn't even feel the movement of his breathing muscles, John should catch up to him quickly.

Maren rang the Villisca's doorbell repeatedly, but there was no response. Puzzled and a bit worried she called the VNA office and learned that Guy had taken Sylvia to the doctor's office. Home Health visits were often unpredictable due to medical complications. She wrote the note on her VNA form that would be dropped off with the rest of her notes at the end of the week. She had one more patient to evaluate before seeing Cole, and she was not looking forward to it. It was a woman with brain cancer.

The diagnosis of brain cancer was essentially a death sentence. Maren wanted some music to cheer her on her ride to Dexum, but she quickly tired of hearing the holiday song Santa Baby. She switched to an a.m. station. The news did nothing to cheer her. After predictions about the coming war with Iraq, the newscaster covered the latest from Afghanistan. A grenade was thrown into a jeep carrying two U.S. Special Forces soldiers driving through Kabul. One suffered an eye injury and the other a leg injury. Their Afghan interpreter also was injured. A suspect taken into custody revealed that he had received terror training at a camp inside Afghanistan, near Pakistan. Five of the students had traveled to Kabul looking for American targets.

It was the first time the daily news included a specific item where Paul's team might have been involved. Maren switched off the radio and forced herself to think about the session she was about to begin with Cole.

Maren was trying to calm her nerves by baking biscuits while she waited for Matt's arrival. An after school snack of cheese and grapes had staved off hunger for the younger McClouds, but soon they would be ready for a real meal. For now they were happily playing in their rooms. For two weeks she had been imagining Matt's homecoming as a significant break with Sydney. Until he started traveling for Botna Enterprises he could stay with his adopted siblings while Maren accomplished some Christmas shopping. It would be like old times, when he lived at home. He finally pulled his station wagon and trailer into the driveway at six-thirty He didn't come in right away, so she opened the overhead garage door. He was standing in the driveway, talking on his cell phone. He waved and a minute later slid the phone into his pocket, but in that minute her hunger for dinner had been replaced with an unsettled feeling.

Danl and Zoe came running at the sound of the garage door. The blast of cold air didn't stop them. They propelled themselves through the garage and affectionately plowed into their big brother. He came into the house with an arm around each child. "Smells good in here. Sorry to be so late. There was snow in Iowa, and Sydney called almost every hour to make sure I was okay." *Sounds like an over-protective mother. I didn't even do that.* Maren felt a tinge of guilt that she hadn't checked with him, but there had really been no time. She gave him a long hug. He was home. That would have t o be enough for today.

The meal and the evening passed pleasantly, without mention of Sydney. Zoe drew pictures for Matt to tape to the walls of his bedroom while Danl challenged him to a game of checkers. When Zoe and Danl went to bed Maren thought she and Matt would have a chance to talk, but after Sydney's second call she gave up. She was sure his phone had caller ID and an off option. She was forced to admit that Matt was still not ready to sever the relationship. Discouraged, she went to her bedroom and watched TV until she fell asleep.

While Matt had the luxury of sleeping late, the school and work schedules remained the same for the rest of the family. Zoe and Danl were finishing their cereal and juice, and Maren was slicing pecan rolls from the Village Café when the doorbell rang. Although Maren had forgotten, Zoe had not.

"There's Mr. Marc, just in time for pecan rolls."

"Oh, that's right. I promised coffee."

"I'll let him in," volunteered Danl.

"I'm coming, too," said Zoe, jumping down from the tall counter stool.

In the excitement of Matt's homecoming, the promised get acquainted coffee time had been driven from her memory. She allowed Zoe's chatter to entertain Marc in the entryway while she dumped the two-day old pecan rolls on a dinner plate and put them in the microwave for twenty seconds to soften them. *Maybe he'll take a cup of tea.* She met the children and their guest as they were coming through the dining area. Marc's expression was still hard to read. *Is he shy or what?* He looked to be about Maren's age, so shy didn't quite fit.

"I was just about to put the coffee on, or I've got tea."

"Tea is fine. I'll have coffee later, when I really need it."

"That's what I always do," she said, startled that a man would have a similar habit. "In fact I don't usually make coffee. I get a morning cup at the Village Café. If you want to get to know the locals, that's the place to do it."

He smiled his stiff smile. "I'll remember that." They all sat in the barrel shaped chairs at the round glass table in dinette area. The guilty toaster that had not yet been brought back inside was clearly visible through the back window. The children finished their rolls and milk while the adults made small talk. Maren learned only that his magazine had commissioned an extensive report on civil war sites in the Midwest, not battlefields, but cemeteries, documents, artifacts, and the underground railroad.

"Someone told me that the Dexum Inn was part of the underground railroad. I know that Gene and Emma Caufield own the Inn and are raising money to reconstruct it."

"That's right. In fact Della said the digging has already started. I haven't noticed anything. I guess they work after the restaurant closes. I've only met the Caufield's once. They live in the antique-looking house on the other side of the cemetery. Peter Winslow is on this side of the cemetery—almost directly across from you. He's been in this area almost all his life, so he should know the history of the inn better than anyone."

Zoe and Danl came back from washing their hands in the half-bath just off the kitchen, and Marc took his cue. He would see them again another time.

"I'll bring the rolls next time," he offered.

"When my dad's here we get chocolate chip cookies for breakfast," asserted Danl.

"He's in Afghanistan," said Zoe.

Marc looked up at Maren almost tenderly, but before he could speak she ushered the children into their coats and out the front door to catch their bus. He pulled on his jacket and stood by the stairs, watching the loving goodbyes. Maren closed the door and turned in time to see Matt tromping noisily down the stairs directly behind their new neighbor. Marc visibly jumped, obviously startled that someone else was in the house. But there was something else... a certain body tension. It was familiar somehow, and it took a moment for her to place it. Marc Vincent responded to the sudden noise behind him exactly the way Jack used to react to unexpected noise or movement when he was first discharged from the army.

Maren had left a message on the Villisca's answering machine that she would stop by first thing in the morning, so she skipped the Village Café and drove straight to their Vagabond House. Guy answered the door and told Maren that Sylvia had been taken to the hospital. She had come down with influenza and become dehydrated. Maren offered her sympathy and told Guy she would wait until she heard from Sue Williston before calling to set up new appointments.

After making calls to new patients to schedule evaluation times, Maren drove to the Sapien mansion. Alice greeted her with a smile and excitedly reported, "George is speaking so much better. The kids can understand him more. I can understand him almost all the time. He's starting to use his old vocabulary, words he hasn't used in months. Our children have been reluctant to phone or even talk to him since he got out of the hospital, for fear they wouldn't understand him. Now I tell them that if they don't know what he says they should ask him to repeat it. We are all so grateful for the progress, but now he's so loud."

They had walked into George's study. He was seated and ready to work, waving some pages he wanted to share with her. Maren had asked George to memorize or read a poem or a prayer to practice his articulation. Predictably he had chosen a classic sports related poem, "The outlook wasn't brilliant for the Mudville Nine that day. The score stood four to two, with but one inning more to play."

Maren was surprised at how loudly he spoke, although his voice was still a throaty monotone. His rate was very slow; but intelligibility was definitely, dramatically improved. *It has to be all the work on respiratory support.*

"I just take a breath and my voice booms out," he told her.

"It must be all the breathing exercises we've worked on," Alice said. "Working on breathing is the most important thing we've ever done." He continued reading, "And then when Cooney died at first, and Barrows did the same, a sickly silence fell upon the patrons of the game."

It certainly wasn't perfect, but Maren heard speech sounds they had never worked on, /k, g, ch,/ and /r/. *Just getting him to pull his tongue in for the tongue tip sounds had improved the phonemes formed with the middle and back of his tongue.* Maren was impressed. Their work on tongue placement had paid big dividends.

"I can see a difference in the way he breathes all the time, not just for speech," Alice reported. "I even see a difference in breathing when he's sleeping. His articulation is so much better, too. Working on tongue placement was one of the best things we've ever done." Whatever they worked on was in Alice's estimation the most important therapy they had ever done. "But can you do something about his voice? His voice is so low. He always had a higher voice than he does now."

"You've definitely passed an important milestone with breathing and articulation, George. I can see you're still pushing against the old trach site, though. When the stoma was open you learned different techniques for speaking. Now you will have to unlearn those." *Resonant voice therapy should be just the thing for him.* "George, let me hear you say mmm."

It took quite a few attempts before he mastered pushing the air all the way to his nose for the /m/ sound. Maren asked him to keep the whinny sound in a vowel as well. "Mmmeee," she demonstrated. "Mmmay... mmmy... mmmoh... mmmoo." He got the idea, but he wasn't good at it. Fortunately, Alice was. "Here's something you can do together. The articulation and breathing he can do on his own." She constructed some sentences peppered with the nasal sounds, /m, n,/ and /ing/. As always, Maren left an abundance of home exercises. They devoured whatever she gave them and asked for more.

Filled with high expectations Maren arrived at the Harrisons' home. She had systematically presented vowel sounds and many consonants to Stephanie and her mom. Every week Stephanie was saying more words. Her language development was quite delayed, since one needs words in order to construct phrases and sentences. Maren wanted to push hard today for more words with /s, f,/ and /sh/, and maybe she could elicit some phrases. Joanne greeted Maren at the door with a warning, "We've all been passing a cold virus around, and Stephanie was awake in the night. She might be a little crabby today. I think she's getting it."

Disappointed, Maren re-thought her goals for the session and lowered her hopes. Stephanie broke into tears several times, in spite of Maren's attempts to make the hour fun.

"Should I work with her this week while she has a cold," Joanne wanted to know.

"Not if she has a fever or sore throat," Maren advised. "We don't want therapy to be a punishment. If she doesn't feel well you might be tempted to push too hard, and she could develop a bad attitude about talking." The written report from the hospital evaluation had finally arrived, so Maren took some time to go over it with Joanne. The surgeon had examined Joanne's mouth and throat while they were there and had found a notch at the end of her hard palate. That meant that Stephanie might be predisposed to having some anomaly—a short velum or sub-mucous cleft of the hard palate. The report didn't state that. It just implied the possibility. "The good news is that in a very short time her vocabulary has increased to over one hundred words. Originally, she had only seven speech sounds. Now she has more than ten."

"Not all of her sounds are correct, though," said Joanne.

"That's true, but her loudness has increased and she's talking more."

"We do understand her more. Actually, everyone understands her more."

While Joanne went to wipe Stephanie's nose, Maren collected her belongings and let herself out. *Tomorrow is another day,* she consoled herself. She knew therapy did not always happen in leaps and bounds. Most often it was a matter of just keeping at it.

Sue Williston had left a message on Maren's voice mail saying the two new patients who were in need of evaluation had been ill for several days. They could wait until next week. December flu season had definitely arrived. Maren spent the extra time at the outlet mall in Edgelawn doing some Christmas shopping and getting a quick lunch. She drove back to Dexum to finish her afternoon visits for the day with John Spencer.

When Maren drove up Crescent Avenue at the end of her work day, she was surprised to see Matt walking a small black dog on a leash. Zoe and Danl had just gotten off the school bus and were running to meet Matt's new four-footed friend. She lowered the window of the van and called to Matt. "Isn't that Peter Winslow's dog?" She was hoping it was, and not an animal Matt planned to keep.

"Yeah, this is Baker. I met Mr. Winslow while he was walking his new pet. I got the feeling immediately that a dog had not been on his radar. His daughter insisted on giving it to him. He took to me right away."

"Baker or Mr. Winslow?" Maren was relieved that the dog wasn't about to move into her house. Matt had acquired a part time job walking the dog, and another contact had been made that might help wean him from his relationship with Sydney. Maren encouraged the children to enjoy petting Baker who was literally lapping up the attention. When she called them, she reminded them to wash their hands and faces for dinner.

"I won't be here for dinner Mom. I'm getting a bite to eat with a friend. You know her, Laurel Haynes. When Maren gave him a puzzled look he explained," You know, the painter. She's also a part time student."

After the younger McClouds were in bed, Maren got out a package of small plain index cards and began making line drawings—a circle representing a face on each one. There were just dots for eyes, a line for each eyebrow, and a line for a nose. No ears or hair. It was on the mouth and neck she focused special attention. She printed a letter on each card and tried to illustrate how the mouth would look while saying each sound. For /e/ the smile was wide, showing teeth. For /m/ the lips were closed. The /s/ showed arrows representing air coming from a smiling mouth. She was disappointed at the result. Something was missing.

She was at the kitchen counter working on the card for /sh/ when the Matt came in through the garage. She knew immediately he was not alone. The clicking on the hard wood floor could only be animal paws. A smiling Matt looked happier than she had seen him for months. "Mr. Winslow was out with Baker when I drove in. I told him I'd take Baker for his evening walk and return him in half an hour." Matt knelt on the floor, rubbed behind Baker's ears, and allowed the puppy to give him doggy kisses all over his face. Baker looked up at Maren and whimpered, then yelped once, trying his best to win her approval.

"Shh," said Matt, holding his finger in front of his puckered lips. "Quiet boy, you'll wake the kids and get us both in trouble." Baker promptly sat down and looked silently at Matt. "Okay, Baker, let's go out. See you in half hour, Mom." When the puppy whined at the door, Matt put his finger to his lips and shushed him again. The dog was instantly quiet. "He's smart, isn't he Mom?"

"Yes he is, and you two have given me a good idea for my project. See you after your walk." She returned to her articulation cards and drew lines to represent fingers on some of them—to depict the way she had often given patients a touch cue for various speech sounds-- the air moving towards fingers. *These should help Cole see and feel the difference between the phonemes. It might even help with his reading.*

It was close to an hour before Matt returned. He had been visiting with Mr. Winslow, and told her all he had learned and admired about Peter Winslow. "Did you know he's a professor emeritus from Edgelawn University? He taught and did research in biology there and was at Cambridge for a short time. I read some of his articles." Matt was obviously captivated not only by the canine neighbor, but also by the dog's owner. There was no mention of the date with Laurel, and neither of them brought up Sydney's name. Maren noticed one other thing, Matt's cell phone didn't ring all evening. *Maybe he turned it off during his meal with Laurel and forgot to turn it on again. Or better yet, maybe he finally told her to get lost.* He gave Maren a goodnight hug. "I've got a lot of reading to do before my training session tomorrow." He hummed a tune all the way to his room. She sent email to Paul and went to bed with a smile in her heart.

So let adventures roll,
Some fun; some take a toll.
Events and mentors each a key
God gives to guide my soul.

CHAPTER 15

Christmas was less than a week away and there was no word from Paul about when or if he would be home. He had emailed that he had treated a number of eye injuries, some were soldiers, some children. There were other physicians who had treated similar injuries from land mine explosions or car bombings. Maren thought Paul seemed remote, disengaged, absent not only physically but emotionally as well. He was being the rock in his world, that's how Maren had come to think of it, while she was the rock in hers. She sometimes wondered about his frequent references to his colleague Bev. She had asked him once if John and Bev were married. He had written that John's wife lives in London, but that Bev had never married. Pushing the troublesome thoughts from her mind, she gathered her files and supplies and drove to the Village Café.

Paul looked around the rudimentary operating room at patients who tolerated the intolerable. *It's always the poor and weak who suffer the most.* These people were so grateful for the smallest kindness. They assumed life would be painful, and they were not disappointed. They seemed surprised by aid and comfort. *It's good to be here, to be part of all this,* he thought, *to put my skills to use to help alleviate real suffering.* His satisfaction grew each day, bit by bit obliterating the confusion and complexities of his original decision, leaving in its place a simpler, purer altruistic motive. He had written to Maren only this morning about the head and neck injuries he had treated. He didn't tell her about the man who had three limbs blown off by an exploding mine.

Suddenly the walls moved around him, as if he was the fish in a swirling bowl of water. He grabbed a table; and in a few seconds he was outside the fish bowl again, the walls appropriately anchored. There had been no earthquake, no rocket blast, and this was the second time he had experienced vertigo in the past week. *Whoa, I need to get more sleep.* He promised himself that after his duty day was completed he would send Maren a long email and turn in early.

"Hello there," Vance Davidson greeted, as he lumbered over to Maren's table by the window. He sat down, invited by Maren's smile. Della approached with a coffee pot in each hand, regular in the right, decaf in the left.

"Looks like you're playing cards," said Vance.

"It's for speech therapy, but I'm not a very good artist."

"Is it something you're going to use with the Evans boy," asked Della.

"Yes, and others." Most of the village knew which homes Maren was visiting. She didn't have to refrain from using names; although she would never breach confidentiality by talking about patients, except in a general way.

"That could be done by computer. It would make it clearer and they could be printed out quickly when you need more. I'll make you a sample of some tonight, if you like."

Maren gave Della a few to try on the computer, but kept some to introduce to Cole during the afternoon session. It was busy in the café. Della pocketed the cards and kept moving. "How are the kids doing," Vance wanted to know. He was such a good listener that Maren found herself reporting on the entire family to the retired pastor.

"I'm sorry to say we haven't been back to church very often."

"Pastor Thomas is sick, you know. I'm going to be filling in until he returns. I'm hoping there isn't a mass exodus. People often get pretty attached to their shepherd."

Maren hadn't heard. She wondered if Vance was asking her to help keep the pews filled. Whether or not that was his intent, she made an appointment to talk with him later in the week. Danl and Zoe had never been dedicated or baptized. She had some questions and needed another viewpoint to help her thought process along, before discussing it with Paul.

"Britain and the United States could take military action against Iraq without a United Nations ruling," the voice announced through the radio. Maren tensed and pushed the CD button to play Christmas music. She, along with most of the country was increasingly convinced that there would be an invasion of Iraq. Selfishly, she was grateful Paul was not in that unfortunate country.

Julie Spencer answered the door. Once again she had arranged for a substitute to take her students, so she could see how John was progressing in therapy. Maren took off her coat. She felt immediately uncomfortable. She sensed negative vibrations between the patient and his wife. It was more than vibrations, she decided. It was definitely tension, and it was contagious. She started by reviewing the exercises she had asked John to work on four, five, or even six times a day. There hadn't really been any progress thus far. If anything, he was worse. She looked at John without smiling.

"Do you notice any improvement, either of you?"

"Maybe a little if I ask him to use his breathing. Mostly though it's the same." Julie was more concerned about something else. "He actually seems to be dragging his right leg more. I've asked for more tests."

John shrugged his shoulders and looked down at his trembling fingers. It was very quiet in the room while Maren struggled with how to discuss the reason for the failure of his therapy.

"How many times a day are you working on the exercises?"

"Good question," said Julie evenly.

"Tired," John managed, indicating a total lack of effort.

"From what, exactly?" He was a home bound patient. It was not like he was holding down a full time job. Maren clenched her teeth. She had little patience for non-compliance.

"Ah ha duh puh suh nuh tay nuh."

There was that statement again. She still couldn't understand what he said and looked quizzically at Julie.

"He's telling you that he has a personal trainer that comes here every day. They work three or four hours some days."

"What about the other hours," Maren asked, without sympathy.

John looked abashed that he didn't get a pardon from her.

"You're both educated people. Usually that means patients make good progress—you know—do homework, follow directions."

"Well, you see John is a pilot, a captain and a coach. He's used to giving the orders and depending on someone else to make it all happen. He did well with therapy in the hospital. They worked with him three times a day. He didn't have to do anything on his own. But shouldn't he be at least maintaining? He actually seems to be regressing."

"Hmmm," said Maren, giving herself time to sift any judgment from her voice. She had to assume there was no medical problem. The VA hospital had discharged him. With a smile she said, "Well John, you can't delegate this. If you want to talk better and be understood there's only one way to make it happen. You will have to work on your own, and it will not be easy."

Maren went over the exercises again with Julie present. When she left she reminded John that she wouldn't give him additional activities until he had gained some control of his breathing. She had seen him perform better. She knew he could do it, if only he would.

No radio or music on the drive to the Harrison home. Maren was analyzing the session with John and shifting her focus to Stephanie. Joanne met her at the door. "Stephanie has a strep infection. She started antibiotics today, so she may be contagious for another day." Since Maren was susceptible to strep infections, and didn't wish to be a carrier to her children, she opted out of their scheduled session.

The Sapiens had let her know that they had a medical appointment at one of the Chicago area hospitals today. They were looking into the new electrical therapy for his swallow. Tiny electrical jolts to the neck near the larynx tended to force a tight swallow. They hoped the electrical stimulation would give him a stronger swallow, so that he would swallow more completely. But they went into it knowing it was controversial.

The canceled appointments gave Maren time to see Cole a second time for the week. Chris and Tanya were planning to take the boys to Florida for Christmas vacation and had asked if she could squeeze in an extra session. Noreen was happy to watch the children an extra time. After practicing some phrases with Cole, Maren put the sound pressure level meter away and got out the articulation cue cards she had drawn. She introduced vowels first, hoping they would be easy. "Ah" showed a mouth wide open, the chin dropped as far as it could go. For the long /u/ sound the lips were puckered as much as they possibly could pucker. For /e/ the mouth showed lips as wide as possible. She demonstrated each and had him try them. She used some of the consonant cards, too. "Puh" was easy, but for some reason the breathy "huh" was a challenge. She held up her hand and huffed on it. He had a blank expression and made no attempt. She took his hand and huffed on it, "huh." His eyes lit as he felt her breath, and then he huffed on his hand.

Her drawings were rough, but once she demonstrated and he practiced they served the purpose. She left some vowel cards and a few consonant cards for them to use. *Next time he'll be able to combine some to make syllables and maybe a few words.* She hoped that providing a visual cue for speech would give him more confidence. She put him through all the exercises again, wrote the directions on a five by seven note sheet, and packed up her things. She was already wondering how Matt and the children were doing.

It had been a week of cold, damp weather, during which Maren had been in and out of the van multiple times a day and exposed to a variety of viruses in every home she visited. She had developed the threat of a cold but no Christmas spirit. The cheery Christmas music on her CDs didn't cheer her. The fact that she had argued with Matt didn't help her mood, either. She had realized that Matt was still keeping in touch with Sydney and had even agreed to see her. Neither of them had the money for a plane ticket, so they planned to each drive to Denver. Afterwards, Sydney would join her father in Cheyenne for Christmas. Maren was so afraid that Matt would go with her that she hadn't handled their conversation well. She knew fear usually makes things worse. She should have known better.

The headache behind her eyes was beginning to spread. She had a little time before she had to pick up Zoe and Danl. Her van seemed to steer itself into the parking lot at the Village Café. Della was alone in the restaurant, waiting for time to pass so she could leave. She was grateful to see a familiar face come through the door. "It's almost the big day," she greeted Maren exuberantly.

"How dare you be so cheerful," Maren returned with a weak smile. "It's cold and gloomy; the world's full of terrorists; another war is about to start; and we're both alone in an empty restaurant." Realizing she sounded like the Grinch, she tried to be more friendly, "Why don't you join me for a cup of coffee."

"I'll make fresh if that's what you want, but I'd be glad to share my homemade Christmas tea with you."

"Wonderful," was all Maren could answer. She was near tears.

For the next half hour the two women enjoyed the warm, sweet, spiced tea and visited as openly as two long-parted friends. Della, Maren learned, had been an administrative assistant to the CEOs of several corporations in Chicago, as well as at a small medical clinic in Albright. "I'm too efficient," she explained. "As soon as they figure that out they want me to assume more and more responsibility. And I do. I try to meet unreasonable demands and impossible deadlines until I'm so stressed I'm ready for a nervous breakdown. Not good for me, my family, or the company. So I quit."

"So, you took a job as a waitress to decompress."

"Exactly. It's hard work, but at least there's no administrative pressure. The Caufields are great to work for. They're generous benefactors of several community ventures, not just the reconstruction of the Underground Railroad."

"Have you met Marc Vincent, yet? He's a free lance writer for *Beyond Our Past Magazine*. He's researching Civil War events in this area."

"He was in here. I introduced him to Ross and Meredith Winston. Do you think he'll write about them?"

"I don't know why he would. Did you show him the basement tunnel and tell him about the plans?"

"No, he didn't ask about the history of the place, more about the politicians who hang out here. Besides, I was pretty busy when he was here."

The tea was gone, and Maren's disposition was enough improved to wish Della a hearty Merry Christmas. She told herself she wouldn't submit to being ill for the big family gathering. She was no longer certain either Paul or Matt would make it for the family celebration. She had to be well.

Maren picked up the children and drove home. Knowing Matt would not be there depressed her all over again. She wished she hadn't argued with him, hadn't tried to make his decision; but she hadn't been able to stop herself from pointing out Sydney's shortcomings. She realized she was angry at both Matt and Paul.

Not being free to express it or resolve it made her increasingly irritable. She knew she was short tempered with the kids and was feeling tired most of the time.

The phone was ringing as they opened the door. Danl got to it first. "It's Dr. Paul." The children got first dibs at talking with him while Maren took off her coat and eavesdropped. When they turned the handset over to Maren and went to their toys, Maren braced herself for what she thought might be a difficult conversation. She still hadn't really managed to forgive him.

"This is a rare treat," she greeted him. The treat quickly turned sour. Paul could only talk about the need for him to stay there, how overwhelming the human suffering was that he confronted every day, and how he couldn't leave Bev short-handed.

"But you can't change the whole situation," she reasoned. "You can only alleviate it for the time you can be there. You need time off, too."

"I don't see how I can leave right now, knowing my family is well and happy ...."

"We're not, Paul," she interrupted. "We need you here."

"But Maren you must realize the children here are in a life and death situation."

"What about your own children? They are growing up without a father, a presence you promised when we adopted them."

"You're there with them. They're safe and healthy and well-cared for. I belong here."

"I'm selfish. I admit it. I want you home for myself, but putting that aside I would think you would want to be home with us." *Unless being with Bev is more satisfying,* she thought. Maren became aware that she had raised her voice to an emotionally charged level, as she heard someone urgently calling for Dr. McCloud. He turned away from the phone to give orders, allowing her a moment to calm herself. When he returned they each had lost the thread of their conversation.

"I need to go, Maren. I do miss you. I miss the boys and Zoe. Give everyone a hug for me." The brief connection, so rare these days, had been marred by both electrical and emotional static, and had ended abruptly, with the push of a button on the other side of the world.

Paul got even less sleep than usual that night. As an ENT surgeon he was called out at all hours for adult head and neck surgery, auditory trauma, and to treat the pediatric patients he loved. His conversation with Maren did cause him to review every step yet another time. No matter how he looked at it, or how many times he went over it, he didn't see that he could have done anything differently.

There was no time during the following day to dwell on their argument. His private thoughts were precluded by patient after patient until suddenly the ground rushed towards him. Instantly realizing it was the vertigo again, he leaned against a chair to steady himself. This week was worse than last. Not a day had passed that he didn't have to hold onto some structure to keep his balance. Fortunately, as long as he stood still his hands were steady. Probably congestion causing an inner ear disturbance, he reasoned. He would take more decongestant when he finished his duty period.

"Dr. McCloud, you look tired." It was Bev. The fact that he was addressed by title rather than first name should have tipped him that this was an official conversation, but he was too preoccupied. "No more than anyone else," he responded absently, leaning harder into the chair.

Maren had promised that while Matt was gone she would take Baker for his morning walk. Peter would take care of the evening outing. She ate breakfast alone when she returned, again brooding about the tone of her conversation with Paul. School was out for the holidays, and she didn't have to think of home visits until after Christmas. She would only provide for Stanton House, so she could focus on her home duties. And there were plenty of those.

A few flakes of white were drifting lazily through the bare Maple trees in the back yard, but there was not enough light beyond the black window pane to attract her attention to them. Her mood was as dark as the window glass. The man she had married seemed more distant than she would have thought possible. It reminded her of her relationship with her father when she was a young girl. She had known that he loved her and was providing for her, but he had been only a shadow in her life, not warm flesh and blood. In a way her marriage was a mirror of the primary relationship. She had originally known love as a dependable if unemotional existence, but Paul had blasted through her old duty bound concept of love. With him there was emotion. It had frightened her at the beginning. Now she feared Paul was slipping into the shadows... away from her and the children, back to the realm of required chores. *Maybe it was just too good to last.*

She forced herself to concentrate on writing a lengthy grocery list. She had invited Paul's parents and Penny and Jim and their children for Christmas Eve, whether Paul and Matt were there or not. Nick and Carrie would definitely be overnight guests. At least Nick and Carrie were only a three hour's drive away. Matt was now twelve to fifteen hours away, and driving by himself if he came home at all.

She retrieved the local paper which carried mostly village news. The morning headlines were mainly human interest stories.

Nationally, things were also quiet two days before the holiday. The senate was talking about the newly elected Senator Frist as Senate majority leader for the 108th Congress. Thankfully, no war news.

Maren and the children went to the supermarket early, while the snowfall was light. She was losing herself in cooking and cleaning duties, unaware how deep the white stuff had become, when Danl asked where to get a shovel. "Mr. Marc said he would clear our driveway. I'm going to help him." She looked out the door and through the garage to see Marc Vincent, snow shovel in hand, was making short work of the accumulation in the drive and along the sidewalk. "I told Mr. Winslow I'd be glad to do his," he called when he saw her. "Figured I might as well do yours while I'm at it." Maren thanked him, grateful for such a good neighbor, and returned to the house to answer the ringing phone. It was Nick. "The house smells really good," he teased, knowing there would be something good happening in the kitchen.

"Danl and Zoe made seven layer bars," she told him, grateful to talk with a son who was not in crisis. "Are you getting here tomorrow morning?"

"No. I'm really sorry Mom, but I've got a problem. My lap top locked up and died, taking a research paper with it. One of the associate professors offered to help retrieve it from the hard drive, but it will take some time. We won't be in until Christmas Eve dinner." He said again how sorry he was, but graduate school was competitive and demanding. He couldn't afford to fail this class. Maren was amazed that someone as sharp about computers as Nick didn't have a back-up file, but she didn't argue. Stranger things happened every day. At least they would still arrive by dinner time.

When Maren walked Baker on Christmas Eve morning, Mr. Winslow asked about Matt's return. "I am going to a reunion with my old army buddies right after Christmas, and I need someone to look after Baker and the house." He would be away until after the new year. His plants would require care at least every other day. "With my son-in-law going to Washington the first of the year, my daughter won't be around to help anymore." Maren was delighted to have a reason to call Matt, and assured Peter they would make sure Baker, the house and the plants were cared for. *Maybe Marc will help keep the sidewalk clear,* she thought, feeling the weight of taking on more and more responsibility. "Merry Christmas Peter. We'll work it out somehow."

Matt answered on the first ring and after hearing Peter Winslow's request explained his situation. "Mom, I started back last night. I had to stop in Lincoln to rest. I got a sandwich and a coke at a truck stop and asked about a place to get a room for the night. I should have taken the southern route. There's quite a storm out here. Snow is blowing and visibility is bad. This big, burly trucker named Les was eating chili and drinking coffee. He asked where I was headed and said he was going all the way to Chicago. He said he'd make a path for me with his rig, that I could just stay close and drive in his tracks. So that's what I did. I lost him somehow, but the roads are clear now, and I'm only a couple of hours away."

Maren was relieved and excited that he was almost home. She wondered if he had taken the northern route to visit Sydney's dad with her, but she asked no questions. There had been no mention of Sydney. Now she could focus on food preparation.

Lunch was long over when Matt—badly in need of sleep—arrived. Danl and Zoe were so thrilled they could hardly let him eat. They went with him to get instructions for the care and feeding of Peter's plants and dog and to obtain a key to his house. After that Matt went to bed. Talk could come later.

CHAPTER 16

Christmas Eve day arrived and Maren hadn't heard from Paul since their latest argument. She had emailed, but got no response. She kept the kitchen radio on, listening for ominous news; but there was none. She organized Danl and Zoe to do some last minute gift wrapping while she accomplished as much as she could in the kitchen.

Penny, Jim and the girls arrived at four, bringing a tray of vegetables, a stack of gifts for the cousins, and several tins of cookies she and the girls had made. Nick phoned about the same time to say his file had been retrieved, and the roads south of Dexum were in fine shape. He and Carrie were on the way and would be there in time for dinner, but just barely. Gloria and Bob arrived at five, bringing their tradition... fresh, boiled, seasoned shrimp for an appetizer.

The table was set, complete with short, white candles in small decorative ceramic holders at each place. Maren's Christmas Eve meal used to be a pauper's meal, something simple. That was before she and Paul were married. It was one of the few traditions Maren and the boys had honored from Grandma Kepple, Jack's mom. It was never as simple once the families were combined, but her candle tradition remained the same. Tonight, after the appetizers, there would be hearty vegetable soup, homemade bread, a tray of fresh vegetables and fruit. Of course the children would serve dessert—the cookies they had made during the previous weeks. It would be the first Christmas without Paul. Maybe the first of many; one never knew. She had to be the rock until he could be there to share the load.

Maren was putting the Christmas candle in an evergreen wreath for a centerpiece when the doorbell rang. Carrie needed help getting through the door. She had an armload of gifts and several tins of brownies. Nick was getting luggage from the trunk, so Matt ran out to help his brother. It seemed to take them a long time to get a couple of bags. Maren couldn't wait any longer. She ladled the soup into the old family tureen and was putting it on the table when the boys came through the door. They said "Merry Christmas," but neither looked at her. They were obviously already in brotherly conversation. They set the bags in the library while the family waited in the dining area and entry way.

"Oh, wait Mom. I forgot. I've got one more thing to bring in," Nick said. He opened the front door, reached out, grabbed a handful of overcoat, and pulled Paul into the warmth of their home. Zoe squealed with delight, and Danl began to shout, "Hooray, welcome home." Evidently Bob, Gloria, and Penny were in on the surprise for they just smiled and were quiet. Maren could only stare, too stunned to comprehend how they could have pulled this off. A tight knot in her throat prevented words. And then the tears came, tears held back for weeks spilled out. She could only see Paul hazily, but he could see all of them quite clearly.

"Group hug, group hug," their children insisted, joyously pulling everyone together with Paul and Maren in the middle. After a moment they all stood back and watched in silence, while Paul continued to hold Maren tightly against him, his own eyes now closed, his face hidden in her hair where his own tears could slip out unseen.

After that, they all held hands around the table and said the Lord's prayer; and the food was passed. As they ate they followed Grandma Kepple's tradition. One at a time, in no special order, someone would tip the small personal candle next to their dinner plate and light it from the large Christmas candle in the center of the table. That person would then relate to the others some incident or event that had brought the spirit of Christmas alive this year. Grandma Kepple called the incidents Christmas moments. Often it was simply hearing a song, attending a concert, or spending time with a friend. It didn't matter. No matter how small or seemingly insignificant the individual moment seemed, the collection of stories became something greater when shared.

Zoe went first telling about how her teacher Lois Smith was her special angel, always extra nice when Zoe was sad. "I'm always sad on the days Dad goes back to work." Penny's moment was at Erin's school program. Erin told them being the angel in the school play was her special moment. Little Colleen claimed it was hers, as well.

Matt told about his encounter with Les, the "angel" trucker. "Just east of Lincoln there was a white out. There were times I couldn't see anything except the red dots of his tail lights. And then," he finished dramatically, "even the tail lights disappeared. I could feel a strong gust of wind against the car, and suddenly I could see daylight. The snow tapered off. I had driven through the storm."

"Did you get a chance to thank him?" Penny asked

"That's the odd thing. Although the visibility got better and better, I never saw the rig again. There were lots of vehicles off the road. I hope he didn't go in a ditch."

Nick, the family pragmatist chimed in, "Aw, he probably headed for a rest stop once it cleared up. That truck stop coffee and chili is potent stuff." Everyone laughed.

Maren lit her candle and told about having Christmas tea with Della Mason. Danl held his candle to the flame. "I didn't think I was going to have a Christmas moment to share," he started somberly, "until tonight when Dad came home."

The room was quiet. Maren and Paul exchanged a private glance, while tears stung their eyes again. It was the first time Danl had ever called Paul, Dad. "The band played, *I'll be home for Christmas* at the holiday concert at school," Danl continued. "That was our first mom's favorite. I remember her telling us it was important to be home for Christmas. Now I know what she meant. When Dad came in, I felt it—in my heart."

Finally, everyone's candle was burning but Paul's. All eyes turned to him, hoping to hear what had happened that allowed him to be home with them. Slowly, he tipped his candle into the flame of the Christmas candle. Carefully, he set it down and continued to look into the flame as he spoke. "I got pretty stressed the past few weeks. I thought everyone had lost their perspective but me." He looked apologetically at Maren. "The truth is I lost my balance. I missed... I needed all of you so much that I tried to fill the empty place by keeping busy helping others. You can only do that so long before you..." He paused, shuffling his feet back and forth on the carpet beneath the table, while he searched for the right words. "...before something breaks. I..." His voice cracked with emotion. "I had episodes of vertigo which, as it turns out, was stress induced. Fortunately, my supervisors are very familiar with stress symptoms. It was Bev who spoke to me, but the words seemed to be amplified, like they were coming from another source. 'Go home. Stop taking care of everyone else. Go home and rest.' It was a ..." He hesitated again, groping for how to describe such an experience. He gave up as his throat tightened and just looked to Maren for help. She reached for his hand. "It was a Christmas moment," she finished for him.

Little Colleen looked around the table. "Well, all the candles are burning. May we have cookies now?"

"Absolutely," boomed Paul, regaining his good humor. He jumped up and turned off the overhead light. "We'll eat cookies by candlelight. It'll be a tasty Christmas moment."

The day after Christmas Nick and Carrie left. Matt resumed his training with the Botnas and assumed his house-sitting duties for Peter Winslow. Paul enjoyed life at home, while Maren returned to doing a few home visits. She was trying to rid her mind of the horrible breaking news. She had done so well at avoiding reading, hearing, and seeing the news while Paul was away. But now that he was home, Paul turned it on. He wanted, needed to stay informed.

The morning news reported that Central Intelligence agents had confirmed the Washington Post's story that the United States was using so-called "stress and duress" interrogation techniques. Human rights activists called the acts, torture. The anonymous agents defended the practice as necessary in light of the September eleventh terrorist attacks. Publicly, U.S. government officials were denying the charges, while declining to address specifics. Privately, however, one official justified human rights violations as being a necessary part of the job. Paul's only comment was, "As General Sherman said during the Civil War...'War is hell.'"

Maren's first visit of the day was with little Stephanie. Joanne had a gift for Maren when she arrived, a recording of Stephanie singing "Away in a Manger." As they listened to it together, both parent and therapist were in tears. The tremendous struggle and effort of that little girl made each sign of progress precious. It assured Maren that some good happens every day, regardless of world news.

George and Alice Sapien's home was still filled with family members who were visiting from out of town. George seemed to be improving, but had trouble concentrating with the distracting activity in the house. He and Alice believed his swallow was stronger. His voice wasn't consistent, but with effort it sounded clearer. Practice was understandably sporadic during the holiday weeks. Maren hoped he could just hold on to the status quo until January. Then he would start to really focus again.

Wendy Mercer did not shout, "Come in," as she usually did when Maren rang the doorbell. Cautiously, Maren pushed through the door, calling Wendy's name. The living room was strewn with newspapers, shoes, and tinsel from an absent Christmas tree. Finally, Maren did hear a response. It was subdued and from the bedroom, "I'm in here." Maren walked through the hallway to the master bedroom.

"What are you doing in bed? Aren't you feeling well?"

"I've been crying again, since about six o'clock when Brad left for work."

"Wendy, it's almost lunch time." The room was dark and smelled stale. "How about getting up and we'll talk in the kitchen. Have you had any coffee yet today."

"No, not yet, and I usually get coffee when Brad leaves."

"I could use a cup," Maren lied. She had already had coffee with Paul. "Let's make some."

It took some doing to get Wendy out of bed, and Maren insisted that she wash her face and hands and brush her hair before sitting down to the table. Maren knew where to find the filters and coffee, but she filled the pot with water while Wendy gave directions. Soon the aroma of fresh brewing coffee and Maren's cheery presence made the effort worthwhile. After Wendy sipped a half cup of black coffee, Maren began probing to find out more about the tears. "What started you crying?"

"I asked Brad why he married me."

"Oh, what did he say?"

"He said it was the way I looked."

"That's pretty normal."

"But what makes him stay," she wondered.

Maren knew Wendy must be wondering beyond that question to, "Will he always stay or is he getting tired of taking care of an invalid wife? Will he leave?" Instead of pursuing that line of thinking Maren wanted to know more about how often Wendy cried and for how long. Did she think about dying? Did she want to die? Hearing Wendy readily admit to both, frightened Maren. She was afraid to ask the next obvious question, and very carefully, quietly formed the words, "Have you ever thought about doing something to end your life?"

"Yes, sometimes I do. It just seems like it would be better for everyone."

The woman seemed to be clinically depressed, not just a little sad. Sue needed to get a counselor out to the house and soon. And then Wendy had a question for Maren. "What does it look like? I mean what happens when I... when there's a seizure?"

As gently as she could Maren described how the seizure appeared to bystanders. She tried to say it in short, simple terms that wouldn't confirm Wendy's worst fears. Wendy didn't have any follow-up questions. She was satisfied for the moment.

Amazingly, some cognitive therapy was actually accomplished, and since Wendy's daughter would be home from work by mid-afternoon, Maren felt it safe to leave. She sat in the van making notes and calling the VNA office. Sue promised to have a psychiatric nurse at the Mercer residence the following morning. Maren wrote in her notes that she recommended outpatient therapy as soon as possible.

The Panera was more crowded than usual with return shoppers. It looked like everything purchased before Christmas was being exchanged. Maren looked around the restaurant for a table or someone she knew who would invite her to join them. She decided not to join the cozy couple she recognized at the coffee counter. It was Matt and Laurel, laughing as they seasoned their cups of coffee. The restaurant was noisy, but she wondered if their heads were close of necessity to hear each other or something else. Maren opted for water as her beverage and stayed as far from them as possible. She found a small table with one chair in the corner of the room opposite the coffee containers. They were on their way out with their to-go cups anyway and didn't see her. She watched as their hands brushed and saw Matt catch her fingers in his. It was turning into a pretty good day. When she got back in her van she played her CDs on the drive to Stanton House and home.

The following morning a very solemn Jared Spencer who would be ten years old in a few weeks, answered the door and led Maren to the family room where his dad sat in his old lounge chair. Maren expected the house to be in disarray during Christmas week, but it was clean and tidy. Jared had been playing a video game on the TV. John insisted the boy turn it off to respond to an introduction to Maren. "Yes, sir," he answered with military precision. Justine heard a newcomer in the house and shyly came out from her bedroom. Another introduction. Jared said a grave "Hello, glad to meet you;" but Justine put her head down and refused to speak.

Julie had gone to the mall, along with half the population of Dexum, to return or exchange some clothing her parents had sent for the children. Both children were left in John's care, something Maren had not previously pictured. They understood John better than Maren did and obeyed him without a question. She wondered if it was out of love, respect, or fear. They had been through some sobering experiences with their dad during the past few months. They had watched their athletic, articulate, competent father go off to war. The burn injuries were bad enough, but he could have recovered from those. The brain injury left this new dad who couldn't even walk or talk without help. At least John was alive. Still, it was an emotionally devastating roller coaster for the family.

John seemed to have made some progress, in spite of the holiday disruption to everyone's schedule. Julie had told her though that she felt his right side was getting weaker. She had contacted doctors again, asking for more tests. Today John's speech was frequently more connected, not consistently that syllable- by-syllable pattern as it had been. It was instructive for Maren to see him with his children. Little Justine stood by his side, unwilling to risk getting too close to the stranger. John reached over the arm of the lounge chair and lifted the tall four-year-old onto his lap. She was the image of her mother with long blond hair, the color Julie's must have been at that age. John's speech was quieter while holding his little girl. What he could not accomplish during therapy sessions seemed to come automatically, as he protected her there. *The motivation and magic of love,* Maren thought.

"Can I go play now?" Justine had been reassured in his arms. She felt safe to go to her room. His powerful arms easily lifted her up and over the arm of the chair. He set her gently on the floor. He saw Maren watching him. "I am luck-y. Still have arms and legs." Then he spoke to Jared. Maren wasn't sure the boy understand every word—she didn't—but he comprehended enough to know that he should turn off the game and play quietly in his bedroom while John had therapy.

Maren complimented him on his control of loudness. "How did you do that?" She challenged him to analyze and verbalize so that he could master the pattern. He had a twinkle in his eyes when he answered in his reedy voice, "Prac- tice." She told him that his was the most orderly home she had been in all week, including her own.

"Is that Julie's influence or ..."

"Mine," he interrupted firmly. "I... am ... lissapined... disciplined one."

It was a paraphasia. Not just the slurred speech that was his dysarthria, but a sign of aphasia, a *new* symptom. She noticed several other occurrences during the session. She felt fear for him, for the family. She would recommend that he be given a new CT scan or MRI immediately. It was a good session though. By the time Maren left the house she knew there was a strong bond of love between John and his family. In spite of his disability, he could still be a powerful influence in their lives... unless something else was occurring in his brain.

When Maren turned off Maple Grove onto Crescent the street lights were just turning on. She noticed a vehicle parked in front of Peter Winslow's house, directly across from Marc's place. She was pretty sure she knew who owned it, but Sydney was not in sight. Maren pulled in the garage and hurried into the house.

"Is Sydney in here?" Paul's look told her he didn't know what she was talking about. Matt drove up just then and recognized Sydney's old Explorer immediately. He started walking toward it as she was coming through Pete's yard, between the house and the old cemetery next to it. Maren and Paul were in the driveway in time to witness the argument which followed. It got louder with each exchange.

"What are you doing here, Sydney?"

"Visiting an old friend. Where have you been?"

"At work."

"You told me you worked for Peter Winslow."

"I have two jobs."

"I saw you with her in the mall. Did you spend the day with her."

"I've been at work. I told you that."

"And she's your secretary, right?"

"Sydney, let it go. You and I are just going in different directions."

"Don't think you can just dump me and not suffer as much pain and humiliation as you caused me."

She opened the door of her car and reached inside for something. Matt knew she kept several guns with her at all times. He stopped walking. "Sydney, don't do something you'll regret."

She turned back toward him. "Me regret? You are the one who will regret your actions Matthew Kepple." She was screaming now. "You are going to be sorry you ever lived. You can't two-time me and get away with it."

Marc Vincent walked out of his front door in time to hear part of the argument and all of the threat. He had pulled on his black leather jacket, but didn't take time to fasten it.

"What's going on, kids?"

"I'm not a kid. You just go back in your house where you'll be safe and mind your own business, while I deliver a present." She now had a small gift-wrapped box in her hand. Marc continued to walk toward the car, talking quietly as he walked.

"Sydney, is that your name? This is a quiet neighborhood, Sydney. You're getting kind of loud here, maybe scaring some of the folks. How about taking your conversation off the street. Why don't you let me deliver that present to Matt. You two can talk this out someplace else, later."

"I don't need your help. I'll deliver my own presents." She hurled the box at Matt and reached under the front seat with her right hand, holding the door open with her left. Marc lunged against the door, pinning her there. He immediately grabbed her arm, released the door, and whirled her away from her car. She barely managed to remain on her feet, but the ring of keys she had retrieved from under the front seat were flung out of her hand and onto the street.

"Pick up your keys and drive out of here, Sydney. Go home." He spoke quietly, calmly. He held the door open while she collected the keys. Obviously shaken, she obeyed without a word. He closed her car door once she was inside and stood in the middle of Crescent Avenue, watching as she started the engine and drove off. Waving casually to the McClouds, as if he'd just come out to get the evening newspaper, Marc turned and went back inside his house.

As her fear receded Maren was left feeling an odd mixture of relief and pride. She swallowed hard. "That's our new neighbor," she told Paul.

They debated about opening the package. Matt laughed at their concerns that it contained a bomb or poison. He ripped it open in the yard, just in case. It was filled with rocks, twigs, and bandages, supposedly predicting that Matt would be injured, thus the sticks and stones, and need to bandage his wounds. A short note stated that Cloris, Paul's aunt, thus Matt's great aunt, and now Matt had been cruel to her—pretending to be friends and then turning her out. She wished she had never have given him the time of day, let alone all the gifts and affection. She wanted all the gifts back immediately. The note ended with the threat that Matt would pay for his cruelty. He laughed, said that where relationships were concerned Sydney was about as mature as a thirteen-year-old, and threw the package in the trash. "She wants the gifts back so she can use them again on some other guy, or sell them to pay bills." Clearly his admiration for her had been destroyed by her behavior.

After dinner Matt went to walk Baker and water the plants. "I'll be awhile. Pete has a great library and said I could borrow whatever I want. I'll stay there for a while to read and keep Baker company." He saw the look of concern on Maren's face. "I'll keep my cell phone on. Call me if you want."

Matt did stay out late, and Maren had gone to bed, but couldn't sleep until she heard him come in. Paul was still catching up on rest. He had fallen asleep on the couch, but woke when Matt returned. The two men stayed up talking until one a.m. Consequently, Maren ate breakfast with Danl and Zoe, told them to play quietly until the night owls woke up, and promised to be back no later than lunchtime. It was an easy day. There was only one evaluation at Stanton House and Cole Evans to see before their Disney World trip. Thankfully, there were no VNA patients.

Tanya answered the door, since Chris was already at the pharmacy. The three sat at the kitchen table to work. Cole greeted her with a mumble. Less patient than usual, Maren asked him for a louder hello. He grunted a little sound that had no particular articulation. "Try again, a little louder. I just can't hear you." She spoke more sharply than she had intended. Cole's mouth opened and groping gestures were evident, but no sound at all came forth. Alarmed that she was causing him to have a stuttering block, she stopped and took a long breath, hoping to be inspired. Chris had reported previously that this inability to speak occurred periodically when he was put on the spot to talk.

"Cole, I'm wondering why you don't speak louder when we know that you can." The young boy, appearing as puzzled as Maren, shrugged his shoulders and eyebrows. "Maybe you're shy," she pressed. He shook his head. He seemed to be searching for possibilities, too. Tanya interrupted, "I don't think he's shy. He's really pretty social." Maren was puzzled. No ideas came.

"Cole, how do you make your voice loud?" She tried to get him to demonstrate, but he could not. The same sheepish expression covered his face while his shoulders and eyebrows shrugged once more. When he could be heard his speech sounded almost as dysarthric as George Sapien's and John Spencer's. Maren asked him to lie on the couch in the living room. She showed Tanya how Cole's diaphragm, ribs and abdominal muscles should work for speech. Tanya put her fingers on the boy's abdomen while he pushed against them with his "stomach." Maren told him to hold a book up with his stomach muscles while he said the days of the week. The response was exactly what she had hoped. His voice was louder and articulation was more precise. Maren used the sound pressure level meter to display his loudness. He smiled when she showed it to him. He knew he had done well. He performed well for over half an hour, using the meter to provide visual feedback.

Chris had purchased the sound-pressure level meter but they hadn't figured out all the buttons. Maren showed Tanya and Cole how to use it. She wrote a number of exercises for them on a five by seven sheet. Her name and phone number were typed at the top. She hoped the day would come when Cole would call her, and she would be able to hear and understand every word. "Next time," she promised, "we'll work on some more speech sounds. I need to make some new cue cards."

After dinner, consisting of a stir-fry that Paul fixed at Maren's request, Matt studied for half an hour before going to walk Baker. Danl and Zoe begged to go, but Maren vetoed the request.

"You aren't the dog walkers," she pointed out.

"He could bring Baker back here for a while. Baker needs someone to play with." It was Danl's idea.

"Sounds like a good solution to me," Paul said.

"I guess I can bring a couple of books here to read while you guys entertain Baker."

Within a few minutes they were in the house, the furry pet obviously enjoyed children. And everyone enjoyed the dog. Even Maren had to admit he was a pretty well behaved animal. At ten-thirty Matt put on his parka and pulled the hood up. A heavy snowfall had started that was predicted to continue all night. He fastened the leash on Baker's collar. "Time to take you home, boy."

Matt was surprised to see the garage door open and Peter's hybrid car inside. He found Peter sitting in his favorite chair with a book in his lap. "I got some kind of flu or food poisoning, I guess. Just didn't feel good, so I decided to come home early. I figured you had Baker at your place." Matt told him that, not only did Baker get his exercise, but the kids got plenty of exercise too. Pete assured Matt that he didn't need any help, just a good night's sleep in his own bed. Promising to return at seven for Baker's morning walk, Matt left Peter sitting in his old oak rocker, a wool throw across his legs.

At six-thirty the following morning, Maren answered a knock on the front door. Marc, looking more somber than usual, was on the front step. "There was a little trouble at Pete Winslow's house last night. I wanted to let you know before the police and press come around. Is Matt here?"

"Yes, he's getting ready to go walk Baker. Why? Is Peter okay?"

Marc had come into the entryway and was looking around. "Are the kids still asleep? I want to talk to you alone."

"They were up late playing with Baker. They'll sleep until seven or seven-thirty."

"You had Baker over here last night?"

"For a while. What's going on Marc?"

"Pete was taken to the hospital last night—about midnight."

"Matt said he had some kind of flu. Is he okay?"

"It wasn't because of the flu Maren. Someone fired a gunshot through his window, into the back of the chair where he was sitting. Fortunately for him, the chair is solid oak. He'll be okay. He's more concerned about his splintered, antique chair than his shoulder. He said Baker barked like a regular guard dog before it happened—maybe scared the intruder into firing accidentally."

"Probably a robbery attempt. I've heard there have been quite a few in the area."

"Maybe, but not the typical pattern of a burglar. A burglar wouldn't want to make noise, wake people up, you know. And the house wasn't entered. Nothing stolen."

"Maybe Baker did scare them away. We didn't hear anything."

"It was just the one shot. Pete's quite a guy. His old army training kicked in. He rolled to the floor and yanked the plug on the lamp. Then he called the police and reported what had happened. He even asked them to make a quiet run, not disturb the neighbors. The lights were flashing though. That's what got my attention. Would you get Matt. I'd like to talk with him before the police get here. Maren, you may have to tell the police what happened here yesterday. You don't have to tell the reporters anything, though. If you want to keep Matt out of it, just don't volunteer anything."

"What happened yesterday.... Oh, Sydney!"

"Yeah, Sydney. She did have a gun under the front seat. I saw it while she was picking up her keys. Couldn't tell what kind though."

Maren invited Marc to pour himself a cup of coffee while she went to get Matt and wake Paul. Marc repeated the information to Matt, giving Maren a chance to digest the reality that the perfect, peaceful village she loved was part of the real world after all. Either a burglar had bungled his latest attempt, or Sydney thought Matt was sitting and reading in that rocker as he had the previous nights. Maren preferred the former theory but feared it was the latter.

Matt immediately and emphatically said he didn't believe it was Sydney, for a lot of reasons. Sure she was emotionally immature, but definitely not capable of shooting anyone. She was too respectful of firearms and had too much self-control, usually. Threats and gifts of stones and bandages were a long way from shooting at someone. It was the word "usually" that concerned Maren. Sydney would, Matt predicted, find psychological ways to extract her revenge.

Marc suggested Matt get Baker before the police showed up and impounded him, and offered to walk along. By the time they got back Sergeant Dave Mulligan had arrived and was questioning Maren and Paul. Other neighbors had evidently observed the street scene from their windows the previous day and shared the story of Matt, Sydney, and Marc with police. Of course Sergeant Mulligan wanted to talk to Matt about Sydney and their quarrel.

Danl and Zoe were just coming downstairs and began asking their own questions. When Matt told them that Baker would be staying with them for a few days all their questions dissolved in arms full of soft, black fur and wet doggie kisses. Maren and Paul made new, strict rules about how they were to respond to anyone they saw who was not *regularly* in the neighborhood.

CHAPTER 17

Everyone seemed to have an extended bout of post holiday blues. Even George Sapien was close to tears. Instead of a return to more rapid progress Maren had predicted, he had lost ground and then plateaued. "But you've made so much progress since we began," Maren pointed out, thinking he was discouraged about therapy. "He misses the kids," Alice explained. "It'll take a week or so to get back in our own rhythm of life. He's really a very emotional man." Maren needed to find something to motivate George again. *I wonder how he would like being a coach for John.* "George, I have another patient I'm working with who could use some encouragement. If he's willing, would you consider meeting with him, sharing some of your experiences?" George's face looked brighter immediately as he nodded his assent. He was ready to focus on therapy if he could help someone else.

George had regressed to the point of biting his tongue again when saying /t/words. Maren started by having him say the sound in isolation, using careful placement. She proceeded to syllables, and then words with /t/ at the beginning, at the end, and in the middle. He improved rapidly during the session. She tried to get him to produce his voice with front focus—not pushing air against his old stoma site. "Say mmmeee," she modeled, continuing the nasal sound from the /m/ into the vowel. His attempt sounded more like "be."

"He was doing that very well in our practices before Christmas," Alice reported, much to George's chagrin.

"Put your finger on the side of your nose, George. Feel it vibrate when you say /mmmm/. Then make the /e/ vibrate, too." He did much better on the second attempt. Soon he was saying phrases using a nasal monotone voice that Maren modeled for him. "Mmmy nnnamme is nnot Mmamme." His face showed he was displeased with the way his voice sounded. Maren assured him repeatedly that she would not leave him sounding like a whinny kid. "This is just an exercise, a step in the process. It will get you to project the air for your voice higher than the back of your throat." Maren wrote out instructions for them and promised to call after she spoke with John.

The last visit for the day was at Stanton House, a swallowing evaluation. "Hey," called Noreen as she was getting into her car to go home. "Aren't you running late?" Maren acknowledged that she was late and that she was concerned about the children getting home before she got there.

"Matt's out of town for the night, Wisconsin, for his new job."

"I'll meet their bus for you. Do you want me to take them to my house?"

Maren was grateful for the offer. Having a robber, or possibly the jealous Sydney around, kept her on edge. "No, would you stay at my place until I get there? We're keeping Peter Winslow's dog, and he'll need to be let out. Danl can put him on the leash in the back yard. You could make a cup of tea until I get there. I shouldn't be long"

Noreen supervised an after school snack of peanut butter and jelly bread and a glass of milk while Baker was outdoors. He insisted on getting back inside to be with Zoe and Danl just as soon as he finished what he went out to do. Baker and his two buddies were playing tug-of-war with an old towel when Maren arrived. The aroma of steaming cinnamon tea greeted her as she came through the back door.

"How do you make it smell so good?" she asked her friend.

"The secret is simple. Actually boil the water and pour it over the bag. Don't microwave it. It's best if you eliminate the bag and use tea leaves in a tea ball, but I didn't find one."

"That's because I don't own one." They sat at the round, glass table in the dinette area waiting for the tea to cool. "I heard about Mr. Winslow. How is he? Have they any leads?" The details Maren didn't feel comfortable revealing in a public conversation with Della at the Village Café came spilling out in the privacy of her own home. She told Noreen about Matt breaking up with Sydney and Sydney's hysterical reaction."Sydney is a prize winning sharp shooter," Maren said, her brave face melting in front of her friend.

"But you don't know it was Sydney. It could be a random robbery attempt."

"That doesn't make me feel any better. A competent robber would be bad enough in the neighborhood, but this one is evidently incompetent."

Noreen laughed. "Listen to yourself. You're telling me you would feel better if the village thief was more proficient."

"It does sound funny when you put it that way, but Paul didn't think it was funny. He was actually reluctant to go back to Afghanistan, even though Marc told us the police would be keeping an eye on our area." Paul's reaction was the only part of the incident that actually cheered her. It reassured her that she and the kids still came first. She almost shared these intimate facts with Noreen, but couldn't quite bring herself to go over all the details, not yet, not with Noreen. Noreen never questioned Randy's loyalty. "They did pick Sydney up and questioned her before she got out of state. She was released, of course. There was no evidence to hold her. The snow that night obliterated all the footprints. And I'm sure she's smart enough to have gotten rid of the weapon if she did it."

"How does Marc find out all this information?"

"Maybe he qualifies as press. I'm just glad he keeps us posted."

They both agreed they wouldn't relax until an arrest was made.

"My friend Jenny who lives out by the new mall, said there was another robbery near her house. She saw a white panel truck cruising the neighborhood the day before. Any trucks around here?"

"The only trucks in Dexum are the painters. They haven't been out this way, though. How's Randy."

Noreen winced. "He told me troops are moving into Iraq. He thinks he'll be leaving Afghanistan soon, even though the troops want to stay there. It's still up in the air."

"You cope with the uncertainty, so well. I need to have everything planned. I can't even handle a burglar in the neighborhood."

Noreen left Maren with some of the wisdom she had accumulated over the years. "Don't focus on your fears. It magnifies them. Force yourself to think about something good every day. And personally, I do a lot of praying."

The phone rang as Noreen was leaving. It was Meredith Winslow Winston. "Unfortunately, Dad's wound developed an infection.

He'll be fine, but we want him in D.C. where I can keep an eye on him for a few weeks. Could I pay you to keep Baker until he returns?" Maren watched the children playing with the dog. She assured Meredith that no pay was necessary. Her concern was that after another few days of doggie bliss she would have to buy the dog.

Two weeks somehow whisked by. During that time she had not been able to visit John Spencer. He had been admitted to the hospital in Edgelawn. Julie had refused to have him go to the VA hospital, preferring to keep him close; so that she could keep an eye one him. The radiologist who read his most recent brain scan told her John had some bleeders in his brain that had probably been there all along—and that they were getting worse. He required immediate surgery. PT and speech therapies would undoubtedly be prescribed.

As Maren was packing her therapy bag for the day Baker barked sharply. He was better than a doorbell. Marc Vincent stood on the front walk, a white bakery bag in hand. "Sorry I'm too late to see the kids. I brought cinnamon rolls." Maren had been about to leave, but invited him in. Maybe he had news. In the kitchen she made tea quickly with a bag, not tea leaves in the tea ball Noreen had given her. Marc seemed to have no news. "How's Paul," he asked courteously.

"He's going to have a long weekend off in February." She hesitated. "He wants me to meet him in London. It seems the headquarters for Pediatric Possibilities has been changed from the states to London. That means his shorter times off will be spent in England, not Illinois—something he neglected to tell me when he was home." Anger rose up in her throat, along with fear.

"It's a great opportunity. Go."

"It's not that simple. I'm worried about leaving the kids, Marc. Maybe Sydney will come back."

"She won't." He seemed so certain.

"She's writing letters to Matt's employers, trying to discredit him." Marc wanted to hear the details, and Maren could sense him taking mental notes as she talked.

"If she's trying to punish him that way, Matt is probably right—it's unlikely she would shoot anyone."

"Don't you think she intended to either hit or frighten Matt, thinking he was sitting there, and accidently hit Pete?"

"No. I don't think so." He spoke with conviction.

"Then it was a robber. I can't leave the kids in danger. If Matt could be here it would be easier, but he travels."

"Maren, if Matt was able to be here you would say it would attract her to come back."

Marc was starting to read her the way Paul could. It surprised her and confronted her with her own thoughts. She sat in a fear-filled silence. Verbalizing her fears seemed to intensify them. It wasn't supposed to work that way according to counselors, but Maren had repressed for so long expression was like opening the dike. A river of anxiety spilled over in the form of tears. "I don't know what I'm going to do. Paul says he needs me, but some things have happened that make me doubt that. I know the children need me. My patients need me. I've tried to think positively and logically, but I'm afraid." Why she could share her fears with Marc, but not Noreen she didn't know. Maybe she just needed to have a male sounding board. Her intellectual self abruptly vanished. She put both hands to her forehead to hide the raw emotions on her face, emotions that unexpectedly took over.

Marc didn't answer. His own face betrayed no emotion. He stepped away from the table, got the box of tissues from the kitchen desk, and put them in front of her. It gave him a moment to consider what he was about to do. He couldn't fight in the most recent foreign war, but he could provide some comfort for those who were involved, for Paul and Maren. He sat down next to her.

"The shooter might not be Sydney or a robber." He took one of her hands in his and pulled it away from her face. "Maren, look at me." She felt as if she was obeying a brother her parents had never provided. She needed his strength, so that for just a moment she wouldn't have to be the rock.

"Maren." He spoke carefully, quietly. "We have reason to believe there's a very different reason why shots were fired into Pete's house." He continued holding her hand, watching as she processed what he was telling her. "We think the incident was very likely politically motivated."

She stopped crying, pulled her hand back, and stared hard at him while clues from the past weeks came back to her. Her intellectual self returned. "Who are you?"

"We're not supposed to tell." His smile was a sheepish grin. "I can tell you there were credible threats against Ross Winston and his family. And I'm not the only one in Dexum here to investigate. I promise you, I will personally keep your kids safe while you're in London with Paul. But I need your promise that you won't blow my cover. You can't tell anyone, not even Matt." *Especially not Matt,* he thought. He reached into an inner pocket of his jacket, and placed his federal identification badge on the table in front of her.

Paul's team had been able to move from their tents to an old hotel, and after a Memorandum of Understanding had been signed between Pediatric Possibilities and the local Ministry of

Health they were able to take over an old building. While it was being renovated the physicians were already working in two of the rooms. It was Possibilities' first primary health clinic in Afghanistan. They hoped to expand the center eventually to a 90 bed hospital. For now it was an emergency surgical center for treating civilian war victims. Since the country had been at war for thirty years that included just about everyone. Oddly, vehicle accidents caused many of the injuries. But explosions of abandoned weapons ranked right up there for causing pain.

There were more pressing needs in outlying areas, but for now Possibilities was too small an organization to consider another site. Paul was looking forward to seeing more of the country, its people, and its children. The more they learned about Afghanistan the more goals he and his colleagues set. They could foresee setting up health clinics wherever there was a military base, sometime in the future, if the peace could be maintained.

He had heard that an invasion of Iraq was imminent, and wondered what would happen if troops were called out of Afghanistan. There always seemed to be another group of terrorists, not so much in Kabul this month as in England. British police had revealed more details of the discovery of the toxin Ricin in Northern London. The deadly poison looked like innocent talcum powder, but a few grains could easily kill an adult. Prime Minister Tony Blair was frequently on the radio, reporting on the war on terrorism. So far fourteen terrorists had been arrested in the Ricin scare. No one had been injured. Paul hoped the story would be history by the time he and Maren rendezvoused in London in a few weeks.

Two weeks went by like the flash of a camera. Sudden, intense. John Spencer, just out of the hospital, was back on Maren's schedule. Surgery had been successful in cauterizing the bleeders in his brain. Hopefully, there would be no more setbacks in his recovery. He was alone when she arrived, and from the way his face drooped Maren guessed he was feeling lonely. "Pretty day out. Sidewalks are dry. Maybe we should have therapy outdoors."

"No..." He said something else. She had to ask for several repetitions. "I said it doesn't matter. The result is the same."

"Oh, 'doesn't.' John, try not to use contractions. Say, 'does not, is not, was not.'"

His expression told her he was beyond caring. "You sound discouraged." The last surgery should have been encouraging. Something that could be done to stop his regression. John was in a funk though. It was one more blow in a long list. One too many.

"I am not a father any more. Can-not," he emphasized, "go to games, coach, drive a car..." His voice drifted off.

She didn't try to talk him out of his feelings, but didn't intend to allow him to focus only on his limitations. "You can't do some things, that's true; but you are still the most important influence in your children's lives. You can still be the most important role model in the world for them. You can show them how to face adversity. You can shape their character. That's really the most important part of parenting. No one else can do that, John. No one else can love them like you do. Now is not the time to give up. It might take many more weeks to come back from the bleed, but more recovery is possible now than I initially thought likely."

He was silent. Maren had watched him struggle with his body's limitations. Now while she watched she knew the struggle was in his soul. He had to make a choice—a decision to go on or to give up. She could think of nothing else to say. She waited and silently prayed. He hung his head. The silence grew longer.

Finally, he raised his eyes to hers. "What do we do next Coach?"

As Maren drove away, her cell phone chimed. She pulled over to the curb to answer the call from Sue at the VNA office. Wendy Mercer had been taken off the list of patients for VNA. She had the fixator removed from her leg last week and registered at the hospital for outpatient therapy. The psychiatric nurse had recommended increased antidepressant medication and that Wendy should have opportunities to get out of the house. Outpatient speech and physical therapies would help. Friends from church would be able to transport her.

Maren's brain agreed with the decision—she had recommended it—but her heart felt a door slam. No chance for real closure with a woman she had grown to like and admire. No visit to say goodbye to her, Brad or Marlo. Not even paperwork to finish. The Mercers would continue their lives without Maren's help, not giving her a second thought. It was Maren who would grieve the loss of contact with the courageous, dedicated family. *That's the way progress works*, she consoled herself. *It will free up time for me to plan the London trip.*

Maren found the Villiscas in good humor. "Plan," Sylvia told her. Guy smiled and nodded. "Yes, we have made a plan. We are going to move to Charlotte, North Carolina to be near our daughter Beth and her family. We should have done it years ago, but we were both so attached to this house. When Sylvia was in the hospital, I was at home with the flu. Beth had to fly up here to look after us, and that decided it. We're ready to go now." Sylvia nodded her head. "New hum." she said, meaning home. She winced and tried again, "New home."

Maren sat in her regular place, the soft arm chair across the coffee table from the couple on the couch. Guy picked up the poetry volume they had used in therapy. "We are so grateful that you got Sylvia talking and reading so quickly. It made a huge difference having you in our home. You found the key to motivate both of us. We'll keep working on it in Charlotte, but we will never forget..." His deep baritone voice cracked. "...what you've done for us." He handed her what looked like a report with a clear plastic cover. Guy had typed the poem Vagabond's House by Don Blanding, and Sylvia had used water colors to paint beautiful illustrations of every verse, a painstaking effort as she regained control of her right hand.

"I... I didn't really do that much for you," Maren protested honestly. She had worked much harder with others who were often unaware.

"You'll never know how much your visits meant to our family."

"Thank you," added Sylvia.

Maren looked through the pages at the artistry she hadn't known Sylvia possessed. "And I will never forget you," she promised.

On the way home Maren stopped at the Village Café, mainly to visit with Della. Maren wanted to enlist her help. Some kind of construction trucks, not the painters' trucks, were in the small parking lot. "They are making substantial progress on the underground railroad passageway," Della explained. "Your neighbor Marc Vincent was here, finally interested in it. I guess we'll all be famous when he writes his article. You do know where it comes out don't you?" She was talking about the tunnel. "Two doors from your house in the cemetery. Kinda creepy. I think the escaping slaves came up through a fake grave."

After listening to a few more details of how the passage was in better condition than they could have hoped, Maren slipped in a comment that sometimes articles, for one reason or another, don't make it to publication. Abruptly, she changed the topic. "I need to talk to you about some therapy that is going to take place here in the café next week."

Maren told Della about the meeting between John and George. Alice would bring George, but would leave him alone for the meeting. John would have the experience of scheduling a ride with the county ride service, since Julie would be at work. They would all arrive mid morning and stay for at least an hour. "I'll be here first. If it works out though, they may want to come back without me. I wanted you to know that they will be hard to understand and may look odd, but they are both very intelligent men."

CHAPTER 18

The Boeing 777 squeaked onto the runway at six-thirty. Maren had flown through the night and watched the dawn over the Atlantic. It was already Friday morning in England. Her first view of Heathrow was not what she had expected. There were no rain slick runways or lights of the airport reflecting from a wet tarmac. No London fog moved in from dark edges of the field, as she had seen in movies. It was a blue-sky, sun-filled day. Following the flow of passengers through the jetway, she pulled her wheeled bag behind her, a lightweight tote slung over her shoulder. Fellow passengers seemed to evaporate, some into restrooms; while returning locals and experienced international travelers hustled confidently to the main terminal. Only a few fellow Americans straggled along the window lined corridor. She was so distracted watching jets from various countries coming and going that she missed seeing an overhead sign. She had to ask for directions twice in order to find the tube station where she was to meet Paul.

She soon caught up with the crowd of travelers making their way through the darker passageway to purchase tickets for the underground train. For an instant she felt totally alone—lost.

And then she saw him hurrying across the room towards her. Everything else faded from sight. In spite of their recent quarrel and her suspicions about his friendship with Bev, her heart leaped in her chest; and the room seemed suddenly brighter. He engulfed her in his embrace. They stood wrapped in each others' arms, like two tangled branches, while a river of busy travelers swirled around them. Finally, Paul pulled back to drink her in with thirsty eyes. His breath caught in his throat. Neither of them could speak, only hold on. Paul took a deep breath and swallowed hard to contain his emotions. "Welcome to London." He took charge of her luggage with one hand and guided her to a Piccadilly Line car with the other. "Mind the gap," he said, referring to the opening between the pavement and the train the way the British did. There were initially plenty of vacant seats in their car, but after a few stops the train offered standing room only.

Paul began talking and didn't stop until they reached Hammersmith Station. "You may hit the wall tomorrow, but today you will have a grand adventure," he promised. "We'll start with breakfast at the flat, but I have tickets for us on the Big Red Bus. We'll start at Buckingham palace and be tourists all day. We'll walk through St. James Park and over to Westminster Abbey. If you like, we'll take a River Thames cruise this afternoon. The boat goes under all the famous bridges and lets you off at the London Eye. That's near the Tower of London. You might be tired this afternoon, but if you have enough energy we can tour it, see the crown jewels and the spot where Ann Boleyn lost her head."

When they arrived at Hammersmith Station Paul offered her the choice of walking a few blocks to the flat or catching a bus. She opted for exercise. He had used a couple of plastic cards to get them onto the underground train, and now gave one to her. "It's called an Oyster Card. It's a debit card. Touch it to the sensor at the turnstile when we go out." After a short walk past buildings of various sizes that housed department stores, offices, and restaurants they came to an ancient, ornate, green bridge. It had castle-like spires and a walkway for pedestrians. Maren had never seen anything quite like it. Here she was, actually walking across the Thames River. The novel sights, foreign languages and accents all around her, the English architecture, and Paul's running commentary so immersed Maren in the city's culture that it seemed she had left Dexum days ago.

While they walked, Paul continued his monologue and they enjoyed the view. "It's low tide now. See the boats resting on the mud. Wait until you see it at high tide when they all ride high in the water and pull at their anchors." Maren felt the warmth of the sun on her shoulders. Forty-nine degrees seemed like spring after the freezing daily highs in Illinois. "Tonight, you will finally meet John and Bev over dinner at a quiet café near here, where your food will be served on Wedgewood China." Maren felt a twinge of anxiety at the prospect of meeting the famous Beverly Skelton. She stopped walking. She had unconsciously pulled her hand to her stomach.

"You okay, Maren?"

"Just excited and hungry," she told him.

Paul took her up the steps to the front door of the two level flat. They went directly down stairs to the kitchen. He cooked omelets and served her coffee, a scone, and some berries; while she tried to anchor herself to her reality by talking about her work. He listened and smiled as she downloaded her thoughts from the events of the previous few days. It was reminiscent of the way she had shared her news and concerns years ago in his small house in Chicago. Her anger began to thaw, as they reclaimed patterns from their past.

"Big George Sapien ducked through the doorway of the café and made his way across the room with a new cane. Alice followed him, carrying his laptop for him; because he wanted to teach John some applications that would help him type. John was late. He had a terrible experience with the ride service. The driver headed for Albright instead of the village and wouldn't pay any attention to John, although John knew the way. The man didn't speak much English, and when John is flustered he is still very hard to understand. There was a total communication breakdown until they picked up another rider who intervened.

"John doesn't wear a jacket, just a sweat shirt and warm up pants. He's always in tennis shoes and a baseball cap. I'm guessing he's going to wear a cap for a long time, since his hair still isn't growing back after his surgery. He pushed his wheeled walker over to our booth. I saw he was carrying an unsheathed, curved therapy knife in one hand, pressed against the hand rail of the walker. You've seen them, haven't you? It looks wicked, like something a hunter would use. He needs the large handle and curved blade to help him cut his food. He slammed it on the table, backed up against the seat of the booth, glared at George, and without a greeting or attempting to control his loudness stated, 'They think I am dumb.' He almost scared the life out of the bus boy who was carrying three glasses of water. The glasses didn't break, but water sloshed all over the table when he dropped them onto the table. The napkins were soaked. George understood John immediately and soon had him talking sports. He quickly got John to focus on how to use a computer with hands that tremble. The bus boy never did return to clean up the mess, so Della took over."

"Why the hand tremor?"

"Side effect of the meds, I guess. Hopefully it will resolve eventually."

"I may know of a drug that would eliminate that. Don't let me forget to look into it. I think you did both of those men a huge service." Paul was impressed all over again at the magic Maren worked with her patients. He half listened to more details of the soldier's recuperation.

"You don't think he'll work again, do you?"

"Maybe not, but who knows what kind of opportunities might open up for him. He at least needs some adult interaction. It's important for him to be with people who recognize his intelligence."

As he watched and listened, Paul too was taken back to the early days of their relationship. He had always been amazed at Maren's gift for healing. *She has such great insight to each patient. Every person in her care benefits...* Suddenly, he realized what that elusive fact was that he had lost touch with. He remembered standing in the hospital elevator before they were married thinking, promising himself that he would never do anything to interfere with her use of her gifts, a promise he had discounted when he had become absorbed in his own dilemma. He silently re-committed himself to be a more supportive husband.

After her story, it was Paul's turn to talk about his work; but he put his stories through a filter. Only the mildly traumatic could flow through. No gory details. No mention of fear. He told her that through cooperation with the International Red Cross a new central heating system had been obtained and installed in their clinic. Workers were now fixing the roof and repairing windows and doors. "The water supply system has already been improved and the new wiring is almost complete. The walls will be plastered and painted and some of the floors will get new tiles. A private donation allowed us to buy two generators."

She noticed he didn't say much about those he was treating, only that their plight was desperate. He did describe a two year old child who had been injured by flying debris when someone stepped on a land mine. He didn't disclose that the someone was the child's brother who had died instantly. He revealed only that the toddler's face was damaged by the fragments. Fortunately, Paul's skill as a head and neck surgeon was available. "The people are so grateful, so thankful for the simplest treatment, the smallest kindness. What we do is often the difference between life and death." He finished with a sigh, obviously not wanting to dwell on the hardships of the people or the continuing danger. Neither of them wanted sadness to mar their time together, so Maren asked no questions. He directed her to rest on the bed while he cleaned up the kitchen. "You'll need all your strength for later," he said, leaving her to wonder if he meant for sight-seeing, meeting Bev, or making love.

She was asleep as soon as her head met the pillow, so they didn't make it to Buckingham Palace. Instead they dawdled through St. James Park and Westminster Abbey. Maren wanted to explore each chapel and read every placard of the famous cathedral. She expressed amazement at the simplicity of the simple wooden throne that had been used for centuries. She walked on the graves of kings and poets. The Poet's Corner was her favorite, and near it Paul pointed out the memorial plaque honoring Franklin D. Roosevelt for being a dependable friend to Great Britain during World War II. The rest of their sight-seeing was accomplished via the Big Red Bus. They got on and off a few times, but primarily enjoyed the running commentary of the docent. By the time they reached the stop for the Tower of London, Paul knew they didn't have time to go in. "More tomorrow," he promised.

Tired but happy, they returned to the flat and made a check-up call to Bob and Gloria. Paul's parents had readily agreed to stay in Dexum with the children. They assured Paul and Maren that everyone was having a great time. Bob was enjoying Baker as much as the children. On Saturday they planned to visit Navy Pier. And they would all attend the little white church in the village on Sunday.

After Maren showered and changed clothes they walked a few long blocks to the restaurant. To her surprise the aroma of curry greeted her at the entrance. An Indian menu was featured. As Paul was describing his favorite dishes, two men approached the table. He stood to greet them. "Oh, good, you came together. Maren this is John Westlake," Paul said, indicating the shorter man. "And this is Beverly Skelton." The tall, thin Englishman reached across the table to take her hand when John had released it. She was flustered, but managed to respond. "Paul has told me so much about you. It's great to finally meet you."

It wasn't until dessert that she summoned the courage to ask about his name. "I must admit I'm curious about your name— Beverly." She gave Paul a sideward glance. She was quite sure he had never bothered to tell her that Bev Skelton was a male doctor; but then she had not really asked him, other than to inquire if Dr. Skelton was married.

Bev was gracious in his explanation. "I know that my name confuses a lot of you Yanks. It's an old English boy's name and also a family name. My father was named Beverly, as was his great-grandfather." The moment passed, and the conversation turned to a discussion of London's museums. "They are all free, Maren;

and each is quite intriguing. Do take in one or two of the less well known ones tomorrow. Perhaps the Florence Nightingale or the Foundling Museum." Maren had not heard of The Foundling. "It's quite fascinating; it was the first children's charity and first public art gallery. It explores the way artists have improved children's lives for over two hundred seventy years." The physicians couldn't talk long, though without returning to their passion, providing medical treatment to the children of the world, particularly Afghanistan.

They talked about the need in Anabah a village in the Panjshir Valley, and Lashkar-gah, in Helmand province where there was a complete lack of specialized surgical facilities. They argued about how to use their resources. Should they also go to Rowanda or concentrate in Afghanistan. They acknowledged that while there was incredible need in Iraq, they couldn't get into that country until the war was underway. They spoke of it as if there was no doubt it would begin soon.

Maren mostly listened and watched her husband. Paul was changing, and she could see why. Ruth had warned her that Calvin had changed. Their work was engrossing, she had said, even addictive. Maren found the conversation fascinating. Maren had never felt so close to people who lived on the other side of an ocean from her. She was developing a greater appreciation for Paul's awe of the dedicated individuals who were directing Pediatric Possibilities' efforts in Asia.

On the walk back, Paul led her beyond the hedge in front of their building to a small, walled garden nearby. "I know it's cold, but I wanted to show you where I used to stand thinking about you, even though there are no flowers here now. It's where I remembered the words from Stardust—they just seemed to come to me." They shared a kiss by the wall, and afterwards walked up the stairs hand in hand. Now it seemed as if they had never been parted. They both rated climbing into bed together as the best part of a fantastic day. They reached for each other under the covers, hungry for the assurance that their love was still very much alive. It was well past midnight before they dropped off to sleep in each other's arms.

The aroma of bacon cooking wafted upstairs waking Maren. The heavy bedroom drapes had protected the lovers from being robbed of much needed rest, but by mid morning Paul had felt refreshed and ready to begin the day. He started breakfast while she dressed. Bacon was a special treat for Maren. She never cooked it at home. They made plans for the day during a leisurely breakfast and discussed the future.

"This is wonderful, Paul. Until yesterday you hadn't cooked breakfast for us in a long time." "Really? I cook lots of mornings when I'm home."

"I mean for just the two of us. We haven't had a leisurely, private breakfast since we got the children. Something about being parents has changed us, changed the way you relate to me. It's more like I'm a mom, not your wife. It was never that way before."

"How can you say that after...?"

"Yes, we make love, but the way you talk to me and the things you share, or don't share, has changed. I started noticing it when you kept discouraging me from working. But looking back, it's more than the work. It's a change in your whole attitude. It's like I'm an assistant—like you are now the one in charge, and I have to ask permission to do things."

Paul was silent, considering. Could it be that he had transferred his concept of parenting from his mom to Maren when they adopted the children. Was there a deeper motivation in his desire to keep the details of his departure from the hospital secret than he had told himself. She didn't interrupt the silence with any questions. *Maybe he's finally ready to hear me,* she thought hopefully. "Maren, I never thought... Maybe I just didn't have any other role models... I mean I promise to be more understanding of your needs—" But he had needs too, needs he didn't totally understand. "—But I think you could be more supportive of me, too. I want you to really be an equal partner with me..." She bristled and raised her eyebrows. "I mean for us to be equal partners."

Maren didn't defend herself. After all, she had thought he was having an affair with a woman named Bev. She understood him better than she had twenty-four hours earlier, and was able to forgive his lack of trust. He finally seemed to appreciate what she had been trying to tell him since the move to Dexum. Forgiveness was a great healer. Maybe now each could start again.

Their day of sight-seeing was at a slower pace than the previous, with stops for lunch and tea. They spent most of the afternoon at the Tower of London and ended the day with a visit to St. Paul's Cathedral. Paul told her it was considered a lasting monument to the glory of God and a symbol of the hope, resilience and strength of the city of London and the United Kingdom. Maren thought it must be the most beautiful building in all of England. Standing in front of it, she remembered how Paul was able to offer hope to the child with the facial injury and quite likely to many others whose injuries were so horrendous he wouldn't talk about them.

On Sunday morning, during breakfast at their flat, Paul was determined to totally clean the slate. "I've been thinking about what you said yesterday—about maybe I think of you as the kids' mom more than my partner. When I was growing up, Dad was in the service; so we traveled a lot. If Mom ever had a job during that time, I don't remember it. They married right out of high school. She's smart, but never had the luxury of a college education. Her job, her career, was us. I wonder now if she ever resented that, Never thought about that before. She followed Dad, supported him, took care of us. She seemed happy. Dad seemed happy. Maybe I did expect us to slip into the same pattern. I realize now how fragile a marriage can be, how it needs to be nourished as much as the children—maybe more. I'll try to work harder at our relationship, but I'm a guy. I may need…some help.

He really was trying. She smiled. He thought that was a good sign. "Maybe you were right, after all. Maybe we will learn to love each other better from a distance." He assured her again that John Westlake and Bev Skelton take very good care of their physicians. "I'll be home for Easter," he promised. He picked up her luggage and escorted her to Heathrow. They had touched on all the topics that had concerned each of them. Once they had re-established their priorities for their relationship every other question was quickly resolved. They had decided to ask Vance Davidson to baptize Danl and Zoe when Paul returned in April. If Uncle Frank could arrange to be in the area, he and Vance could work out the details of a combined ceremony. All the family would be invited. Paul agreed that when his commitment to Pediatric Possibilities had been met he would try to find a position with an ENT practice in the states. They were both feeling more at peace. They had been tested as they never would have been in Colorado, and they had not only survived, they were stronger for it.

Matt met Maren at the airport, and filled her in on the latest news during the dark drive home. "Sydney sent more letters— not just to the Botnas this time—to their clients in every state where they do business—warning that I have a police record in California and that I am an unstable, undependable person."

"Did they call her on it?"

"Oh, she didn't sign her name or give any contact information, but I know she did it."

"Well your employment history and lack of police record should be easy to verify."

"Yee-ah, except it seems I left California with an unpaid traffic violation on my record."

"Parking ticket?"

"Speeding. She made it sound like drunk driving though, and until they get the response from the California State Police and I pay the fine Louise and Will asked me to take some time off work. It embarrasses them and puts them in a bind. They're being great about it," he assured her. "They said they trust me, but for the sake of clients it would be best if I stay in Dexum until the whole thing is cleared up." Matt turned his new Subaru onto Crescent Drive and drove slowly to the driveway. As he was about to turn in, he stopped.

"What's wrong?"

"I saw something move in the cemetery, by Pete's house."

"Could be a fox. They've been around this winter."

"Not unless it's wearing a metal collar. I saw my headlights reflect off something, something moving… could have been a flashlight." There were no other cars on the road. "Whoever is in there either walked from our neighborhood or left a car at the end of the creek path in the village." He pulled in the driveway next to Bob and Gloria's new red Honda minivan and turned around. "At this hour it shouldn't be hard to spot a strange car in the village." He was right. Dexum rolled up the sidewalks when the library closed at nine. After the Village Café closed at seven and the lone sports bar at eleven no one was on the streets. Matt drove back to Maple Grove and into the village.

By the time he got to Lincoln Street where the path came out he saw someone approaching a dark SUV. "Hey, you. Stop," he shouted as he opened his door. The person was small, dressed in dark clothes and a dark, knit hat; but something glinted in the Subaru's headlights.

"Matt stop. That could be a gun or a knife."

"Or a wrist watch or flash light," Matt said as he got back into the car and followed the vehicle. The SUV drove out Lincoln to Main and turned right. There in the street lights Matt could tell the vehicle was an Explorer, without a license plate. He couldn't tell the year, though. Both drivers ran a traffic light and made left turns through a quiet neighborhood. "Matt, he knows we're following him. " *Where are the police and what about all that protection Marc promised.*

"Maybe it's a she, not a he," Matt said as he narrowed the distance between them. They chased the SUV through the narrow streets, running stop signs and lights until they were out of town. On the wider road the chase accelerated. Maren watched the speedometer climb quickly to sixty-five in a forty-five zone. There were only a few cars on the four lane road, and Matt was continuing to accelerate, changing lanes to get around another vehicle.

Suddenly a light colored sporty car shot out from a side street on their left. It accelerated in the inside lane for oncoming traffic. "Look out," Maren screamed as it cut in front of Matt's Subaru, forcing them over. Matt jammed both feet on the brake and cranked the wheel hard to the right. The Subaru jumped the curb and stopped on a sidewalk in front of a renovated two story house. "Walker Insurance," said the sign planted in the grass just inches from Matt's front bumper. Fortunately, the air bags did not inflate. Maren's heart was racing. Matt turned on the overhead light to make sure his mom was okay. She noticed he wore a stunned expression. "I think that was Laurel's Hyundai." It was now nowhere in sight, and the Explorer was also long gone. "I hope the rims aren't bent," Matt worried about his new car. "I'll have to get the tires balanced for sure."

Bob and Gloria had already turned in by the time Maren and Matt got back to the house. It had taken hours for Maren to get to sleep. She was glad she had arranged to have an extra day off work after the London trip. She had expected she would be jet lagged, but without enough sleep it took extra effort this morning to organize her thoughts and plan for the coming week. She made a list, but she knew what she needed to do first. Once the children were properly hugged and fed, she drove them to school. Bob and Gloria were more than ready to get back to their own home as soon as she returned, saving Maren from a conversation she wasn't ready to pursue. Matt was bound to sleep in, no doubt brooding over his poor choices of girl friends and his now unbalanced tires. Baker would pounce on him sooner or later, begging for a walk.

A call to Sue resulted in the assignment of two new patients. One was a mild stroke, a right hemi paresis CVA. The other was a wheelchair bound woman with dysphonia, a voice disorder. It had been years since Maren had seen any voice patients. She'd need to brush up, make sure she was current on the latest research and best practices. She scheduled appointments for each and for her ongoing case load.

She also arranged to meet Marc, but not in Dexum—in the Edgelawn mall at lunch time. By mid morning Matt was stirring.

She let him know she was leaving and stopped first at the Village Café. It seemed like she had been away for weeks. She needed a cup of real coffee and a conversation with Della Mason. Della always had a laugh simmering, ready to be served at a moment's notice. It was just what Maren needed with her coffee this morning, a friendly smile. They would soon both be laughing over Maren's foolish fears that Paul was becoming romantically involved with Bev Skelton. She wasn't sure what else she would share.

"Pete Winslow is home," Della said. "Meredith stopped here yesterday. She'll call you in a day or so. She knows you've been gone. I'm guessing she'll want to discuss Baker." Della knew that Maren's entire family had assumed ownership of Baker within a few days. Parting with their adopted pet would be painful.

"Maybe I can offer to buy him and get Peter a new dog."

"You know Greg will be happy to help with that. He's always got an abandoned dog at his clinic. He said a thin, homeless man brought in a young beagle a couple of weeks ago. The guy just couldn't afford to feed her any longer. By the way, Greg said he hoped you and Paul had a great Valentine's Day celebration in London."

"Is nothing a secret in this village?" Maren asked, wondering why no one seemed to know about the car chase or who was prowling around in the cemetery.

"Apparently there are a few secrets," Della said. "I'll tell you this. I'm pretty sure those painters are not painting anything, and I'd be surprised if Marc Vincent writes for *Beyond Our Past*."

"Really! Do you have any facts?"

"Not yet, but I'm working on it."

She didn't want to talk about Marc, afraid she'd say something that would blow his cover. "How's the tunnel coming?"

"The Caufields have been out of town, too. They returned yesterday, a day earlier than they had planned. Last night, right before they locked up, Gene went down to check on the tunnel progress for himself. He said something didn't seem right. He heard noises, thought he saw a light. He didn't have a flashlight, just the workers' bare bulb overhead at the foot of the stairs; so he didn't go in too far. Early this morning he walked the length of the passageway. It's close to being open to the end, but he couldn't walk through. He said only a kid could crawl through to the outside."

"Or a woman," Maren suggested. She then shared the events of the previous night. She thought of mentioning her appointment with Marc but decided against it. She had given him her word. Her promises weren't made lightly.

"Maren, you are jet lagged. That doesn't make any sense. I don't know if it was Sydney in that car last night or not, but think about it. Sydney could get to the cemetery along the creek path from Lincoln Street. Why would she be in the tunnel? One of us would have seen her if she came through here."

As Maren was preparing to leave, Della presented her with a plastic box the size of index cards. "It's a whole set of the cue cards you gave me. I put in three or four of each. When you need more let me know." Maren was amazed at how Della had turned her crude drawings into commercial quality, computer generated cue cards. She had cut and filed them behind tabs for easy access. She refused payment saying she had the time, and the materials were left over from other projects.

Marc got a sandwich, and Maren ordered soup. She got iced tea, while he fixed his coffee. She was feeling much sharper, thanks to the talk with Della and the caffeine. Marc was vague. He either couldn't or wouldn't tell her anything about the previous night. The way he avoided looking at her—focusing on stirring his coffee and replacing the lid not once but several times—made her suspect he was keeping something from her. He did confirm that the cemetery intruder got away.

"It was an Explorer, possibly the same one a village cop reported parked in the village the night of the shooting." This was new information to Maren. She looked at him wide eyed. "There was an Explorer that night, like Sydney's? And you didn't tell me?"

"Maren it was just a bit of information we got from going through notes of on duty cops that night. It might mean nothing. There are lots of Explorers. I did confirm that Sydney was in California last night while you chased another Explorer through town." He got back to the question at hand. "The cop didn't take down the license number the night of the shooting, because the vehicle hadn't been there long. He's sure it had an Illinois plate, though." Marc asked if she had seen a license plate on the vehicle she and Matt had chased, and seemed genuinely disappointed that she couldn't remember whether there was a plate or not. "Without that," he said, "We still can't identify the driver."

She asked specifically about the Hyundai and if he knew Laurel Haynes. He didn't look up or act as if the person in the car was of any interest at all. His expressed opinion was that it was probably someone leaving the pub in the village to drive like that. Maren was disillusioned. She shook her head sadly. "I would have thought a group of federal agents in a small village would be able to be more efficient."

Marc seemed more interested in whether she and Paul had had a good time in London than on following leads. She did tell him about the name mix-up, and he noticed that she blushed when admitting her jealousy. "I'm grateful to you for encouraging me to go, Marc; and I do appreciate your trusting me with your identity."

He didn't want to tell her that he was more than a little nervous that this meeting might compromise his cover. He had made the decision to reveal his identity knowing the risk, and he was glad it had been worth it. Now he re-committed himself to not putting her or other agents at risk in any way. He knew in his gut he needed to be very careful not to let her be further drawn into this assignment or his world.

Maren's last visit for the day was at the Evans' home. She was eager to see if he had made any progress and excited to give them more cue cards. He only had vowels, and a few consonants, /m/, /p/, and /h/. Today she would introduce /t/, /k/, and /s/. Chris greeted her with good news of another sort. Cole had been accepted into a work program that would begin after spring break. "He'll be at Albright Community Hospital every day after school. He'll be helping with carrying supplies and some busing of tables in the cafeteria. His school speech therapist thinks this is a great opportunity for him." Maren agreed, but also realized immediately it meant the end of her work with him. Even if they wanted to continue on the weekend, she would not agree. Her first priority was to be available for her own children.

The session went well, but she discovered he spoke better while walking or playing catch, rather than sitting at a table. It gave her the idea that with her ambulatory patients, field trips would be a good idea. She would take Cole out of the house on the next visit.

Maren was anxious to pick up the children. Matt had cleared his record with the state of California and returned to his travels, so he wouldn't be home. Meredith had, as promised, called and taken Baker to her dad's house. She had offered to pay for the dog's stay, but no pay would have been enough to compensate for the loss of their canine friend. At least he was close by. They could visit him, but it wouldn't be the same.

Noreen had happily resumed her childcare duties. She met the school bus and kept Danl and Zoe at her place until Maren got there. They were happy to be playing with Chauncey. It alleviated some of the pain of losing Baker, and made Zoe's weekly violin lessons easier to schedule.

Danl and Chauncey were playing on the hill in Noreen's front yard. Danl seemed to be skating down the small hill, now barely covered with snow, using a piece of cardboard or something as a skateboard. Chauncey bounced along beside him, delighted that his companion was back. "Time to go home," Maren called as she got out of the van.

"Hi Mom. Did you see that long run I made? It was the longest yet. I need some rope to make ties for my skate, because it's hard to keep my foot on it. Do we have any rope."

"You have a sled at home, Danl."

"But I don't have skates or a skateboard." He held up a rectangle that only a nine-year-old could consider ample enough for a skateboard.

"Put it in the back hatch for now. Matt will be home tonight. We'll ask him to help you make ties tomorrow."

Satisfied, Danl carried the old license plate to the back of the van.

The journey may seem long,
but I will finish strong.
Five keys will open doors until
"I'm home," my grateful song.

CHAPTER 19

Maren pushed off her shoes in the back entryway and set two bags of groceries on the kitchen counter. She went to the computer to look for news from Paul. She always did that first, with her coat on. Once she took off her coat, life got too hectic. She printed an email that was longer than usual. It was something about the capture of Khalid Shaikh Mohammed. Paul's note told her to make an exception and turn on the TV news. She walked to the living room while she read. The master mind of the 9-11 attack was being interrogated. Paul mentioned the excitement of the troops. She hoped, as did nearly everyone else, that the world really was safer.

She was reading the remainder of his email when Matt arrived. "I'm starved," he called from the back entryway. "What's for dinner?"

"Whatever we can make with leftovers," she called. "Hey, good news." She didn't mean news of the arrest. There was something more important. "Paul gets a thirty-day R and R. He'll be home for spring break and stay until the week after Easter." Cheers and yelps sounded throughout the house. Danl and Zoe ran from room to room shouting "Yippee," and "Woo-hoo." They put a red circle around March twenty-third on the kitchen calendar. "We should go out for dinner to celebrate," Matt suggested, hoping to avoid leftovers for dinner. Always the practical one, Maren said they would celebrate when he arrived. She went to the refrigerator and began pulling out covered dishes.

"We'll eat leftovers, but I think I've got some chocolate cake and ice cream in the basement freezer. We'll have a mini celebration. Let's get the table set."

"I wish Baker was here. He loves ice cream." It was Zoe.

"Chauncey likes eating the snow." Danl was trying to cheer her.

"I don't care about that. Chauncey's just a ringer!" Zoe flung the words at him. He stared at her without comprehending. He didn't know what she meant, but it didn't sound flattering. He missed Baker, but it wasn't Chauncey's fault that Baker was gone. As he opened his mouth to argue the point. Matt's cell phone tune interrupted. He answered and motioned them to quiet, mouthing silently, "It's Laurel." He hadn't heard from her, except for a single voice mail, since seeing her car the night of the chase. She had to be out of town, she had told him in the message, to visit her uncle in Maryland. He moved to his bedroom for privacy. Maren sighed. At least it wasn't Sydney.

It was after seven-thirty by the time the mini-celebration was completed. The children were in their rooms, and Maren was loading dishes into the dishwasher when she heard someone knock on the front door. She peeked out the library window. No car in the driveway. It was Marc, looking more serious than usual. "I didn't want the kids to know I'm here. I've got some pictures to show you." He spoke quietly, with an official tone to his voice. They went into the library and closed the doors. He showed her two photos that looked like mug shots of the same man. Maren shook her head before he even asked if she recognized him.

"He was caught going into the Dexum café through the tunnel at quarter to seven tonight. Says he's been sleeping there off and on since it was open enough to crawl through from the cemetery. We think he may have helped that along. He was one of the original excavation crew members, but was laid off at Christmas. Tonight, the police noticed an Explorer parked on Lincoln Street, because it didn't have a plate. They called us."

"Did he have a gun? Was there a gun in the car?"

"No to both questions. Here's his story. His name is Howard Kaboda. He came down here from Edgelawn to take the job with the tunnel project. He went homeless right after being laid off. Claims he found the car abandoned at the strip mall a couple of months ago, right after Christmas. He's not sure of the exact date. It was running, and the keys were locked in it. When no one showed up after a half hour or so, he got the mall security guard to help him open 'his' door. He claims he waited a long time, but the owner never showed.

No theft report has ever been filed. He picked up a stray dog. They both slept in the basement, where he could pilfer enough from the café to feed himself and the beagle. He recently turned the dog over to the local vet. He maintains he doesn't know what happened to the car's owner or the license plate. He's sure it was attached when he acquired the vehicle, but could only say it was an Illinois plate. The VIN number had been filed off. He says he never noticed."

"Why did he run when we saw him?"

"He came out to the cemetery for a smoke... says you spooked him."

"Do you think he shot Pete?"

"Without the plate to find out who owns the SUV and substantiate his story there's no way to tell."

"Co-mon, Marc. You've been doing this a long time. What's your gut feeling?"

For the first time since he came through the door he smiled at her. She was starting to know him better than he had intended, and it confused him. "How do you do that?"

"What?"

"Have that insight into …me?"

"It's the speech-language pathologist in me. We have to be detectives and counselors in addition to therapists. So, what do you think?"

"My gut feeling is that this guy is not the shooter."

"Then where does that leave us?"

"We're getting closer. I would bet this guy or the car—even though it was out east of town—are somehow involved. But I don't think he did the shooting. If you and Matt hadn't interfered the other night when you chased him—if we hadn't been busy protecting you two." He stopped, knowing he had already said too much.

"Protect us. What do you mean?"

"I mean stop you from getting injured or killed in an accident or shooting. You were going forty miles an hour over the speed limit at one point." There was an edge to his voice.

"Marc, were you in that Hyundai?"

"No, Maren. Matt was right. That was Laurel." He hesitated, letting out a long, noisy breath. "Laurel is my daughter. She uses her mom's last name. Her mom and I separated a long time ago. She couldn't handle the stresses of my work and was afraid our son would want to follow in my footsteps. He's a musician. It was Laurel who... It's unusual to be assigned to the same case." Feeling vulnerable, he stopped. He didn't want to explain the whole situation.

She was processing the ramifications of this latest information, what this would mean for Matt, and how having his daughter in danger affected Marc. *All this intrigue and I thought Paul was the one on the front line.*

"You know I won't tell anyone, including Matt."

"That's right." He answered quickly. "You can't. I know she's been seeing him, and not just for business. But it's up to her whether or not she tells him." He hesitated, reminiscing, and then, "How do you cope with it Maren, the strain of Paul being gone so much and in the middle of a war zone?"

"Well, I follow my friend Noreen's advice—I pray a lot and try not to watch the news. Taking care of the kids and investing in my work with patients helps me to focus on others instead of myself. And I pray a lot," she repeated.

On Monday Maren stopped to see John Spencer right after her morning coffee stop at the café. He had forgotten she was coming. The house was quiet and as neat as usual. John was wearing the cardigan sweat shirt he wore instead of a coat. "Where are you going? Do you want to have a therapy field trip?" He told her that his dad would be there any minute to take him for his driving evaluation. He was obviously nervous and excited. "When I can drive I can take the kids to activities and meet George without a hassle."

Maren acknowledged the satisfaction he would feel and that some get-togethers would be helpful for both men. She also sensed that he no longer wanted to have speech therapy at home, if at all. He would be able to chauffer his children to school and their activities, attend parent-teacher conferences, maybe even get a part time job. "I'm thinking about doing flight instruction, in simulators."

While they waited for his dad Maren cautioned him that he needed some way to become what she called "his own therapist." He agreed that he needed something to keep him motivated. He showed her a card that identified him as a member of a wounded veterans' group, and told her he could practice speech there. That gave Maren an idea. Before she left they made plans to start a speech support group for adults. Maren would ask Gene and Emma if they could use the Dexum Café after hours one evening a month. At first it would be John, George, and Maren, but they would invite others. When Ed arrived Maren watched them walk to the car. John's leg no longer dragged. He seemed to be leaning less on the walker. And since the change in medication Paul had researched for him, his hands trembled less than before.

The last visit of Maren's day was with Stephanie Harrison. She had celebrated an important birthday over the weekend. She was now three years old, old enough to be admitted into the pre-school program in the local elementary school. The patients Maren had grown to love were moving on, for one reason or another. There were new evaluations every week, but she had become attached to her first few homebound patients.

Stephanie could now say many words. She used the phonemes for /p/, /b/, /m/, /n/, /t/, /d/, and /s/. She was more proficient at the word level than in phrases, and her phrases were short, but she spoke in short sentences. Although she was precocious intellectually, her language development was falling behind. "If I ask her to tell me what happened when she went out with Daddy, she really can't," Joanne lamented to Maren. "She'll get out a few words and then get frustrated and give up or sometimes get angry, because I can't understand."

"You're saying she's harder to understand now than a couple months ago?"

"Yes! Does that mean she's getting worse?"

"It means she's trying to express more complex messages, and her ability to program her muscles for the speech sounds can't keep up with her thought process."

"Oh, then that's good?"

"Ho, ho. Hum, pay." Stephanie was tired of waiting for Maren's attention. She was substituting the /h/ sound for sounds she couldn't yet produce, /g/ and /k/. She was telling her mom, "Go" and telling Maren, "Come." She didn't have the /l/ sound either, and so simplified the word /play/ to /pay/. Both Joanne and Maren immediately understood Stephanie's message. Her pushing on Joanne and pulling on Maren emphasized her meaning.

As Maren was about to leave she reminded Joanne to take the evaluation reports to their local school and request placement in a preschool class for Stephanie.

"I'm going this week to observe the classes, but Stephanie has been making fantastic progress with you. We just don't know if we want to mess with success."

"Children learn some things better in individual therapy, but other things develop faster in a group. Go observe, and we'll talk about it again."

The March afternoon was sunny, allowing the neighborhood Children to enjoy being outdoors. The memory of the shooting back in January was fading with the retreat of cold weather. The neighbors were more likely to talk about the roundup of al Qaeda leaders than a failed robbery last December. Peter was seen around the village regularly and seemed to be in excellent health, further supporting a sense that it had all been a bad dream. Pete faithfully walked Baker up the street each day to give Danl and Zoe a chance to romp and play chase with him. They would toss a nylon bone and race to see who could get it first. The losers would chase the winner, trying to retrieve it. Maren and Pete watched as they chatted. The only way Zoe had a chance to win was if she faked throwing the bone. She started running and then tossed it in front of her. There were shrieks and yelps of excitement and delight.

"I think Baker is laughing right along with them."

"They all seem pretty happy. Thanks for bringing Baker over. It means a lot to all of us." She was surprised at how much she had missed the furry fellow.

"I think it means more to Baker. He never looks this cheerful at home." Pete hesitated. "I'd like to be able to give Baker to you, if you would take him of course, but Meredith is quite insistent that I keep him until the intruder has been found."

"I hope that will be solved soon."

"The police brought some pictures over, but I couldn't identify the man. Did they contact you and Matt?"

"We saw the photos." Actually, she had seen them twice. Sergeant Mulligan came to show them to Maren and Matt the day after Marc had asked her about them. "We didn't know the man, either." Before Pete could ask any other questions, Emma Caufield drove up, on her way to her home on the other side of the cemetery. She parked at the curb and joined them.

"I left Gene to close up. It's such a nice day I just had to get out of there."

They chatted while the children and Baker wore themselves out. It gave Maren the chance to ask about starting the speech support group at the café. She offered to pay for use of the room. Emma said she would check with Gene, but was sure it would be fine. She asked if they had seen the mug shots.

"Gene saw him when he worked on the tunnel, but no one knew much about him. What concerns Gene and me is that right now he has a place to sleep. When he's released from jail he'll be out on the street again. We won't press charges for taking the food, and there seems to be no connection to the shooting. He'll probably be out soon. They can only ticket him for speeding and driving without a plate. Gene and I are trying to find a way to help him. The Lord may have directed him here for some reason. The village residents seem to think there are no poor or homeless here. Maybe this will be a wakeup call. I think the local churches should get involved."

"Mom, he didn't give me a turn." It was Zoe. The good time was disintegrating into arguments, due to hunger and fatigue. Maren herded them into the house noticing that, as Pete put the leash on Baker and led him away, the sad faced dog kept looking back.

During dinner Danl wanted to know when Mr. Winslow would give Baker to them. Matt came in at that moment and joined them. "Pete's going to give us Baker?" Matt was surprised. "That's pretty cool."

"He's not giving Baker to us."

"I heard him out in the yard," Danl insisted.

"Oh, that." Maren stopped. *Never say things you don't want children to hear. They are always listening,* she reminded herself.

The three stared at her hopefully until she repeated what he had said. She hated to repeat it because she didn't want the children thinking about the shooting, again. She wanted them to feel safe. They hadn't talked about it in weeks. "So, until the intruder is found he feels he must keep Baker at his house."

"Mom, maybe we should pray about it. You always say to ask Jesus for help." It was Zoe's wise beyond her years suggestion.

"Well yes, but I don't know about praying to take Mr. Winslow's dog away from him."

"We won't. We'll pray that the police catch the guy who shot Mr. Winslow."

Maren was confronted with her children's trusting, hopeful faces. Even Matt looked at her expectantly. "Can't hurt to ask," he said. "Okay guys. Lets hold hands and ask for justice." One troubling thought occurred to her. "Remember, when you ask for something you should be willing to be part of the answer."

The week flew past with no further talk of capturing the gunman or acquiring Baker. On Saturday Paul's parents came for an overnight visit. Paul hadn't written them about their decision to have the children baptized at First Church, so it was up to Maren. She started by telling them they had been enjoying attending First Church. Fortunately, Bob and Gloria were pleased and expressed hope that Frank could take part in the ceremony that signified entry into the Christian faith. They were eager to attend the church on Sunday with Maren and their grandchildren.

Bob began talking about Paul's latest e-letter. The military is looking for physicians and nurses to start a clinic near Kandahar's air base. Bob said Paul was more interested than John or Bev. "Paul feels like there are facilities in Kabul now. He thinks it makes more sense to establish a clinic near each military base, than to build another city hospital." Obviously, Paul was sharing more military information with his dad than with Maren. She shooed the children to the playroom, and Bob volunteered to supervise. Maren wondered what the latest bit of news would mean for the family, if anything. *I'll have to do a Google search just to find Kandahar.*

"We're going to get a dog," Zoe announced to Pastor Vance at the door. Vance looked for Maren's cue before answering. She shrugged and nodded while Danl gave the rest of the story. "But the guy who shot Mr. Winslow has to be caught first."

"Yes, " said Zoe, "It should be pretty soon now, because we prayed for it." Maren shrugged and nodded again, indicating it was all basically true.

On Monday the south breezes gave way to strong northern winds, and precipitation that started as rain quickly turned to flakes. Maren finished her session with Cole early and drove cautiously through blowing snow to pick up the children at Noreen's house. Danl was not in a good mood. "You said Matt would make ties for my skateboard, but he didn't." She had forgotten to mention it. In her defense, spring seemed to have arrived, thus eliminating skateboards from the mix of thoughts she constantly juggled. "We'll get it fixed," she promised. "Go get your skate and put it in the van. Matt can fix it tonight. We'll turn on the backyard light and you can try it on our hill after dinner."

It was because of the snow that Matt happened to be home. He was supposed to have been traveling all week, but driving conditions were terrible north of them. As soon as they got home, Maren went straight to the computer to look for word from Paul.

Danl extricated Matt from the book he was reading and dragged him to the garage. When Danl showed him the license plate Matt assumed it was something Noreen had given the kids. It was cold in the garage, and Matt was eager to return to his book. It was a spy story Laurel had recommended. He quickly tied some twine to allow Danl to tie his skate to his foot. "I think I need one for the other foot." Danl had experimented enough to know that the small license plate wouldn't accommodate two feet. Matt was eager to get back to his book. "Why didn't you ask for ice skates or a snowboard for Christmas or your birthday," he asked. Seeing Danl's sad expression, he cast a quick look around the garage and spotted an aluminum frozen casserole pan in the recycling bin. "Buddy, I think I can fix you up. In fact I think this will work better than what you have."

After dinner Maren cleaned up the kitchen while she watched Danl through the window. He seemed to be skating across the lawn and sliding down the gentle slope using both feet. The gentle slope in their yard wasn't as good as the hill at Noreen's, but he was having a good time. When she opened the back door to the deck and called him to come in he held one skate up by a broken tie. It had already worked loose. Maren suddenly realized that his skate was an old license plate.

"Danl, where did you get this?"

"I found it." He was worried that he'd be in trouble. He had crossed the road at Noreen's place to retrieve it. He wasn't supposed to cross the road. He finally admitted it was not even in front of Miss Noreen's house. He had followed Chauncey quite a ways down the road, while Zoe had her violin lesson. Maren tried to get him to remember when he had picked it up, but he hadn't been to

Noreen's for many weeks. When Matt had been home only Zoe had gone there for her violin lesson.

"Danl, this could be a clue that would help find the gunman. Remember when I told you we might have to be part of the answer? I need to take your skate."

After Maren tucked Danl and Zoe into bed, she called Marc. She told him about the present she had a for him and said she would bring it right over. "No, I'll come there. I don't want to make you the subject of gossip while Paul's away. Better if you aren't seen coming in here alone. At least Matt and the kids are there."

"You mean for chaperones?"

"Something like that." He didn't need her to see all the equipment set up in his house, either.

She could tell he was excited about the find, but he cautioned her not to get her hopes up or to tell anyone outside the family. This could be a false lead. They had investigated plenty of those. Still, she was sure that he would make a few calls and within minutes they would know who owned the plate, maybe even have the gunman in hand.

CHAPTER 20

Paul's plane landed on time Sunday night. Maren had allowed Zoe and Danl to ride to the airport even though it was well past their bedtime. That's what made spring break fun as well as challenging, everyone's schedule was relaxed. Maren had accepted only two new patients from VNA in the past month and one child from Early Intervention. To keep her schedule light, she wouldn't add any more, until after Easter when Paul went back to Afghanistan. Spending time together was the first priority for the next month.

Paul pulled his luggage as fast as he could walk, without actually running. He felt no fatigue. Having learned to sleep in just about any place during the past seven months, he found the padded seat of the jetliner over the Atlantic was more than adequate as a bed. The Iraq invasion had finally begun just four days ago, the same day U.S. troops had launched terrorist-seeking raids on villages southeast of Kandahar. Bev had said it was a sign that it was too early to set up a surgery in the area. Paul didn't agree, but didn't argue the point. He was going home, and was relieved that there were no flight delays due to the military action in Iraq.

After excited greetings, he eagerly climbed in the driver's seat for the trip home. The children fell asleep almost immediately, and Maren alternately "rested her eyes" and tried to fill him in on the village news. She was relieved to have him at the wheel, and he felt content being more directly involved with his home and family again.

Everyone woke early, eager to begin their time together. They were all in the kitchen by seven-thirty preparing a family meal. It had now become a tradition to have chocolate chip cookies for breakfast when Paul came home, but he was making omelets as a side dish.

The pace today was to be slow. The days would become increasingly full as the week progressed. With a family party at the house after the baptisms, there were plenty of chores to do. Maren started writing lists and making silent, unilateral decisions while Paul cooked. He glanced at her. "Lay it on me organizer. What's happening this week?"

"We have an appointment with Pastor Vance on Wednesday. Nick and Carrie are coming Friday night to help, but that means we need extra groceries. They'll bring desserts, but no real food. Father Frank will fly in on Saturday and stay until Monday afternoon. Bob and Gloria will bring Elizabeth. Penny. Jim and the girls will come in time for church and spend the day. You need to put the toast in, Paul."

"Now Maren, I've got this covered." He was re-establishing his presence. "Since we have cookies, we won't need toast."

The children giggled, loving how all the rules changed when he was in the kitchen. Maren frowned, but Paul used his thumb and finger tips to push up the corners of her mouth. "Lighten up, Maren. Let's celebrate. Like Nehemiah said, let's eat the fat and drink the sweet wine. It's a holiday."

She allowed the corners of her smile to spread even further as he worked his magic on all of them. *As I live and breathe, it's a miracle. He's been reading the electronic Bible I gave him...but Nehemiah? I have no idea what that's about. I'll have to look that up.*

"Does that mean we get to drink wine?"

"No, Zoe, just the grape juice at communion on Sunday."

Matt watched from the doorway. His mom and Paul were fantastic together. Something inside him ached. He felt empty, and longed to fill the void. He had thought Sydney would fill that empty spot. She was blond, pretty, talented, and intelligent, all things on his list. She had seemed as smitten with him as he was impressed with her, but then there was her jealous, possessive nature, her irresponsibility with money, her manipulative personality. He hadn't seen that in the beginning.

Maybe that wasn't the way it happened, making a list and finding someone that fit the description. He still felt the empty ache and hoped his time was coming. He knew now he needed someone more mature, more responsible, someone with a life of her own, not a leech. Laurel certainly was her own person. She seemed strong, sure of herself. She was almost a mystery to him. There was time. They would take whatever time it took to get to know one another. He would celebrate today, hoping that he was one day closer to his destiny with the right person. A rap on the front door interrupted his thoughts and caused him to turn his back on the joyful kitchen scene to greet Marc on the front step.

"Marc, come on in. Paul's home. You're in time for chocolate chip cookies."

Laughter drifted from the kitchen. "Oh, I forgot that he came in last night. Thanks Matt, but I don't want to intrude on Paul's re-entry. I'll come back later to say goodbye. My assignment here has been canceled until the underground railroad tunnel is complete. My boss is so interested in featuring it that he decided they'll send a writer when it opens. I could be anywhere on another assignment by then." Marc put a hand on Matt's shoulder, and left it there for a long moment. "If I don't see you again Matt, good luck."

As Maren was gathering some therapy materials for use with Stephanie, Matt told her about Marc's news. "Did he say anything about…" She stopped herself. *He must know something, maybe they made an arrest.* Matt didn't know that she had given the license plate to Marc. "Uh, about where he's going?"

"No, just that he'd come by later."

Two days passed without seeing Marc and very little of Matt. When Matt wasn't working he was with Laurel. Maren knew Matt was hoping she would come to the family party on Sunday. Paul took Zoe and Danl on various outings and took himself to the couch for a few naps. Maren met with John and George to work out the details of their new group. John's medications had been adjusted, again. His hands no longer trembled. And something else—his walker had been replaced by a three point cane. She saw the Harrisons and encouraged Joanne to enroll Stephanie in the speech-language preschool class for fall. On Wednesday morning Maren, Paul, Danl, and Zoe met with Pastor Vance.

"You know we practice infant baptism in our tradition, allowing parents and the community to decide for their children that they will be taught to follow Jesus. Children are then included in the church before they can respond with their own confirmation of faith. However, a seven and nine year old are not infants. At your ages you need to have a say in this. That's why I asked you to attend Sunday School and spend time with Kendra our Director of Family Ministries. Kendra tells me that Zoe and Danl have each decided they want to give their hearts to Jesus and follow him. I understand you drew these." He held up drawings each had created to portray opening their hearts to Jesus. Zoe and Danl nodded solemnly.

"Baptism means you are sorry for things you have done wrong, and with God's help you will try to stop being selfish and self-centered." They had often talked about selfishness and being self-centered at home. The children nodded, again. "So we use water to show that God washes away all the bad things you've done when you tell him you're sorry, as if they had never happened."

"And then we get to be brand new." Zoe said, impatient with Vance's slow speech pattern.

It was Vance's turn to nod. "That's right. Now, your uncle Father Frank would like to sprinkle you with water to show everyone that is what's happening. You are each becoming a new person in Christ. But, for the past several years we have given older folks—like you two—the choice of sprinkling or immersion, being dunked all the way under water. If you want to be sprinkled, we would have Father Frank baptize you here during our Sunday worship service. If you want submersion we would go down the street to our sister church with your family and friends after the late service and use their baptistery, a walk-in tub of water."

"That sounds neat." That was Zoe. Danl wasn't so sure. "But we're baptized either way, right?" Vance assured them they would really be baptized either way. He told them to talk it over at home and let him know by Friday morning.

They stopped to pick up a gallon of milk and then straight home. Paul parked the van in the driveway, because the children saw Peter Winslow and Baker in front of his house. They wanted out immediately, and raced to see who could put a hand on Baker first. He was straining at the leash trying to meet them. Maren noticed the purple petals of hyacinths that had emerged near the house the day before. She and Paul admired the signs of spring before unlocking the front door.

Once inside, Maren started for the kitchen to get lunch ready; but Paul caught her arm. "Alone at last," he said in a low, suggestive voice. They were enjoying a long, soft kiss when the doorbell rang. "You'd think a dog could keep them busy longer than that," Paul complained. Instead of children, he found Marc standing on the front step. After greetings and welcoming Paul home, Marc declined their offer for coffee and got to the point of his visit. The three stood in the entryway for the entire conversation.

"I don't know how much you've told Paul," Marc began.

"Everything, Marc. He's my husband."

"I kind of thought you were that kind of couple, no secrets."

Paul winced, silently vowing again to share all his secrets with her in the future. "Thanks for watching out for Maren and the kids."

"It was my pleasure, as well as my assignment. I wanted to let you know we found Donald Cooper, known as DT Cooper, owner of the Explorer and license plate. He's been in prison on other breaking and entering charges since two days after the shooting. He left his SUV running while he broke into a house in back of the strip mall. Unfortunately for him, it was the house of an Albright policeman who happened to be at home. It will hit the news today or tomorrow, and I'll be out of here Friday morning. I've been telling the other neighbors that I've been reassigned. And that is true, just not with the magazine."

"So we were never really in danger. It was just a robbery, not political intrigue, and not Sydney. Did they find the gun?"

"Not yet. He may have tossed it in the river. He's high on alcohol or drugs most of the time. Probably doesn't remember."

"But he remembered being here...shooting Pete?"

"Yeah, he had been breaking into quite a few homes; but never was armed before. Right now he's claiming someone set him up. We know he was here. It was his Explorer parked in the village. This is the most serious charge he's ever faced. He'll try to get out of it anyway he can, but with his record he doesn't stand a chance. No one will believe a word he says."

"I thought I would feel more relieved, but I'm still kind of unsettled."

"That's natural, Maren. It will take time. You've been on edge for months. Now I need to let you folks get back to celebrating. I'm going to say goodbye to Pete and the kids. Thanks for all your help."

"What about Laurel?" Maren felt Marc was hurrying away before they could ask any more questions, and she was concerned for Matt's sake.

"She's leaving tomorrow, Maren... the last of the painters. She stayed around as long as I...as it could be justified."

The item made the evening and early morning news. Peter Winslow was seen on TV telling reporters he felt just fine and was relieved the mystery had been solved. He called his daughter Meredith Thursday morning and Maren in the afternoon. He knew what Zoe and Danl would say. He wanted to check with their parents. Maren's happy response assured him this was the right thing to do. He gathered all of Baker's belongings, put them in his gardening wagon, attached the leash to Baker's collar, and walked him up the street to his new home.

Paul was getting a saucer of cookies for a bedtime snack when Matt came in looking glum. Baker jumped up from his pillow and yelped in excitement. As Matt scratched Baker behind the ears and enjoyed doggie kisses, Maren assured him that Baker was now a permanent part of the family. Matt took a cookie and got a glass of milk while Maren and Paul continued talking. Maren had decided to include a few friends from the neighborhood, in addition to family. Paul talked around a bite of cookie.

"It's okay with me Maren, but let's not include the whole village."

"Just Will and Louise Botna, Vance and his wife, of course Noreen, Peter, and…" She looked toward Matt.

"You can take Laurel's name off the list. She won't be coming." Paul stopped pouring milk and watched. Maren wasn't sure how to answer. She just uttered, "Oh." The look of concern on her face was all the encouragement he needed.

"Mom, she's a federal agent. She told me tonight. She was here with a few others on an assignment. They thought Pete's shooting might be connected with threats to Ross Winston. Now that DT Cooper is in jail, she's been re-assigned. She said she stayed here as long as her boss would allow, but she has to be back in D.C. in the morning. Can you believe that?" Paul focused on filling his glass with milk, leaving Maren to respond. "Oh Matt, I'm sorry. I know you… It is hard to… Imagine, meeting a federal agent right here in Dexum." She looked to Paul for help, but after a quick glance at her he stared into the chocolate milk he was now stirring.

The weekend was to be a wonderful escape from routine, worries, wars, and disappointments; but there was a schedule to be met. Maren was thankful that the shooting mystery had indeed been solved. Seeing Marc Vincent drive past the house in his black Escalade on his way out of town Friday morning left no room for doubt. It was over.

Nick and Carrie arrived in the afternoon, bringing extra bedding and unexpectedly bags of groceries to turn into various salads as well as desserts. Zoe moved into the spare bed in Danl's room, gladly giving up her own space for the brother and sister-in-law she rarely saw. Matt's room would be for Uncle Frank when he arrived, but Matt was as restless as Baker. The McCloud canine seemed nervous at the unusual activity in the house. Matt decided to take the couch in the library a night early to keep Baker company there. Everyone had stayed up late talking, but by two a.m. the house, still filled with the aromas of spaghetti sauce and baked goods, was quiet.

Not an hour later Maren was awakened from a sound sleep. "What's wrong?" Paul was pulling on his robe. "I couldn't sleep. I thought I heard Baker bark." He went to the front of the house where he found Matt standing in the entryway holding Baker's collar with one hand, the door handle with the other. "Don't open the door, Matt," Paul commanded. He ushered Matt and Baker back into the library, where they stood like sentries, one on one side of the window, one on the other, to look up and down the street. The motion detector flood light on the garage turned on just then, as a vehicle going down Crescent Avenue drove too close their driveway.

Maren came in, startling them from behind. "What's going on?"

"Something spooked Baker, Mom. We just saw some cars going by. Kind of unusual for Crescent Avenue at this hour."

"Well it is spring break. Everyone's schedule is different. Look at the extra cars in our driveway." Paul said nothing. Even in the dim light she could tell he was tense. She had a sudden insight into how Afghanistan was carving a mark on him and on thousands of others who had been there. Seeing no other activity outdoors, they returned to bed.

Paul and Matt went to meet Uncle Frank's flight on Saturday morning. The drive provided time for a good visit, during which Matt brought up the subject of his relationship with Laurel. "I see you and mom and Nick and Carrie; you seem so happy, like life just flows along for you. I'm hoping Laurel will bring that special happiness into my life. Well, she already has. She's cautious though. She's only willing to say she's surprised at how fast our relationship has grown. It's like she tried to prevent it, but couldn't. I think that's a sign." Paul assured Matt that there are challenges in every relationship, that life doesn't just roll along without a few bumps in the road.

"Why are you, the longtime bachelor suddenly ready for a life partner?"

"I've been thinking a lot about that. You know, when Nick and Carrie got married, I objected on the grounds that they were too young. I think the truth was that I saw how happy they were, and I couldn't get into their happiness. I mean I didn't have what they did, and had no idea how to make it happen."

"You mean you were jealous?"

"At first I was angry that Nick and I wouldn't get to have any adventures together, like other brothers in their twenties. And then yeah I was jealous. Finally it was just pure envy. It's hard to be the only one in the family without a partner, the only one alone." Paul talked about how close he and Penny had become, long after she and Jim were married. "You never know what might bring you together."

"I just really thought if I could find a wife, Nick and I would have more in common."

"Matt, you can keep your eyes open, but to find the right partner means being open to the unexpected. You can't just interview promising applicants. I'm sure you will find a life partner at precisely the right time. Just don't try to force something."

After lunch Frank played Uno with Danl and Zoe. They had decided to have their great uncle Frank baptize them with sprinkling, mostly because of Danl's reservations about being dunked. Gloria, Bob, and Aunt Elizabeth arrived before breakfast on Sunday. They wanted to see the children before the party. Gloria handed each of them a wrapped gift that was a little over a foot long. They eagerly tore the paper off the odd shaped presents. Each found a large, wooden key-shaped plaque Bob had cut and stained. There was a poem, hand printed on parchment paper affixed to it with a clear glaze. A key chain was attached through a hole at the top of the wooden key, so they could hang it on a wall. Across the crown of the key Bob had carved their initials ZAM for Zoe Ann McCloud and DRM for Danl Robert McCloud.

The children had never been given middle names. When Maren and Paul had discussed it in London, Paul suggested the children choose their own Baptism names. Each had chosen their grandparent's name—Gloria's middle name and Bob's first. Gloria and Bob were the only grandparents the children had ever known, grandparents who loved them unconditionally, who dropped whatever they were doing to be with them when they were ill, who helped them pack and move, stayed overnight with them to keep them comfortable and on schedule, and who took them on exciting field trips. They were grandparents who loved them just as they were and set examples of what they could become. Danl and Zoe couldn't have put their feelings into words, but they expressed their love and appreciation by taking their names.

Gloria had artistically inked the lettering of the poem she had written for them, a poem to guide them in life. She had incorporated the points of Pastor Vance's sermon series, about how to have a happy life. Since she had heard only one of the talks, she had contacted him for notes on the others. Zoe and Danl read it aloud.

Five Keys

A trip to take have I 'cross land and sea and sky,
through waves of doubt and mounts of cheer
'til "Home again," I'll cry.

A craft to choose or win of wing or wheel or fin.
I'll use the keys that Life provides.
The first of course is kin.

Maps be carefully planned;
can't draw the way in sand.
God's Word the key to my True North will be kept close at hand.

Some friends must come aboard to laugh or wield a sword.
Companionship's key number three.
We'll weave a three-strand cord.

So let adventures roll,
Some fun; some take a toll.
Events and mentors each a key God gives to guide my soul.

The journey may seem long, but I will finish strong.
Five keys will open doors until
"I'm home," my grateful song.

The hundred fifty year old church bell rang loud and long, broadcasting the joy of two new creations in Christ to all the village. Everyone invited attended both the church service and the lunch. Each brought something to share and cards or a small gift for the children.

Peter Winslow who was usually seen only in gardening clothes looked like the college professor he had once been, dressed in his best suit. He brought two mustard plants he had started in his greenhouse. They were potted and wrapped with bright paper. "They are Brassica juncea" he told them. In case they hadn't heard the story of the mustard seed that Jesus told, there was a copy of the parable in the gift card. He warned the children that although the seeds were tiny, the plant could grow to be immense, thus reminding them that only a tiny bit of faith is needed to live a wonderful life. "With a little care, just watering each week, they will grow into huge, healthy plants large enough to provide flowers to enjoy, leaves to eat, seeds for flavoring, and even shade from the summer sun."

Zoe received a bracelet with two Christian symbols on it from Penny Jim, and the girls. There was a cross and a fish. Danl got a children's Bible that was beautifully illustrated with colorful paintings.

Uncle Frank offered a short prayer before lunch, giving thanks not only for the food, but for the lives of Danl, Zoe and those who would help guide them through life. Noreen played "Jesu Joy of Man's Desiring" on her violin after the prayer, while folks walked through the food line. As the dessert line formed she played, "What The World Needs Now Is Love." That was when Pastor Vance and Laurie arrived. He had been detained by a new members class at the church, but there was plenty of food from which to chose an ample lunch.

Maren's sister Ruth and Paul's Aunt Cloris phoned to congratulate the children. The conversations were short. Danl and Zoe had been serious as long as could be expected. Maren suggested they change clothes and go into the backyard to play. Erin, Colleen, and Baker eagerly accompanied them.

Will and Louise Botna had phoned before they arrived, asking if it was okay to bring their daughter April. Matt had taken the phone call and assured them that everyone would be glad to meet their little girl. When they came in he saw that April was not as young as he had expected. She was on spring break from the University of Wisconsin where she was pursuing a graduate degree in business management. Paul saw Matt's eyes dilate when he met her. He took in every inch of her smiling, energetic presence. Paul gave him a knowing wink and noticed that Matt was her attentive host all afternoon. He whispered to Maren, "I predict we'll be seeing more of April Botna."

"Maybe," said Maren, "As long as Laurel doesn't return."

By four o'clock the guests were leaving. Maren or Paul walked each to the door. Needing a breath of air, Maren went out to the driveway with Peter Winslow.

"Thanks for coming Peter. We're grateful to have you for a neighbor."

"I'm happy to have you folks here, and so is Baker. It's a good thing you took him, so I didn't have to take him to the motel with me last night."

"Why were you in a motel, Pete?"

"Oh, Marc Vincent asked me to. He said he had a couple of loose ends he needed to wrap up for the preliminary story on the underground railroad. He had a crew come out for the night. They wanted to take night photos in the cemetery, with actors, you know. He had already turned in the keys to his house. I told him I'd stay out of the way, but he said it would be better if I'd go. He put me up at that new hotel in Albright—very nice—pricey too."

"So Marc was in your house last night."

"That's right, and some of his colleagues."

CHAPTER 21

It was eight o'clock before the last of the guests who were leaving actually drove away. The goodbyes between Paul and his parents seemed to take longer and were more tender than in previous years. These days most families were feeling closer. Everyone knew that a single day, a single minute could change everything forever. No one spoke of it, but everyone acknowledged in some way that life is fragile.

Nick, Carrie, and Matt cleaned up the kitchen, while Zoe and Danl played the travel game Aunt Elizabeth had given them. Frank settled into a comfortable, oversized chair with a book he had been trying to finish. Paul thought it might be time for a talk with Maren, but she said she was going to take advantage of the opportunity to take a long, hot bath and turn in early.

Breakfast Monday morning was cold cereal and bagels with cream cheese. Matt had to see a Botna client in Wisconsin, so he dropped Frank at the airport a bit early. Nick and Carrie were packed and on their way by mid-morning. Danl and Zoe were only interested in staying home to enjoy spring break with Baker, so Maren and Paul put on wind breakers and went for a walk. They enjoyed the quiet for ten minutes or so, and then Paul cleared his throat and shuffled his feet.

"Maren, there's something I've been wanting to tell you." She hoped it wasn't about giving up her work. She had severely limited her hours, so that he wouldn't feel she was spreading herself too thin.

"Maren, I want to apologize for criticizing your desire to continue working in your profession. You are incredibly talented, gifted really, and I was just selfish. I wanted you all to myself. I didn't trust you to make good decisions while I was away. I tried to control you, so I wouldn't lose you. I hope you can forgive me."

Maren was surprised and touched. She thought they had made progress on the way they related to one another in London. She hadn't really expected any other discussion. But, here finally was the man she had married, open, vulnerable. Whenever she felt they were drifting apart, he did or said something that softened her heat and filled her with his love. She knew she had something to confess, too.

"Paul, I have to tell you something, too. I never did confess to it when I was in London, but I thought Bev was a woman, and that you were having an affair with her. So, I can't judge you too harshly. I don't get a very high score on trust, either."

They stood near a blooming dogwood tree, put their arms around each other and enjoyed a long, tender kiss. Someone in a passing car honked approval. Maren, never one for public displays of affection, felt entirely comfortable.

Paul left the day after Easter. He was anxious to be back with his colleagues in Kabul, but he thought his heart was ripping when he finally let go of Maren at the airport. "You were right Paul," encouraged Maren, "Being apart has helped us love each other better. We never quarreled before, but we never made up either. We just drifted along, losing our passion for each other." Paul remembered the making up part. He felt very warm just thinking about it. "No more secrets though," he vowed, "Being separated is enough of a test for any couple without secrets." She kissed him one more time. "No more secrets," she agreed.

Two weeks later Maren was still re-building her case load of home patients. She had resumed her routine, if you could call it a routine. Stopping at the Dexum Café, at least that was routine. It was good to be in regular contact with Della, again. "Decaf?" Della asked.

"I'm thinking of switching to tea, like the English."

"That's great iced on a hot day, but it'll never be as satisfying as hot coffee in the morning." She poured the hot coffee into Maren's cup without waiting for a decision. "How is your little private practice doing?"

"It's great. In fact, I'd like to rent an office somewhere. Then I could see more patients without driving all over. I would really like to work more with people with voice disorders, too. Once Paul comes home we could have a joint practice. Voice is a specialty that we're lacking in this area."

"Would he like that?"

"We love working together."

"I meant seeing patients with voice disorders. I thought he wanted a pediatric practice."

"Kids have voice problems, too."

Maren didn't seem to grasp what Della was questioning, but she decided things would work out in time. Meanwhile, she offered to help Maren with billing and typing of reports for her private patients. "By the way, that writer from *Beyond Our Past* was in here yesterday."

"You mean Marc Vincent?"

"Yeah, that guy. He had breakfast and talked to Gene and Emma about the underground railroad. Oh, by the way, remember our homeless excavator Howard Kaboda? He's going to be a docent, give tours, organize groups. Gene says he's a wealth of historical knowledge. He spent a lot of time in the public library to keep warm and read every word in print about this area during the time of the civil war. If he does well, Gene will put him in charge of the whole project."

"It's a good thing Mr. Kaboda met the Caufields. They're both so kind." She finished her coffee, looked around at others coming in, wondered what secrets their lives held and what the real reason was for Marc's visit. There was no time to ask more questions. Patients were waiting.

"Bye Della. See you later."

"This afternoon?"

"No, I promised to take the kids on a bike ride after school."

Maren's work day was short. She was home pulling weeds in the front yard while she waited for the school bus, when a black SUV pulled into her driveway. Marc Vincent opened the door and stepped out. "I thought you would be home this time of day." He almost smiled. She felt as if they were old friends. She pulled off her garden gloves, dropped them on the grass, and went toward him with both hands extended in welcome. He caught her hands in his.

"Ah, here's my silent partner."

"I heard you were back in town."

"I had to testify in federal court in the city this morning."

"When we last said goodbye, you didn't leave."

"I tried to keep that quiet."

"Pete told me. Of course I knew the story you gave him wasn't true. We saw cars coming or going from his place at three in the morning."

"It was my last conversation with you that kept me from leaving. You still wanted the gun to be found, and so did I. But when I heard myself telling you that no one would believe a word DT Cooper said, I decided to re-evaluate all the evidence as if I believed him."

"Did you find the gun?"

"Yes I did, and it did have his fingerprints on it. He fired the shot, but he was telling the truth about someone setting him up."

"Was it Ross Winston's political enemies?"

"No, Maren. It was about me, about revenge. I was responsible for putting a gangster named Anthony Pacielli behind bars for a fifteen year sentence for racketeering. He's just one on a list of half a dozen men who have sworn to pay me back for inconveniencing them." Maren shivered. No wonder Marc's wife hadn't been able to live with him. Paul worked in a dangerous part of the world, but at least his enemies weren't hunting him personally.

"Pacielli was paroled a year ago, but he didn't show up until I was assigned here. When he found out where I was he figured out a way to pay me back without being suspected. He sent some of the threatening letters to Ross Winston, but not the originals. His were the letters that threatened the family. He decided not to kill me. In fact his threat had been that he would take away my life, without killing me. When the department told me he was in the area I was pretty scared. I thought he was going to target Laurel. My first reaction was to send her back to headquarters. She was not happy about that, leaving the job and Matt. She convinced me to let her come back. It turns out he didn't know she's my daughter."

Maren had guessed right. Marc wasn't just one of the agents. He had commanded the Dexum operation.

"Pacielli's plan was to discredit me—make sure I messed up. He paid DT to fire a gun through Pete's window. He told him no one was inside, that it was just a joke. He had no way of knowing Matt was supposed to be there that night, instead of Pete. He didn't really care whether Pete was hit or not. It was the threat he wanted to establish. When Baker barked, it startled DT; and he fired a wild shot. It's a wonder Pete was even hit. DT left the gun in the grass next to the path as instructed, picked up the bag there with his cash, and beat it out of town. Pacielli kept the gun with DT's fingerprints, planning to have it discovered later.

"It would look like DT was the only one involved. He would be arrested for the shooting, and I would pull everyone out. Then he would move in and kill Pete. He hoped I'd be discharged from the agency, or at least demoted. Even if I kept my job, my judgment would always be questioned and I would never be able to forgive myself. He misjudged me, though. I would have left one agent behind, probably Laurel if Pacielli hadn't been in the picture."

"That was because of Matt," Maren said; and Marc nodded.

"Things got pretty mixed up when DT was arrested for a separate crime, and we didn't find him right away. And then Kaboda took DT's car and lost the license plate. But Pacielli could still make his plan work. He just waited for me to leave. As soon as I ordered the other agents out and left Pete unprotected, he planned to break in and... He's a pro Maren. He wouldn't have missed. Pete would be dead, and the fault would have been mine."

"Pete said you spent the night there."

"That's right, three of us did; but we didn't sleep. When Pacielli broke in, we were waiting for him. I told Pete the truth about one thing though, we did get some great pictures. There's enough evidence to put Pacielli away for a long, long time, without parole."

"How did you find out he was involved?"

"Good police work, Maren. That's all I can tell you, but it was through the letters. It wasn't until you got me to give DT Cooper the benefit of the doubt that I figured it all out. There's a record kept of threats, and a profiler rates the probability an individual will act on those threats."

"And Pacielli got high marks?"

"That's right. And now I have to ask you..."

"I know—I can't tell anyone what I know, not even Pete."

"Well, it would help protect my identity if you didn't spread all this around. It may leak out eventually, but please, no email or phone call to Paul. That isn't as secure as you may think. Wait until you can tell him in person."

The school bus stopped and the doors opened. Zoe and Danl jumped out and ran up the driveway to greet Mr. Marc. "Are you moving back," they wanted to know.

"No, I just stopped to say hello. This neighborhood is too quiet for me." They ran in the house to get Baker and bring snacks for the bike ride. Marc took the opportunity to say a final goodbye to Maren. "I'm sorry for the distress for you and your family. It appears that I was the cause of most of your anguish."

"You know that's not true, Marc. There were threats against the Winston family and against Matt. Sydney is obviously emotionally unstable. Who knows what she might have done. I would wish you good luck Marc, but I think you need more than luck. You need to have someone praying for you."

"Can't hurt. Are you volunteering?" The children and Baker were in the garage, packing granola bars and bottles of water in their bike bags and checking tire pressure. "I am, but please take care of yourself." She gave him a hug. He put his hands on her shoulders and pushed her back far enough to kiss her forehead. He took a business card from his shirt pocket and handed it to her. "If you ever need anything Mrs. McCloud, you or Paul, here's where you can reach me."

"So you're off on another dangerous assignment?"

"Maybe so." He actually smiled. "You've inspired me. I'm going to visit Laurel's mom."

New life was bursting forth along the creek path creating peace and beauty, in spite of the dangers in the world. Everywhere Maren turned there were signs of hope... flowers, birds making nests, frogs, and proud young parents showing off their babies in strollers. More al Qaeda leaders had been captured, and Sadaam Hussein was on the run, never again to return to power.

By the time they got to the park the children wanted a snack stop. Zoe and Danl sat in the grass eating, while Maren claimed the park bench facing the lake. Noreen Anderson rode up on her bike and joined her.

"Randy's coming home next month. I think he's finally open to starting a family. He'll go back of course, but he's changing. He said that others are managing families in spite of separations, so maybe we can too. He also said if he doesn't make it home after the war, I should have a part of him to keep. He meant a son or daughter."

They sat in silence, each savoring the day and their hopes for the future. They watched a group of four soft, yellow baby ducks, being led to the water for a swimming lesson. Mrs. Duck waddled proudly in front, across the path toward the lake. Zoe and

Danl noticed and, trying to get a closer look, moved too quickly. The frightened momma duck hurried her babies into the native forbs and grasses near the water. Daddy duck had been urging his family from behind; but now he fluttered his wings noisily, hovered momentarily, and flew off at a low altitude in another direction.

"He's deserting his family," said Maren shaking her head.

"Oh no," corrected Noreen who believed that ducks mate for life, "He's making himself a decoy, leading the enemy away. As soon as the danger is passed, he'll rejoin his family."

In appreciation...

No work is ever accomplished alone. I am grateful to the multitude of patients I have served during three decades of working as a speech-language pathologist in a variety of settings. The patients I was privileged to guide through the therapy process in their homes put their trust in me. They shared their lives with me. It was that powerful, emotional experience in private homes that initially motivated me to write this book. I became a better therapist and a better person for having witnessed the dedication, sacrifice, and perseverance of family members caring for a loved one at home.

My special thanks goes to the patience of readers who waded through draft copies at a stage in writing that was way too early to provide them any real enjoyment. They took their responsibility seriously and offered suggestions that improved the story as well as my writing. They were my guides: Connie Peshia, Jennifer Smith, Judy Crimmin, Karen Young, Lisa McGregor, and Melanie Kobulnicky.

My husband Hank's encouragement and enthusiasm for my writing have given me the confidence to continue, even when life gets in the way.

I am grateful to God that I have a personal relationship with Christ. Because of that I can trust the Holy Spirit to guide my life. My hope is that this story will encourage others to face the obstacles in their lives with new confidence and take bolder steps in their faith journey.

Printed in the United States
By Bookmasters